"So, you w_____ _____ _____, did you?" Her voice had a faint trace of a French accent. "You wished to rid the world of this curse." Her eyes gazed at Steve, then past him at Mary. "And you wished to avenge your brother. You were misled by this . . . insect here. What's wrong, Mr. Smith? Surely with all your muscles you cannot be restrained by a mere woman?"

She had taken out a wooden stake. She turned, and with a graceful, effortless motion, thrust it clean through Smith's belly.

She was over Smith now, one bare foot in the dark water. "So you thought it would be so simple to kill me. You thought I was such a fool. You are an imbecile! No mortal is clever enough to harm me. Did he promise you immortal life? Well, you are not going to live forever. You are going to die here and now. We will have your blood, but not in the manner which you might choose. You will die, and your body will rot in this dark place. The rats and other vermin will feed on your impressive muscles, for after all, they are nothing but meat, plentiful meat. Your bones will warn others who might think I am easy to destroy."

She grabbed his hand, then quickly and deftly cut his wrist to the bone. Red blood gushed out below his palm.

She knelt over him, then seized his arm and began to lap at the blood with her tongue.

BLOOD FEUD
Sam Siciliano

PINNACLE BOOKS
WINDSOR PUBLISHING CORP.

PINNACLE BOOKS

are published by

Windsor Publishing Corp.
475 Park Avenue South
New York, NY 10016

First Printing: April, 1993

Printed in the United States of America

All quotes are from poems in Charles Baudelaire's *Les Fleurs Du Mal, (The Flowers of Evil)*. The author's translations try to convey the literal meaning rather than the rhyme and rhythm of the poetry. Justly revered by the French, Baudelaire is little-known in the United States. Like Poe, he is a spiritual father to all modern horror writers.

This book is dedicated to the Catholics the author has known, and three women in particular, who have sincerely tried to live their faith despite all that the church hierarchy has done to make it difficult for them.

Quand elle eut de mes os sucé toute la moelle,
Et que languissamment je me tournai vers elle
Pour lui rendre un baiser d'amour, je ne vis plus
Qu'une outre aux flancs gluants, toute pleine de
      pus!
Je fermai les deux yeux, dans ma froide épouvante,
Et, quand je les rouvris à la clarté vivante,
A mes côtés, au lieu du mannequin puissant
Qui semblait avoir fait provision de sang,
Tremblaient confusément des débris de squelette,
Qui d'eux-mêmes rendaient le cri d'une girouette
Ou d'une enseigne, au bout d'une tringle de fer,
Que balance le vent pendant les nuits d'hiver.

                "Les Metamorphoses du Vampire"

When she had sucked all the marrow from my
      bones,
And when languidly I turned toward her
To give her a kiss of love, I saw nothing more
Than a goatskin flask with sticky sides, all full of
      pus!
I closed my eyes in cold dread,
And when I opened them again to living clarity,
At my side, instead of a powerful mannequin
Which seemed to have stocked up on blood,
There trembled in confusion the debris of a
      skeleton,
Which of itself gave off the squeal of a
      weathervane
Or of a sign hung at the end of an iron bar,
Which the wind balances during winter nights.

                "The Metamorphoses of the Vampire"

Prologue

The Oregon coast,
August 1982

All afternoon the sun struggled to appear. Patches of white thinned to blue; then the surrounding clouds swallowed up the blue again. The sky seemed filled with fuzzy, warring amoebas swallowing each other up. By five o'clock the sun had lost for another day. The tenuous grayness thickened and dropped, and a fine drizzle began.

Alex came up onto the top of the hill. Wet wind stirred the ferns and other leaves at ground level, breathed softly through the boughs of the firs. Tiny violet flowers were sprinkled across the dark earth, and fungi blotched the tree bark. The air on his face was cool, and when he turned his head he could hear the wind sing in his ears. From below came the murmur of the surf, and he could see sand and the gray water through the dark shapes of the trees.

He wore a T-shirt from a marathon he had run, a nylon windbreaker, and jeans. Not enough—his shoulders

7

jerked upward in a shiver. He should have packed a wool sweater, but he had forgotten how strange the weather at the beach could be. Yesterday it had been ninety-five in Portland, but today it felt more like November than August.

Tracy took his hand. "Cold?" she asked.

He shrugged. "Kind of."

The nylon gym bag she was carrying reminded him they weren't just out for a stroll. The fear which had stalked him for the last few weeks was very close now. She gave his hand a squeeze.

Her long blond hair was pulled back into a pony tail, and her blue-green eyes had a strange intensity. She seemed more excited than scared. Her beauty was still a wonder to him, and other feelings—affection, longing, sadness—briefly drove away fear. At six feet she was a couple of inches taller than he was. Her body was lean and hard like his own. They did five-mile runs together every other day. He'd always been clumsy and shy with girls, but she'd gotten him past that quickly. Naked, she was everything he had ever hoped for. There must have been other men before him, but that didn't matter. If only they were back in the motel together and this were over with. She squeezed his hand again, and he tried to smile.

The path had merged into a gravel road which cut through the firs. In the open they could feel the drizzle and almost see it fall. A chain-link fence with a locked gate and a big No Trespassing sign separated them from the house. She took the wire cutters out of the bag and handed them to him. He climbed the eight-foot fence, cut out pieces of barbed wire along the top, then went on over. She threw the bag to him, then climbed over.

The tip of her tongue, wet and red, flickered across her lower lip. He had watched her put on the pale pink lipstick at the motel. She took his hand.

"This is it," she whispered.

The house—with the Victorian towers and porches, the scalloped wood beneath the ridges, the embellished supports under the eaves—must have been built in the last century. Restored, it would be beautiful, but that would take a lot of work. Much of the white paint was gone; dark wood showed everywhere, and what remained was cracked and blistered. Patches of the roof were obviously rotten, the gray cedar shakes covered with an almost fluorescent, yellow-green moss. Houses on the coast took constant work; otherwise, like this one, they began to rot. A house was, after all, mostly dead wood, and the same insects and fungi, the mists and sea air, which worked upon the forests would eat at a house.

As they walked to the porch Alex felt the fear blossom like a dead flower in his chest. His mouth and throat were the only dry things anywhere within the landscape. He wanted to turn and run.

"He'll be in the basement." Tracy's voice was low and soft. "Once we're finished we can go back to the motel. Then I'll be safe. And I'll always be grateful, Alex." She looked at him, but he couldn't speak.

She took his arm as they went up the steps. His right foot touched the third board, and the rotted wood gave way as soon as he put weight on it. If she hadn't had hold of his arm, he would have backed away. His steps were tentative. You couldn't tell what was solid and what was rotten.

The carved oak door was stained almost black, a

9

knocker in the middle, the face of a gargoyle, the metal weathered green. Above the door was a stained glass window; its blue and crimson panes were dull in the shadow. Tracy opened the door. She laughed. "It isn't even locked. We won't have to break a window or anything."

Alex smelled something musty and faintly putrid, the breath of the dwelling seeping out through its mouth. He didn't think he could make himself go in. He couldn't remember being so afraid, not as an adult. Tracy's story had been fiction until now, mere imagination, but this house and what dwelt here were real.

She must have seen what he felt. Her eyes grew cool like the gray air all around them, and her mouth stiffened. She wore jeans and a navy windbreaker. The pink smear of her mouth and the crimson glass over the door were the only warm colors anywhere. Everything was gray or dark, the browns and greens of the trees subdued, the house a dirty white and gray-brown.

She grasped his wrist. "Come on," she whispered and started inside. She pulled his arm upright, and he let her draw him inside. Cold, dark, and alongside the musty, mildewy smell was something much worse. Cobwebs obscured the corners of the living room. The heavy square furniture was rust-colored, torn, and looked thirty or forty years old. The network of cracks in the plaster wall formed a pattern which seemed somehow designed, intelligent.

She led him to the end of the hallway, let go to open the door, then took the big flashlight out of the bag and handed him the bag. The beam of light brought out all the details of the decay around them. She straightened her shoulders. "Let's get this over with."

10

"I can't." It came out so fast he couldn't hide the fear.

"Alex . . . You promised. I need your help. I can't do this alone. Please." She raised her hand to touch his cheek, but he drew back. "You said you loved me. You promised to help. Maybe . . . maybe you aren't much of a man after all." The melodic quality of her laugh jarred.

Alex felt his eyes go liquid. He couldn't risk talking, but he gave his head a shake, then followed her through the door. The stairs were wood, and the jouncing flashlight beam showed earth at the bottom. The musty smell grew worse. A board cracked underfoot, but this time he didn't trust the stairs, and he was ready.

The joists were only a couple of inches over Tracy's head. The yellow-white light swept the ground around them. The earth was uneven, and it formed mounds and sloped gradually downward. The walls were stone, not brick, and green moss grew on them. Rusty metal posts held up the floor joists. Three small windows along one wall let in beams of gray light, and the cold wet earth below steamed.

"It seems so big," Tracy said. "More like a cave than a basement." She pointed the light at the ground before them and started forward. "Are you okay?"

"Yeah," he murmured.

She stopped before a big flat square piece of wood, outlining it with the flashlight. "Lift it," she said. He didn't move. "Alex . . ."

He knelt down and got his fingers under the wood. It was plywood, the edge faintly rotten. As soon as he raised it the stench hit him. This was its source, that smell of decay, of putrefaction. His fingers slid free, and the board hit the earth with a dull clump.

11

"Lift it up, Alex—all the way. And this time don't drop it."

She was angry, and he couldn't blame her. He was acting like a coward. It wouldn't help for him to fall apart. He had to control himself. If only the fear would go away, but he knew this was only the beginning. He clenched his teeth, then grabbed the board, stood up and flipped it over. The smell made him gag, and he tasted something hot and sour. "Good Christ," he whispered.

A dark-haired woman lay within the shallow grave. She wore a black gown, but her arms, feet, and face were so white they seemed to glow. She was the most beautiful woman he had ever seen besides Tracy, but she was dead. Even though her eyes were open and conscious, she was dead.

"She sees us," he whispered.

"I know. But she can't move. She can't hurt us, not now. Not until dark."

Through the black fabric he could make out the pink of her nipples, then the outline of her rib cage, the mound of her belly with the navel in the center, the dark V of pubic hair. Black locks curled about her face, the ends sweeping out and blending with the dirt. Despite her pallor, her lips were bright red; the lower lip very full, the tips of the canines making tiny indentations. Her brown eyes stared up at Alex, pleading with him. Be kind to me, don't hurt me, and I can reward you.

"Don't look in her eyes." Alex didn't move. Tracy shook him, then slapped him hard across the cheek. The blow stung, the pain for a moment obliterating the fear.

"Hey," he said.

She dug her nails into his arm. "Don't look into their eyes—I warned you about that."

"I forgot."

"Don't, or you'll never leave here alive. Cover her up again. We've got to find him. I think he's supposed to be at the far end from the stairs."

Tracy shone the light on the torso, and Alex was careful not to look at the woman's face while he raised the board. He stared instead at her breasts, the pink smears showing through the fabric—pink like Tracy's mouth. He started to ease down the board.

"Oh, just let it drop!" she said.

He winced. "Not so loud—they'll hear you."

"Who cares! I'm here!" she shouted. "I'm here, you bloodsucking fuckers! What are you going to do about it!"

"Stop it—stop that!"

She glared at him, her mouth contemptuous. Then the anger went out of her. "Sorry. I suppose it did sound rather stupid." She laughed, and its melodic flow again seemed out of place. "Come on."

They headed for the far wall. Every few feet were the wooden surfaces. "God, I thought there'd be coffins," he whispered.

"So did I." She laughed. "Like in the movies, but they're dead so I guess it doesn't matter. They won't rot anymore."

The floor sank gradually, then rose again near the far wall. In some places the earth seemed freshly dug up, but here about this mound it was packed hard.

"Try this one," she said, pointing the flashlight at the edge.

This time he was ready for the smell, but it was even worse. He was glad he hadn't eaten much lunch. He had the board up about two feet when he felt something on

13

his hand. He crouched slightly and saw several black smears—slugs—all over the underside of the wood. Adrenaline made it easy to push the heavy board over. It struck the stone wall and came to rest.

The man was dressed in black, a scar across one eye, the mustache on his white face crooked. Crooked? Looking more carefully Alex realized it wasn't a mustache, but a five-inch slug crawling across the face. The soil around the head was alive with small bugs, the yellow light from the beam glistening off black chitin. The man's eyes showed something of the white-hot anger within him. Alex knew he would be pulled down into the grave to remain there forever with that corpse and all those crawling things. He stepped back and turned, but Tracy caught his arm before he could escape.

"Take it easy!" she said. "Just take it easy." She put the flashlight in her jeans and grabbed him below the shoulders with both hands. The bright light stabbed up between them, making him blink and turn his head. "That's him all right. I know it's awful, but we've got to kill him now. Once we do that it will be safe, and we can get away from here. Do you understand, Alex? Do you?"

He realized sweat was dribbling down his sides even though he felt deathly cold. He fought to control his breathing, to make it part of him again. Finally he nodded. "I understand."

She took the wooden stake out of the bag, put it in his left hand, then used both hands to close his fingers about the wood. The circle of light jumped around on the floorboards overhead. She got out the mallet and put it in his other hand, then shined the light on the dead man's chest.

14

"Come on, Alex."

He turned slowly and took a half step forward. His legs were trembling, and he knew his body wanted to betray him. "Tracy ..." The panic in his voice made him stop to struggle some more. "I ... I don't think I can do this."

She laughed, and he wanted suddenly to hit her for what she was doing to him. "Then we'll die—or we'll become like him. There won't be a place on earth where we can hide. He's seen us now, and he'll hunt us down and destroy us. It's him or us, Alex. You choose."

He tried to make himself move. "But the ... others."

She made an exasperated noise. "I told you—he's the source. Kill him and the others will fall as well. Now choose, and you'd better hurry because it will be dark soon, and he won't just lie there much longer. It's him or us, Alex."

He drew in his breath. Once it was done, he could leave this place—they could go out again into the light and air. He stepped into the grave, straddled the man, then squatted down, raising his right arm. Tracy moved the light, catching the face again briefly. The slug had moved past the mouth, and the eyes glared up at him, hatred bursting upon them like a dark flare. The face was wizened and dead, but not the eyes.

"Don't look!" she yelled, her voice no longer tranquil.

He turned his head, his quivering left hand holding the wooden stake over the man's chest, his right hand faltering.

"Do it!" she screamed. "Do it, you gutless coward! Do it or we're both damned!" Her voice was raw and strained, desperate, deafening in the dark dead place.

He struck. Something cold and wet splattered him,

15

and the thing writhed, its legs moving up to meet him. A scream, something not human, clawed for his brain. The fear that it was coming alive drove him, and he hit at the stake again and again. The wailing had fear and hate and agony in it. When the noise finally ceased and the thing was quiet, the sound still echoed within his skull. He had never heard anything like it. With a sob, he dropped the mallet and staggered back out of the grave.

She grabbed his arm. "Oh, Alex—I knew you could do it! He's dead, really dead!" Her lips brushed at his cheek, but he turned away. She grabbed the hair above his right ear and pulled his face back to her. Her tongue flickered into his mouth and darted about. He shuddered, then put his arms about her and drew her to him. His whole body was trembling. She let the flashlight drop, then whispered, "I knew you could do it." Her right hand slid under his jacket and shirt, gripped at his back, then slipped down under his pants. "It's all right now. It's all right."

But he couldn't stop shaking, and even in the silence he heard the dim echo of the thing screaming as he drove the wooden spike through it. "Let's get out of here," he whispered.

"All right." She kissed him again, then bent to pick up the flashlight. "There's one thing, first."

He had to fight to keep from running. "What . . . thing?"

She opened the bag and took out a big butcher knife, holding it as if she was about to stab someone. "You . . . you have to cut off the head."

"Jesus! Are you crazy! What are you talking about?"

Her voice was soft again, but her shouting had altered

its tone. "Not only the stake, but the head needs to be cut off then, and . . ."

"No!" he shouted. He could scream too. "No! What do you take me for!"

"A man—a *man*. To be sure we must cut off the head, and . . ."

In the dark she looked dead too, like the woman in the ground, and all around him was death and the stink of death. He turned and ran. "Alex!" she cried, and the yellow beam of light careened off the earth about him. His foot struck plywood and gave a dull thud. Halfway up the stairs a board split. He hit his elbow, but clawed his way upward. He ran out the front door and leaped over the stairs, hitting the ground two feet beyond them. Only after he had clambered up over the fence and reached the forest did he stop to rest.

It was so much better outside, the air clear and clean, but he was still frightened. He looked at his watch. About half an hour until dark. The drizzle and mist in the air obscured the fence and made the house look like a mirage or illusion. Gradually his breath slowed down. He wiped his face with his hand, then noticed red smeared all over his knuckles. Looking down he saw red—blood on his hands and all over his jacket. The panic came again, but then he realized the dead man's blood had splattered him when the stake pierced its chest. Alex's left hand throbbed. The mallet must have struck his fingers. He glanced at the house again.

"Tracy," he murmured.

He couldn't leave her there. But he couldn't go back. He couldn't. The mere idea terrified him. He couldn't force himself to do another thing. He paced about, stop-

17

ping to glance at the house. Finally he saw Tracy come out onto the porch.

Relieved, he walked slowly toward the fence. She tossed the nylon bag over the fence before starting to climb. The toes of her Nikes found resting places in the chain links. Near the bottom, she let go and sprang back, landing lightly on her feet. Her face was pale, her eyes still angry. "We'd better do something about that blood all over you." She started for the trail.

Alex picked up the bag, then followed silently. Back in the woods you couldn't see the drizzle, but it hung in the air about them. Alex still felt cold and shaky.

He finally said, "Did you . . . did you . . . ?"

She stopped abruptly and turned. "No—I didn't do anything. I left him there." She ran her tongue across her lower lip. "I . . . I don't like knives." She took his hand and forced a smile. "I think it will be all right. He looked dead—Jesus, he looked dead."

Alex shivered, his hand tightening about hers, then followed her quietly through the forest. The twisted limbs of the trees were like strange bones, yellow-white tendrils of moss hanging from them. All about him, the gray-green world darkened.

Alex lay on the queen-size bed and sipped at some brandy. The noisy heater blew warm air at him, and he could hear the shower running and Tracy humming. The fear had died down at last, but was still very close. He wondered if he could ever forget what he had seen, if his life—if his feelings for Tracy—would ever be the same again. The faces of the dead man with the thing crawling across him and the dead woman seemed seared into his brain, the images fixed forever. He felt cold again, the fear stabbing at his chest, and he finished the brandy, grateful for the distraction of it smoldering down his throat. The hand holding the glass shook. He slammed the glass down on the nightstand and stood up.

He walked over to the sliding door. The drape was drawn, and he wondered, not for the first time, if the dead thing could be standing out there. If it was dead, yet still alive, how could you ever kill it? Perhaps that face was waiting behind the drape. The terror he had struggled so long to subdue was suddenly back, and for an instant he was certain something was out there.

"Stop it," he said aloud, then grabbed the cord and whisked the drapes open.

Drizzle misted at the glass, and he saw the yellow lights shining on the wet black parking lot and the cars below, and further away the red neon Coastal Inn sign with Vacancy in pink light.

He eased his breath out and smiled. So ridiculously ordinary. Who ever heard of a monster at a motel like this? He put his hands against the glass. It felt cool, and he noticed a big crack in the lower right corner. Maybe that was why he couldn't seem to get warm enough.

He drew the drapes, wishing again that he had brought a wool sweater. The skin of his bare arms was prickly. The T-shirt felt thin, and he had hurled his bloody windbreaker out into the surf, not wanting it near him ever again. He went back to the bed and lay down, crossing his ankles and cupping his hands behind his head. He wondered again if it really was dead.

"Please stop," he whispered.

He could get into his car and drive as far away as possible. There would be no sleep for a long time. He could

19

be in California tomorrow or Idaho. Perhaps it wasn't too late to get away.

The shower had stopped, but Tracy was still humming. The door opened, and she stood framed in a steamy mist. A lavender terrycloth robe fell to her feet, and her straight wet hair appeared darker. She smiled. "Feeling better?"

He sat up, shrugging slightly.

"It's all right, Alex—honestly it is."

"Sure."

She sat on the bed and put her hand on his thigh. "It's foolish to worry so. I'm certain he's dead."

Her throat was long and white, and he could see her pulse throb faintly in the hollow between her collarbones. Her mouth was big, the upper lip curving sensuously on either side. He wanted to tell her he didn't want to talk about it, but he wasn't sure he could get the words out. She looked so beautiful sitting there, her skin clean and fresh, faintly pink from the shower. She would be naked under the robe, and normally he would have drawn her to him and kissed her, his hands slipping beneath the robe, but something had changed. He no longer trusted her. She had pulled him into this horror, she had despised him as a coward, and now she pretended nothing had changed and everything was wonderful.

He closed his eyes, fleeing into the darkness, then rolled over onto his stomach.

"Oh, Alex," she murmured, then sighed. "I . . . It will be all right, honestly . . ." The bed creaked slightly, and she stroked his left palm lightly with her fingertips.

Dimly, through the wall, they heard a woman giggling.

20

"I've told you I was sorry, that I know how hard this all was for you and that I didn't mean to snap at you. It will be all right, my darling. Everything will be all right. Only one of the books said anything about the head, and . . ." She must have noticed his body stiffen. "But I want you to forget that. It's finished now."

He felt her hand run along his spine, over his buttocks, then slip between his legs. He heard her whisper into his ear, "I promise." He didn't move. The bed creaked again as she got up, then her robe rustled softly and made a clump like a sigh as it hit the floor.

She got on top of him, stretching her body along his, her hands grasping his shoulders. "My darling," she whispered, "my poor, poor darling." Alex didn't move as she rubbed against him, her lips nuzzling the side of his neck. "I wouldn't blame you for being afraid, for being angry, but it had to be done." He felt her sigh, then she got up off him.

She pulled his T-shirt out, then slipped her hand underneath and touched his spine. He shuddered. "You're so cold. You should take a shower. I told you you should."

Her fingertips massaged him gently, then she moved his shirt and kissed his back while her hands gripped his buttocks through the thick denim of his jeans. Her lips touched him again and again, her flesh and her breath warm, and then she licked his back.

His breathing quickened, and he felt himself relaxing. She slid one hand beneath him. He let her turn him over onto his back. She mumbled something, then undid his jeans and pulled them and his shorts down. "Alex . . ." she whispered, then began kissing and licking him.

"Oh . . ." he moaned. He wished she had picked an-

21

other time—everything was changed, and he felt so sad and strange, distant from his own body, the flesh that stirred under her touch. Still he could hardly ignore what she was doing to him. His hands clutched at the sheets.

She drew back. "Oh, Alex." The bed creaked again as she rose, straddled him, then slid herself down onto him. "Oh, Alex—oh God." Her hands held his sides, and she rocked on her haunches, raising and lowering herself.

Alone in the darkness, Alex thought of the dead woman's face, her eyes. He opened his eyes. Tracy's breasts, the pink aureoles, hung over him, and strands of long wet hair slapped at his face. A red flush showed below her collarbone. Her mouth opened wide, she sat straight up and one hand grabbed at his hair, pulling while she pressed down onto him as hard as she could, her hips twisting.

He clenched his teeth and felt his own loins shudder as he rose to meet her, his back arching. She moaned, her knees hugging his sides, then cried out twice, the second cry an extension of the first. All the breath seemed to go out of her. With a sigh, she used her hands to smooth her wet hair back over her shoulders. Her blue-green eyes stared down at him, her mouth still half open.

"Oh, Alex. What will I ever do with you, my poor darling?"

He said nothing. He had never felt so far away from her, and now that this act was done, nothing more separated him from the night and what lay waiting for him.

"You've gotten me all sweaty again! Naughty boy! I need to go take another shower." She laughed once, then

22

rose slowly and got off the bed. In the yellow-orange light from the pole lamp her sweaty skin gleamed. Her breasts were small and high, her rib cage prominent, her belly flat and hard. Alex knew just how strong she was. She picked up the lavender robe, then bent over and kissed him just below his navel. "Cheer up," she said. She stood and smiled. "And either pull your pants up or take them off. You look rather silly." She let the robe drag on the floor as she headed for the bathroom. The shower clunked, then came the swish of the water.

He pulled off his T-shirt, wiped himself off, then stood and pulled up his jeans. He wondered if she really cared for him, or if he were just a piece of flesh she used to satisfy herself. A living vibrator. He made a noise like a laugh, but his eyes filled with tears. Women were supposed to feel cheap and scuzzy afterwards, not men. He jerked his belt angrily, then threaded it through the loop. He sat down, then lay on his side.

His head throbbed slightly, and he thought longingly of sleep. The heater and shower were like two winds, soft and steady. He closed his eyes tentatively, but the faces did not appear. Last night there were nightmares, but he hadn't known how bad it would be. He had never felt so weary.

The sounds soothed and soon drifted away. He was back in the forest amidst the great dark trees, walking along the path which led to the house behind the fence. This time he jumped the fence, clearing it with a single leap. In the air he felt as if he might float away. The earth no longer held him prisoner.

Inside the house the fear started again, and then he saw the black-haired woman waiting for him. Her dark eyes watched him, her red lips forming a smile. She

23

took his hand and led him upstairs to the bedroom. A candle flickered over the cracked plaster walls, casting dancing shadows. He realized he was naked. The sheets were lavender, and she pulled off the black negligee, revealing the white torso, the pink nipples, and the black patch of hair. She opened her arms to him.

He kissed her, and then they were rolling about the bed, their hands caressing each other. Her eyes turned blue, and he realized it was only Tracy after all, but then he saw the dark hair between her thighs, and he was no longer sure who it was. He groped for her face, but all he could find were legs, breasts, hips, feet, hands. This could not be one woman—there must be two—the dark one beneath him, and Tracy clinging to his back, nuzzling at his shoulder, his ear, while the other woman rolled her tongue about his.

Was ... someone watching ... watching from the shadow? A man. Dread sucked the desire from him, but it didn't touch the women writhing about him. He wanted to run, but the women held him.

Gradually the dead face came into focus, as if he were watching it through a lens and slowly turning the barrel. The eyes were full of hate, and in his hand was the big butcher knife from the bag. Alex tried to get away, but a woman held each of his arms. They began to laugh. Alex couldn't escape, he couldn't even cry out.

Suddenly he recognized the dead man. The corpse's face was lined and old, but the dimple in the chin was his, and the eyes as well—it was Alex's face, his own death mask. He struggled to escape, but the two women held him spreadeagled on the bed.

"I'm going to cut out your heart," the thing whispered, "and then we're going to eat it."

24

The knife rose, light catching the wide blade, then fell. Agony sudden and sharp in his chest, as if he were an insect being speared on a giant pin.

He jerked his eyes open, fleeing the dream, and saw the dark-haired woman in the black gown standing before him in the motel room. A faint smile twitched on her lips. He couldn't quite breathe right, and the pain was still there. Clumsily his hands brushed at his chest, felt the buried shaft, the wooden stake. Bright red blood covered his hands.

He groaned and tried to get up. The thing must have gone completely through him. He gripped the wood with his right hand, but was afraid to pull it free, afraid to leave such a hole in himself. Somehow he had managed to stand, but he couldn't quite see right anymore. The room and the woman wavered, then everything began to dissolve.

"Alex!" Tracy had come out of the bathroom.

The floor hit him, jarring the stake, sending the agony again through his chest. He knew he was dying, and he wished he could see his mother and father, his sister Mary, one last time. He had loved them so much.

"Poor pathetic fool," a woman's voice said. "Now it's your turn."

Tracy's laugh rippled like flowing water. "Did you think I was relying on him for protection?"

Her laugh was the last thing he ever heard. It faded into darkness.

Part One

Rappelez-vous l'objet que nous vîmes, mon âme,
    Ce beau matin d'été si doux:
Au détour d'un sentier une charogne infâme
    Sur un lit semé de cailloux,

Les jambes en l'air, comme une femme lubrique,
    Brûlante et suant les poisons,
Ouvrait d'une façon nonchalante et cynique
    Son ventre plein d'exhalaisons.

.   .   .

Les mouches bourdonnaient sur ce ventre putride,
    D'où sortaient de noirs bataillons
De larves, qui coulaient comme un épais liquid
    Le long de ces vivants haillons.

.   .   .

—Et pourtant vous serez semblable à cette ordure,
    A cette horrible infection,
Étoile de mes yeux, soleil de ma nature,
    Vous, mon ange et ma passion!

Oui! telle vous serez, ô la reine des grâces,
    Après les derniers sacrements,
Quand vous irez, sous l'herbe et les floraisons grasses,
    Moisir parmi les ossements.

Alors, ô ma beauté! dites à la vermine
    Qui vous mangera de baisers,
Que j'ai gardé la forme et l'essence divine
    De mes amours décomposés!

                                        "Une Charogne"

Do you recall the object we saw, my love,
    That beautiful summer morning so mild?
At the turn of the path, a loathsome corpse
    On a bed of dirt scattered with pebbles,

Its legs in the air like a lewd woman,
    Burning and sweating poisons,
Spread open in a nonchalant and cynical way,
    Her womb full of gases.

.   .   .

The flies buzzed over that putrid belly
    Where black batallions of larva marched out,
Flowing like a thick liquid
    Along those human rags.

.   .   .

—And yet you will be like that garbage,
    That horrible infection,
Star of my eyes, sun of being,
    You, my angel and my passion!

Yes! such you will be, oh queen of graces,
    After the last sacrement,
When you go under the grass and the rich flowerings
    To mold among the bones.

Then, my beauty, tell the vermin
    Who will eat you with kisses,
That I guarded the form and divine essence
    Of my decomposed loves!

                                        "A Carrion"

Chapter I

Portland, Oregon
February 1988

The rain had soaked Steve's hair, his Lycra tights, and Brooks shoes. Running into those thousands of falling drops made it hard to see. His hands were clenched into fists, but his knuckles and the backs of his hands felt icy cold. To his left were the Morrison Bridge and the glassy darkness of the river, to his right the grey expanse of turf. The freeway traffic across the river mumbled dissonantly, a continual reminder you were in the middle of a city.

It had been raining forever—for days, months, years—for November and December and January, and 1985 and 1986 and 1988 and—nothing but constant rain or drizzle, and never anything so energetic as a downpour, just this eternal grayness and mists and cold and dribbling. He remembered suddenly that part of Dante's hell was cold, not hot, and that took him all the way back to a literature class his freshman year at the University of Oregon about eleven years ago. He had never gotten used to this climate, and this winter was the worst yet. Why didn't he get away from here once and for all?

His left knee hurt. He had tried to think of blood flowing through it and clearing away the toxins, but the tendons were just not convinced. He was into his fifth mile, and each time his left foot hit the ground the ache sharpened, as if someone were twisting the joint. Cutting back to three miles hadn't helped, so he had decided to go back to five. A mistake—it felt worse than ever.

A dull anger burned low in his ribs. He wasn't even thirty yet. He'd always stretched and trained gradually and worn the best shoes. Your goddamn knees weren't supposed to give out on you this early. He knew runners in their fifties who had no problems at all, and he had always assumed he could keep this up indefinitely. Now, within a couple of minutes of starting, the pain began.

He tried to ignore the ache, but then he was back in the afternoon meeting trying to explain to Peter that the project was behind schedule and that Peter was making them both look bad. Peter kept nodding thoughtfully, but you could see in his eyes that he didn't buy any of it, that he would continue to behave like an arrogant little asshole.

Steve decided thinking about the pain was preferable. His knee had thrown off his stride. Part of the secret of running long distances was finding and keeping a rhythm, but he couldn't seem to do that anymore. Hell, his whole life was that way. Ever since Brenda had left him he stumbled around, unable to find a rhythm, a pattern, that made any sense. And being a supervisor had turned into a disaster. He just couldn't handle people like Peter. He concentrated on his legs, on the sensation of movement, on the feel of each foot striking the wet concrete.

Poor sad little yuppie, he thought.

The Hawthorne bridge, fifty yards away, was his stopping point. He forced his legs to move faster, ignoring the burning in his chest and the pain in his knee, and took great breaths of air. Almost there—a little more, a little longer. When he reached the dark shadow of the bridge, he let his arms drop and stood for a minute feeling his chest rise and fall, his heart beat. God, it did feel good to stop. He had forgotten everything for a few seconds there.

He started walking back in the other direction, the gray concrete retaining wall between him and the river. The rain had let up some, but under the nylon pullover his T-shirt was soaked with sweat. Passing under a light, he glanced at his watch. 6:30 already.

The sternwheeler went by, red lights strung along its deck, the paddles churning the water white behind it. People waved. He waved back, then put his hands on the concrete wall and looked down. A few thick timbers set into the side, then the black water flecked with yellow light. The boat's wake made the water slap at the side. The river would be very cold this time of year. Even a good swimmer might not make it to the other side. Something floated several yards out beyond the light. Last summer they had found various parts of a body drifting in the river.

He shivered, then turned and started across the grass. Don't start that, he thought. Just don't start. Late at night about two years ago, shortly after Brenda had left, he had understood with absolute certainty that he was

33

going to die some day. Time would pass, it would rush by as the end came closer. No one escaped death. The knowledge that came to him that night cast a long shadow.

He crossed Front Street, went up a block, then rode the escalator up to the bridge level and the main entrance to the building. You could cut through the underground parking lot, but someone had been attacked there a couple of months ago. The guard at the desk nodded at him.

"Must be pretty miserable out there. Ever think about switching to some indoor recreation?"

"All the time."

In the fitness room Bill Kowalski was doing bench presses on the universal gym, but the locker room was deserted. Steve showered and dressed quickly. His knee had begun to throb in earnest.

He took the elevator up to the eighth floor, got the ice pack and aspirin out of a desk drawer, and went to the refrigerator in the coffee room. His hands twisted the plastic tray, and the ice cubes broke loose with a loud crack. He took two aspirin, then headed back to his desk with the ice pack. He rolled up the dark grey wool of his left trouser leg, then swung a brown wingtip up onto the bookcase. His breath hissed out between his teeth as the icy rubber touched his bare knee. With a sigh he sank back into the chair and closed his eyes. There was so much to do, but it could wait.

He dozed for fifteen or twenty minutes, probably just enough to keep him up all night. He must be tired if he could sleep with an icepack on his leg. Peter's report and memo were next to the terminal. The clock overhead said 7:15. The report would take an hour to review.

He started through the memo. Abruptly, he grabbed the top of the paper with his right hand and tore it in two, then crumpled up the halves. The ice bag fell off his knee, and his foot slipped off the bookcase. He glared at the paper wads, then laughed once.

"Oh, screw it." He was hungry, and no one else worked the hours he did. Maybe he was a fool to do it. He threw away the paper, rolled down his pants leg, then went and emptied out the ice bag. After straightening his desk, he put on his trenchcoat and grabbed his umbrella.

Outside the rain had begun again. Or had it ever really ended? He opened the umbrella. The street was shiny with rain, reflecting back the downtown lights, and the car tires made soft, sibilant noises. His knee still felt numb from the ice, but by tomorrow he'd be limping again. How would he ever keep his sanity if he had to stop running? Throwing fits at Peter's memo—a bad sign.

As usual, he walked down Second toward the parking lot under the Morrison Bridge. Boringly predictable, like everything else in his life. Even the rain was getting to him. Maybe he should go back to Colorado. There wasn't a soul in Portland who would really care.

"Excuse me. Excuse me."

The voice finally registered. A woman stared at him through the half-opened window of a car. He walked over to her.

"Do you know anything about motors?"

In the yellowish light from the streetlamp he could see her long brown hair, the oval of the face with the pink, sensual-looking mouth, the large eyes and slightly turned-up nose.

"A little. What's the matter?"

She laughed, the sound pitched higher than her speaking voice. "It won't go!"

"Pop the hood for me."

The car was a gray Toyota Camry, new-looking. He had to put down his umbrella so he could use both hands to get the hood up.

"Let me hold that for you." She was right beside him, very tall, about his height. A dark wool coat with padded shoulders hid her shape, but he could smell perfume. She held the umbrella over them. He looked down at the engine, surprised by his own sudden desire. It had been such a long dry spell, and after Brenda he was wary of beautiful women.

"Thanks," he said. "Does it turn over?"

"Yes, but it won't start."

"Go ahead and try it again."

"But you'll get wet," she said, as if it mattered very much.

"It won't be the first time. It's not raining that hard."

He took the umbrella and stood around to the side. He had learned from his dad that you never stood in front of a car while someone started it. She smiled from behind the windshield, then the starter RRRRRed and the engine bucked. He couldn't smell gas, so it probably wasn't flooded. Better check the wires and see if she was getting a spark. Maybe the coil was bad.

"Woah," he said. "Wait a minute." He found the coil and the distributor, then frowned. That was simple enough. He slammed the hood shut.

She got out. "Couldn't find anything?" A car honked at her and swerved aside.

Steve took her arm, shielding them both with the umbrella. "Let's get out of the street." Once on the sidewalk, he let go, but she didn't back away. "Do you have any, uh, enemies or anything?"

She laughed. "Nothing out of the ordinary. An ex-husband who's a bastard, but he's far away."

"Someone's taken your coil wire. You can crank all day, and the car will never start."

"Is that serious?"

"Not really. It's a simple cheap part to get, but most of your auto parts stores are closed now."

She shook her head. "Why would anybody do that?"

Steve licked at his lips, shrugged, and looked around. Maybe this was some kind of . . . setup, and he'd spoiled things by coming along when he did. Foot traffic was light on Second this time of night. He didn't want to frighten her, but it might be good to get away.

"I belong to Triple A. Maybe I should just call them."

Steve looked at her face again. God, she was beautiful. He had gotten himself in a bind—afraid to approach attractive women, unwilling to go out with plain ones. "Listen, I'm parked just a couple blocks away. We could probably find you a coil wire. G.I. Joe's at Delta Park is open until ten, and they would probably have one."

She touched his arm, smiling. "Oh, thanks, but that seems like too much trouble to put you to. I'll just call Triple A in the morning. I'm too tired to mess with it now. I can tell them I'm missing a coil wire. If it wouldn't be too much trouble, though, I could sure use a ride home. I live fairly close and . . ."

"That's no problem. I'd be glad to. I'm parked under the Morrison Bridge." She was rather trusting for a woman, but he probably looked pretty safe dressed in formal business garb.

"Thanks." She laughed. "Who says chivalry is dead?"

"You'd better lock your car."

"Oh, yes!" She locked the doors, slung her big purse over her shoulder, then smiled at him. They started down the street. "I really am grateful, you know. I wish I knew something about cars. What's your name, by the way?"

"Steve Ryan."

"Glad to meet you, Steve." She stopped abruptly, shook his hand, then slid both hands back into her coat pockets. Her hand was big, white and strong. She wore dark spiked heels, but the coat hid most of her legs. "My name's Sarah. Sarah Whitney. Would you mind if . . . ?" She hesitated.

"Mind what?"

"Well, I've had a dreadful day, and this is simply the last straw. I could use a drink, and Guido's does make good Margaritas. Would you let me buy you a drink? It seems the least I can do, anyway."

"Oh, I can buy my own drink."

She laughed and touched his arm. "Don't go all macho on me, all right? The drinks are on me."

Steve shrugged, then smiled. "Okay, you convinced me."

Guido's was right on the corner. Steve liked the place. It was warm and quiet inside, the booths made of oak stained dark. The glass candle holders at each table flickered red. Steve helped her off with the heavy coat and hung it on the coat tree by the door. She wore a charcoal gray wool skirt and jacket, and a pale gray blouse which left a V of white skin exposed in front. Steve hung up his own coat and watched her walk away. The skirt fell below her knees, a respectable length, but a slit in the back alternately revealed something of each thigh as she walked. She was slightly built, but her hips filled the skirt nicely. He thought of slipping off her shoes, then putting his hands under that skirt and pulling down her panty hose and panties. Her legs would be so long and white.

She slid into the booth, fussed briefly at her hair with her fingertips, then lay one hand over the other on the oak table. "God, it's been quite a day." She turned to the waiter. "I'd like a large Margarita, and this gentleman will have . . ." She glanced at Steve. Her eyes were gray, her eyebrows darker than her hair.

"I'll have the same."

"And bring us the fancy nacho plate, the big one with all the goodies on it." After the waiter was gone she said, "I'm starving to death."

"I'm pretty hungry myself." His eyes wandered about the room, which was nearly empty. She was so beautiful he found it better not to stare at her.

She rubbed her hands against each other. They were big, her fingers very long, the nails colored a bright red. "It's so nice and warm in here. So tell me about yourself, Steve. What do you do when you're not busy rescuing damsels in distress?"

"I'm a supervisor in Systems Development at Willamette Power."

"Ah, a rising young manager."

"Christ—I hope not."

She laughed. "It is a terrible rat race, isn't it?" She paused for an instant. "Married?"

He glanced down at the table. "Not any longer." He was glad he could finally keep his voice fairly neutral.

"You, too. Any kids?"

"No." He looked up at her. "And you?"

"No—thank God. Not that I wouldn't mind having children with the right person."

She ran the tip of her tongue along the rim of the glass. tasting the salt, then took a healthy swallow. "I work for a public relations firm, Hutchenson and Associates. Let me give you an official card." She fumbled around in the big purse until she found a wallet. "Here you go."

He glanced at it. "You're only a couple blocks from where I work."

The waiter set down an enormous plate of nachos covered with melted cheddar, diced peppers, salsa, and ground meat. Sarah used both hands to brush her hair back over her shoulders. Light brown, wavy along its entire length, it was obviously permed. A tiny diamond sparkled on each earlobe. She pulled off two nachos clumped together and ate them both, then licked her fingers. "Delicious, but I wasn't planning on devouring all of these. I need your help. Not that I'm not hungry enough to eat them all, but there's my figure to think about."

Steve smiled. "I'm hungry myself." The cheese was still hot, and the salsa was just spicy enough. "They do taste good." He started to cross his legs, winced, and thought better of it.

"What's the matter?"

"Matter? Oh, nothing. My leg's a little sore. It's decided running doesn't agree with it."

"Oh, do you run? I do five miles three or four times a week. It keeps me in shape for eating nachos."

He laughed. "It seems to agree with you. You look like you're in pretty good shape."

She chewed thoughtfully. "So do you." He met her gaze for a few seconds, then looked away. "I started running after my husband left. It's all that kept me together, I'm afraid."

Steve stared, drawn to her as much by the suggestion of vulnerability as by her beauty. "You took it pretty hard?"

"It's no fun losing someone you love to another person, even if your lover does turn out to be rather despicable."

"I know exactly what you mean. Exactly." He would never forget that night Brenda had told him about Tom. He couldn't believe her at first, couldn't imagine that she could do such a thing and deceive him for so long.

"Hey," she said.

His eyes came back into focus, and he realized she was squeezing his hand. She waited an instant, then let go. "You look like you're still grieving."

He licked his lips. "I suppose I am."

"Well, don't. I'm sure she's not worth it."

"Yeah." He grabbed more nachos. She was awfully nice for someone so beautiful. And she seemed interested—more than interested. God, it would be wonderful to make love to her. Maybe he could exorcise Brenda once and for all. He was certainly behaving like a zombie tonight. Women like her didn't come along very often. He took a big swallow of the Margarita. "How do you like working in the public relations business?"

Her eyes were playful. "It sucks." They both laughed. "But it pays well."

"Like the fast-paced world of data processing. Are you from around here, Sarah?"

41

"Yes, I'm a native webfoot. Born and raised in southeast Portland. I even like the rain."

He shook his head. "You do?"

"Yes. I think . . . there's something . . . fake about sunshine. Our summers are much more boring than our winters. I like gray days and mists and dark green forests and big ferns. I even kind of like slugs, and I like building a big fire in the fireplace on a wet, nasty day and watching the flames dance about while the rain splatters against the windows. Life is . . . rather desolate, after all, and there's something more truthful about gray misty days than the false cheerfulness of sunshine. I'd go crazy if I had to live somewhere like Hawaii." She drank Margarita, and Steve watched the muscles ripple along the white expanse of her throat.

"I never quite thought of it that way."

She laughed. "Don't mind me—I'm full of romantic nonsense. Now you tell me something about yourself. Tell me something secret, something no one at work knows about you." His smile slowly faded. She put her hand on his and squeezed. "Say it. Say it."

"I'm lonely. I'm very lonely." He laughed once. "I suppose that's not particularly odd, though."

She stared straight at him. "So am I. You don't know . . . what real loneliness can be until . . . We all live in our separate, isolated worlds, but the master I serve—I mean, the goals I follow—require so much from me. So much." She forced a smile, but there was a wariness, a vulnerability, which didn't fit so attractive and self-assured a woman. "I . . . let's just say I know what you mean. We could do something about that loneliness, you and I."

They stared at each other. Steve wished they were

alone somewhere. "Could we?" His voice sounded faintly hoarse.

She took his hand. "Yes. Oh, yes."

He put his other hand on top of hers. "You're very beautiful, you know. I . . ."

"You're very attractive yourself, especially your eyes, but there is one thing, one . . . problem."

He frowned, running his fingertips across her knuckles. "Problem?"

"I can't . . . I need help. I need help badly, Steve, and you have a right to know that from the start. I don't want to bother you with my troubles now—it can wait— but I . . . I do need your help."

"Is it your husband—your ex-husband?"

She shook her head. "No, it's nothing like that. There's no one else, I promise you. I'm a fool to bring it up now when we hardly know each other. You must think I'm crazy. Promise me—promise me you'll forget I said anything, that you won't ask me about the problem. When . . . when we know each other better I'll explain, but not now—not tonight. Promise me you won't ask me what I mean."

He kept stroking her knuckles with his fingertips. "Are you sure? You seem to want to talk about it."

She shook her head vigorously, her hair eclipsing the glistening diamonds in her ears. "No. Not now. Not tonight. Promise me."

He shrugged. "Okay. I promise."

She sighed and then laughed, regaining her composure. "You must be thinking you landed a real nut case tonight."

He shook his head. He hadn't let go of her hand. "I

wasn't thinking that at all. I was thinking . . . that my luck had finally changed."

She turned her hand and slid her fingertips up under his shirt cuff. "You're very sweet."

The waiter appeared, hovering at a discreet distance from the table. "Need refills on the Margaritas?"

"Yes." Sarah pushed her glass toward the edge of the table with her left hand.

"More nachos too?"

"Sure." Sarah nodded, then turned to Steve. "You'll help me eat them, won't you? We can work them off, I'm sure."

Steve said nothing. He rubbed his fingertips back and forth over Sarah's hand. The Margarita had loosened him up just enough. Even his knee felt better. This was like some dream come true, some crazy dream, and he was content to savor it rather than try to wake up. He liked just looking at her. He knew she wanted him, and he felt a kind of achy desire in his chest.

"Are you sure you don't think I'm some kind of weirdo?"

He shook his head. "No."

"This has been such a strange day that it had to get better. Maybe you took my coil wire. If you did, you can give it back to me now."

He laughed. "I didn't take it."

"I know." She stroked his palm with the tip of her forefinger. "How long have you been living alone?"

"A couple years."

"You don't like it, do you?"

"Not really. How about you?"

"Peter was such an asshole that it seems something of an improvement."

44

Steve stared at her. "Peter—Peter was his name? Peter what?"

"Russell."

He laughed. "I have an asshole named Peter who works for me, but he's married, come to think of it, to some long-suffering woman." He shook his head at the Margaritas the waiter set down. "Christ, those things are big. I haven't done any serious drinking in a long time."

"We'll have to savor these instead of bolting them down. Here's to mechanically apt supervisors who help out women in need." She raised her glass.

"Here's to women in need." They clinked glasses.

Steve sipped the Margarita, but his eyes stayed on her. They were still holding hands, and his tightened about hers. A faint flush showed on her cheeks. "You look rather . . . hungry, Steve. And not for nachos."

"It's that obvious?"

"Yes. I'm hungry too. Ravenous." The waiter put the platter of nachos on the table. She pulled one free. "We'd better eat these, though. Food is supposed to build strong healthy bodies, and this is my dinner."

"Mine too."

"I can see you need to develop better eating habits. I'll bet you skip breakfast."

He shook his head. "Wrong. I eat a bran muffin."

Her nose and upper lip moved upward. "Disgusting. I like big gooey sweet rolls with raisins and melted butter on them."

"I haven't had one of those in years."

"Well, we'll have to fix that. Why do you run except so you can eat all the wicked foods?" She licked at the salt on the edge of the glass, then took another sip. "How long have you lived in Portland?"

He told her about growing up in Colorado Springs where the weather was dry and sunny even for much of the winter and about coming to the University of Oregon, and then they talked about work, all the hassles of an eight-to-five job. As they talked, their hands stroked and touched one another. They moved about in the booth, shifting position, crossing or uncrossing their legs, but they kept a grip on each other.

They had finished the nachos and most of the Margaritas and the clock over the bar showed nine-fifty when the waiter appeared. "Steve Ryan?"

Steve frowned. "Yeah?"

"Phone call for you."

"Me?" He stared at Sarah. "That's impossible. No one knows I'm here."

The waiter shook his head. "Wrong. Somebody does. They described you and the lady to a T."

"But . . . I wonder if it's someone from work. Christ, I hope it's not a production problem."

"Phone's behind the bar."

"Okay, I'll get it." Steve gave her hand a final squeeze, then raised both his arms to stretch. "How could anybody . . . ?"

Sarah pushed her hair back over shoulders. "Ditch them. Tell them it's a family emergency." She put her big purse on the table. "It's late, and it's time to go home."

"Tired?" he asked.

She looked straight at him. "No. But I am ready for bed."

He licked his lips. He couldn't believe his luck could change so fast. "Yeah. I'll see who it is." He stood up, took a step, and winced at the pain in his left knee.

Her hand shot out and grasped his wrist. "Hurry, okay?" She stood. "I guess I need to use the bathroom." She held his hand on the way to the bar, gave it a final squeeze before walking away. He watched her hips move, and again the slit in her skirt bared the back of one leg, then the other.

Easing out his breath he stepped behind the counter and found the phone with the receiver beside it.

"Hello, this is Steve."

"Steve Ryan?"

He didn't recognize the woman's voice. "Yes."

"I called to warn you that the woman you're with may be dangerous. She was involved in the disappearance of a young man. He may have been . . . murdered."

"All right, who is this?"

"A . . . friend."

"You have a funny way of showing it—who is this? How can you . . . ? Do you think you can just tell me something like that over the phone and I'll believe you? I think you're a liar. What do you have against her?"

"I'm not lying!"

"Then tell me your name." He wanted to slam down the phone.

"All right, I will. This is Mary Connely, Alex's sister. You met me once at our house when you stayed for a few days with Alex."

Sadness settled about his heart, enfolding it. "Alex," he whispered. "Did you ever . . . ?"

"We never found him." He could hear the sorrow in her voice. "He was with her—with that woman who calls herself Sarah now—when he disappeared."

"That can't be true. It can't be."

"But it is—I'm certain."

He felt his eyes fill with tears. This didn't hurt so bad as with Brenda, but it was the same thing—betrayal. If it were true—*if*.

"Steve, are you still there?"

"Yeah, I'm still here."

"Listen, I know she's attractive and seems very nice, but don't trust her. I'm really afraid she may have killed Alex, and I don't want her to hurt anyone else. Are you listening?"

"Yeah." Sarah came out of the restroom and smiled at him. He smiled back, then turned away where she couldn't see his face. "You must be mistaken—she's someone else."

"No."

"I . . . I just don't believe you."

He heard her draw in her breath. "Steve, I am sorry, but I don't want anyone else to ever go through what my family went through. Do this much for me—don't go anywhere with her tonight. Just . . . stay away from her until we have a chance to talk. I can see you tomorrow. We've met, and I think you'll remember me. I won't be just a voice over the phone. That's not too much to ask, is it? Please."

"Okay."

Her sigh sounded ragged. "Thank God. Is the address for you in the phone book the right one?"

"Yes."

"Then I'll see you tomorrow afternoon. What time can I come over?"

"I'm home by five."

"All right." She hesitated. "I am sorry, Steve."

"Yeah."

"I'll see you tomorrow. Take care." She hung up.

He gripped the phone and fought to calm himself. "Thanks a lot," he whispered. At least this time things hadn't really gotten started. Could Sarah be such a monster—a murderer, even? Christ, that was impossible! But coil wires didn't just vanish, after all, and it made no sense to steal one. Who was setting up who? Maybe she'd removed it and then sat waiting for him. Fear suddenly thrust its cold fingers through his sadness.

He needed some story to tell her. Work—that was it. This was a call from work. He drew in his breath. Get yourself together—you've had to keep going when you hurt far worse than this.

At the other end of the bar the waiter ran up the tab while Sarah got her wallet out of her purse. She looked at Steve, and her smile vanished. The waiter counted aloud as he put green bills in her hand.

"Why don't you let me pay for it?" he asked.

Her gray eyes were fixed on him. "What's wrong? What's the matter?"

"Things . . . have kind of gone to hell at work, I'm afraid. The payroll run is printing goofy checks. I'll have to go in."

"Oh, no."

They stopped near the door, and he helped her on with her coat. "You should have let me pay for it."

"I said the drinks were on me, remember?"

The rain had stopped, but clouds of mist obscured the yellow streetlights. She slipped her hand about his arm just above the elbow. "You couldn't ditch them, huh?"

He forced a laugh. "Payroll's the one system you can't ignore. Everyone in the company gets mad if they don't get their check on time, especially the CEO."

"How did they know you were here?"

"I don't know. Maybe one of the operators stopped by for a quick one before work and saw us. The night shift starts at ten."

"I suppose I could take a cab home."

"Hell, no. I'll drop you off and come back. That's the least I can do."

She gave his arm a squeeze. "Thanks."

Whatever Mary Connely thought, he doubted Sarah would kill him in his own car. Christ, Alex had been going with that girl for a long time before he disappeared. He remembered suddenly that the sister had red hair. She had sat around drinking beer with them one night. The girl friend had been a blond. Tall and very attractive. Like Sarah. She had been out of town that time he had stayed with Alex. He swallowed, grateful for once for the mist and darkness around them.

"Steve . . . Are you okay?" She drew closer to him, her hand tightening on his arm.

"Sure, sure. Just wondering . . . which subroutine could have gone nutso—if I'm lucky and it's only one."

Maybe Mary was full of shit or badly deranged. Maybe her brother's death had driven her over the edge. He would just have to wait until tomorrow to see. And just how exactly had she known he was at Guido's with Sarah?

He always parked his Taurus near a light hoping to discourage car thieves. A big crow sat on the streetlight arm. He unlocked the door for Sarah, then closed it once she was inside. The parking lot was almost empty. He got in. The rain started again, the drips running down the windshield. The Taurus had a split bench seat in front, and Sarah slid over close to him. The green lights of the dash came on, and the car started right up.

"Where to?" he asked.

"I live over by Mount Tabor. Get on the Banfield and take the Fifty-eighth Street exit."

Once they were on the freeway her hand gently touched his knee. Her coat had opened up, and a half inch of her slip showed, a lacy white strip between the dark nylons and the wool skirt. Steve's mind paced restlessly round and round as he tried to figure things out, but there were no answers, only mysteries. He couldn't shake the feeling that the past was repeating itself, that he was being betrayed a second time.

"It's the gray house with the swing on the front porch."

The Taurus pulled into the narrow driveway. The house was a small, older one-story with a tiny garage, typical of the neighborhood. Behind it rose the dark shadow of Mount Tabor, firs hidden in blackness.

"We're practically neighbors," Steve said. "I only live half a mile or so away."

"That's convenient." She sighed, her hand closing about his knee. They listened to the wipers swish. "What is it, Steve?"

He hesitated, his mind going round and round again. "I . . . I'm just worried about this payroll thing. It may take all night to fix."

"Sounds awful. I wish . . . I wish you could come in for a minute."

"I do too." He didn't have to feign sadness.

"Some competition." She laughed. "A lousy computer program." Her voice had an ironic edge, and she slid away from him across the seat and seized the door handle.

He grabbed her other hand, and she turned, her beau-

51

tiful face staring at him in the dim light. "I'll . . . I'll make it up to you."

"Promise?"

"Christ, yes."

She slid closer, and they got their arms around each other. Sarah's tongue felt thin and agile as it rolled about his and probed deep in his mouth. Her lips were hot, her long fingers very strong. Steve opened his mouth wider and slipped his hand under her hair, grasping the nape of her neck.

Finally she drew away. They were both breathing hard. "Are you sure you wouldn't like to come?" He hesitated. "I don't bite, you know. Not unless that's what you like."

"I really need to get back. Can I . . . can I see you tomorrow?"

"If you don't get back here tonight, you'd damn well better show up tomorrow."

"Maybe we could meet for dinner?"

"Oh no, I won't risk having someone call you again. You come over here and don't tell anyone where you're going. I can cook, and to make doubly sure I'll leave the phone off the hook. Is six all right?"

"Seven might be better."

"Fine." She slid away from him and put her hand on the door handle. "You know, if you solve your problem early, you can always come back." Her voice had an ironic edge again, but he couldn't bear to look at her.

He squeezed her hand. "Yeah. I . . . it sounded serious."

"All right, then." She stroked his chin with her fingertips, then grabbed a lock of hair over his ear and pulled him toward her.

"Ow," he said, but then her mouth closed about his, and the pain vanished in a surge of longing.

She drew back, but her fingers were still in the hair at the side of his head. "I like men with long hair." She gave a final tug. "Good night." The door slammed shut behind her.

The porch light was on. She unlocked the door, smiled at him and raised her hand, then went inside. Steve hit the steering wheel with both hands. "Goddamnit!" He could still go in. He wanted to go in. Instead he put the car in reverse, backed up, and drove away.

Later, as he lay in bed, he thought over and over about getting up and going to her. The phone started ringing about eleven, but he didn't answer it. When he finally fell asleep around three, she was waiting for him, naked, in his dreams. They kissed and stroked one another, but he was never satisfied, and he knew, even in the dream, that she wasn't real.

Chapter 2

Mary hung up the phone. Her skin was naturally pale with a few freckles, but now her face was flushed. It was all so embarrassing. She wore no makeup, and her red hair hung halfway down her back. She put her hands in her parka pockets and walked from the phone booth back to her car.

The detective had called from Guido's. Mary had come over immediately, and the two women had sat in a dark corner. Mary never thought the man would be someone she knew. Anyone in the bar could see what was happening between Steve and Tracy. Mary drank her beer and left quickly, unable to bear watching. Memories of Alex and Tracy came rushing back, too vivid, things she thought she had forgotten.

Not that she could ever forget Tracy's face, even though her hair was colored and styled differently. Her height and that big curvy mouth couldn't be disguised. A month ago, when Mary saw her sitting in a car at an intersection downtown, she had immediately written down the license number and called the first woman private investigator listed in the yellow pages.

Mrs. Hughes had no trouble tracing the car. "Sarah Whitney" had registered it when she moved to Portland six months before. Her routine never changed: eight to ten hours at work, then various forms of exercise, mostly running and swimming. Mary's own life was monotonously regular—and celibate—except she disliked fitness exercise. "Sarah" apparently had no men in her life—until tonight. That was why Mary had rushed over to Guido's.

She closed the right car door, then slid across the seat and put the key in the ignition. (Ever since a minor accident a few months back, the left door wouldn't open.) The rain had intensified; all the water on the windshield blurred the outside world, hiding it. A man and woman sharing an umbrella walked by.

Mary rubbed at her eyes. Her hands felt trembly. This was the first time, except for the brief glance at the intersection, that she had seen Tracy again. Her brother's presence seemed to hover about the woman, as though he might materialize again, but Mary did not believe in ghosts. She knew Alex was dead. She had believed that all along. The police and even her parents thought the two of them had run away together, but she knew Alex better than that. Seeing Tracy alone reopened all the old wounds. Mary had loved Alex so much, and she still missed him. She missed her father too, but he'd been sixty, not twenty-one.

The same thing was happening to Steve. Men could behave so stupidly. They were such easy prey for women like Tracy. They sat there like great stunned fish as the net was drawn about them and they were hauled in. Women wouldn't fall so easily for a pretty face.

It had happened just as fast to Alex. He'd never had

a girlfriend in high school or the first couple of years in college, then suddenly he had appeared with Tracy hanging about him. Mary never much cared for her, but she had tried to like her for Alex's sake.

What would she tell Steve tomorrow? The whole thing was so embarrassing. She had only met him a couple of times: at that race where Alex won and Steve came in second, then again at the house. He probably wouldn't even recognize her. He certainly hadn't noticed her at the bar, but then that was the idea. He had been preoccupied, and she had sat with her parka hood pulled up, hiding her red hair. What was she supposed to do now—tell him never to let this incredibly beautiful woman near his bed? Maybe she had kept them apart for tonight—*maybe*—but Tracy, or Sarah, or whoever she was, had obviously had plenty of practice with men.

Mrs. Hughes said Tracy had sat in the car for an hour before Steve came along. Still, could Mary really prove anything? Even that Tracy and Sarah were the same person? This couldn't continue much longer. On a college instructor's salary, Mary didn't have the money to pay an investigator. She was halfway through her meager savings. She could go to the police, but they were notoriously overworked and undermanned. The last thing they would be interested in was a five-year-old missing person's case. Besides, they had been both worthless and insensitive the last time.

She turned the key. The engine whirred, and the old Ford coughed feebly and shook. "Don't do this—not now!" She decided to risk flooring the pedal, although that might flood the engine. It stammered, sputtered and finally caught. She was going to have to get a tune-up soon, and if she ever finished her dissertation, she was going to sign up for a car class at the community college.

If only her dad had spent some time teaching her about cars. He and Alex had spent hours in the garage, then they would come in, hands black with grease, and mess up the sink and several towels cleaning up. She laughed once, then the tears came.

"I miss you both," she whispered. "I miss you so much."

She drove home in the rain. Her two black cats, Cesare and Schedoni, were waiting by the door. She poured Friskies from the bag into their bowls, set a stack of freshmen themes on the kitchen table, and took two cartons of Chinese food out of the refrigerator. The kung pao chicken and sweet and sour pork had tasted better yesterday. Sharon's paper about her boyfriend was so painfully bad Mary slipped it to the bottom of the pile, then speared pieces of pineapple, green pepper, and pork on her fork. The sauce on the batter-thickened meat was an incandescent pinkish red.

Steve hadn't changed much. He was still darkly good-looking; he had a little less hair in front and dressed like a businessman, although the pink paisley tie was rather wild and his hair came down over his ears. He and Tracy made a rather stunning couple, the perfect yuppie pair. All they needed was a Volvo station wagon and a baby named Whitmore Hansen Ryan in a hundred-dollar stroller.

She laughed once, then thought, God, you do sound bitter.

After all that had happened, the themes were unbearable. The one-bedroom house was so small that it didn't lend itself to pacing. She peered out the front window, but it was pouring again. Walking alone in the neighborhood wasn't safe, but she did it sometimes anyway. Tonight it wouldn't be worth it. She smashed down the garbage, then put in the empty cartons. The fork joined its brethren and three days worth of dishes in the sink.

The work area for her dissertation, an old desk covered with books and papers, was next to her bed. She dropped her jeans on a pile of clothes by the desk, then pulled off the turtleneck, slipped the straps off her shoulders and turned the bra around so she could unfasten it. Goosebumps prickled her shoulders and arms. She covered her tiny breasts with her long slender fingers and wondered what it would be like to have breasts and hips like Tracy. She put on an old flannel nightgown faded to a color between pink and beige, then got into bed. As soon as she closed her eyes, the face appeared with its large sensuous mouth and the wavy, permed hair. Steve watched Tracy, his desire for her so obvious.

Mary opened her eyes, turned, and sat up. If only she could take a walk, but no, it had been raining forever, and women who walked alone were asking for trouble. Dear God, she thought, what am I supposed to do now? What does any of this mean?

She couldn't sleep for a long time, and the next morning the themes didn't read any better, and the tiny house was still a messy little prison. Going out to breakfast usually cheered her up, and after eating bacon, eggs, and hashbrowns, drinking two cups of coffee and reading the *Oregonian*, she did feel better. It lasted until she reached the parking lot at Maryglenn College by Riley Hall. Then she recalled abruptly that she was teaching four sessions of freshman composition in the second year of a fixed two-year contract at her old alma mater and being paid twenty thousand dollars a year. Her dissertation was half done at best, and even if she were finished, her prospects without a published book and several articles were very dim. And tonight she had to go see Steve Ryan and somehow persuade him that the voluptuous Sarah Whitney was a very bad business. Maybe her mother was right. Maybe she should perm her hair and find a nice Catholic professional man to take care of her.

Outside her office door waited a short version of Arnold Schwarzenegger dressed in black. He had a bristly crewcut, the hair forming a tiny wall above his broad forehead. His eyes were dark with a few lines under them, and he had a thin black mustache like the bad guy in an old movie. "Professor Connely?"

"I'm an instructor, not a professor, but you have the name right."

"Very well, Miss Connely. May I speak with you for a few minutes? It's an important business matter."

"It's not life insurance or Amway?"

"No."

"I suppose so, then." Father Tom Donaldson came wandering down the hallway in the usual yellow cardigan with his pottery coffee cup in hand. She nodded at him, then unlocked her door and gestured at the opening with her right hand.

The room was little bigger than a closet, and as low person on the totem pole, she didn't get a window. A massive old desk and two sturdy chairs of oak and leather took up most of the floor space, while the wall behind the desk was all bookcase. Mary's chair creaked as she sat. The man took off his black windbreaker, set his attaché case on his lap and popped the catches. His tight short-sleeved shirt showed off his biceps. His chest was nearly as thick from front to back as it was wide. Mary was not impressed. She didn't like flabby men, but the Mr. Universe types always struck her as grotesque. She preferred the leaner fitness of the triathloners like Alex. Or Steve.

"What is this about, anyway? I have a class in an hour and . . ."

"This won't take long." He glanced over his shoulder. "Could we close the door?"

Mary shook her head. "The door always stays open." His mouth drew into a disapproving line. "There's no one in the offices on either side of me right now. Keep your voice down, and no one will hear you."

"Very well. Here's my card." Eggshell colored, it said, Roland Smith, Private Investigator. He took a manila folder out of the attaché case, set it on the desk, then closed the case. "Miss Connely, what I'm going to tell you may seem unbelievable, but I hope you'll bear with me. My client, an elderly man in poor health, had one son. Over two years ago while away at college, his son became involved with a woman named Sharon Lawrence. Shortly afterwards, his son disappeared."

"Dear God," Mary whispered.

"This is a picture of my client's son and the woman." He took a five-by-seven photograph out of the folder.

Mary felt cold and, for the first time, truly afraid. "It's her—oh God, it's Tracy."

"Yes, Miss Connely. And now you understand why I'm here."

Mary swallowed once and nodded.

Smith leaned back in the chair and took a pack of

60

cigarettes out of his shirt pocket. "Do you mind if I smoke?"

"Yes."

Annoyed, he put the cigarettes back in his pocket. "Tell me, Miss Connely, have you ever had any dealings with the occult? No? Well, are you familiar with stories about various supernatural beings like werewolves, ghouls, vampires?"

"My dissertation is on the Gothic element in certain late Victorian novels, so yes, I know what you're talking about."

Smith stared at her. His eyes were strangely expressionless. "So you'd know the book *Dracula?*"

"Of course—but will you please get to the point."

"Okay, Miss Connely. I'll just let it fly. We believe my client's son and your brother were murdered by a vampire."

Mary pointed at the photograph. "You mean . . . ?"

Smith shook his head. "No, not her. If you know the stories you know vampires are immobile during the day."

"Yes. Then how . . . ?"

Smith took a smaller picture out of the folder, a reconstruction of an older photo, done in brownish sepia tones. Mary had seen enough Victorian daguerreotypes to date it to about 1860 by the dress with the high lace collar and double row of buttons. The woman's hair photographed white and was piled on top of the head. She had an aquiline nose, high cheekbones, a disdainful curve to the mouth, the lips pinched looking. Her eyes were large and gazed rather angrily at the camera.

"This is the vampire."

"A *woman?*"

"Yes."

"But you can't photograph a vampire. A lens won't capture their image anymore than a mirror would."

"Very good, Miss Connely. This photograph was taken some years before she became a vampire. Her name is Francoise de Rambouillet. She was well-known among Parisian literary circles during the eighteen sixties. She knew the poet Baudelaire."

"How could you possibly know all this?"

Smith sat back, pulled out his cigarettes, then put them back in his pocket. "My client is very wealthy. He's had a number of people working on this business for over two years. It took a lot of bucks to piece all of this together."

"But how does Tracy—or Sharon—fit with this?"

"She's the vampire's helper. She can be active during the day while the vampire has to stay in her coffin."

Mary pointed at the old photo again. "You mean she's *here*—somewhere close by?"

Smith nodded.

"Oh, God." Mary felt light headed, then she thought of something so horrible it made her stop breathing for a couple of seconds. "If this is true—if a vampire killed them—they would become vampires too."

"Yeah, but . . . We don't think that's what happened. We think they were murdered first, then drained of their blood. It's only if the vampire sucks it out of you while you're still alive that you become a vampire."

Mary laughed. "All right, if this is your idea of a joke, I'm not amused. You've scared me half to death, so you can just stop now and tell me who put you up to this." Her voice was shaky.

"Sorry, this is no joke. No joke at all." Smith's face

was an unfeeling blank. He hardly looked the type to be involved in so grotesque a ruse. "I have another picture in here, but I don't think I'll show it to you. It's my client's son. They found him a couple months after he disappeared. The body had decomposed, but you can still see his throat was cut."

Mary opened her mouth, but nothing came out. She had spent a lot of time wondering about Alex. Sometimes she tried to imagine him alive and happy, but more often she thought about how he might have died and she hoped he hadn't suffered. The image of a knife cutting open his throat and the red blood spurting out was so vivid that the fear seemed to paralyze her chest. She shook her head, aware of the tears running down her cheeks.

"I'm sorry," Smith said grimly.

"Close the door," she managed to say. While he was shutting it, she got Kleenex out of her purse and wiped her eyes. "How do I know you're telling the truth? How do I know you're not making this all up?"

Smith sat down and tapped his knee with the pack of cigarettes. As he drew in his breath, his massive chest swelled. "You can see for yourself. My client is old and sick, but he wants his revenge. He's hired me to take care of this vampire, to keep it from ever hurting anyone again."

"How?"

Smith stopped tapping at his knee. Something related to a smile pulled at his mouth. "The old fashioned way, like in the movies—the stake through the heart."

"You're crazy!" Mary realized she had stood up.

Smith shook his head. "Uh, uh." He watched her as she slowly sank back down in the chair. "If you've read

63

Dracula, you know how it's got to be done. And you understand, of course, why we can't involve the police."

Mary shook her head. "I don't believe you—I don't believe any of this."

"Oh, you believe me. Like I said, my client's old and sick, but he thought you might like to come along."

"What?"

"For revenge. My client would like to drive the stake into this thing's heart himself, but he can hardly move anymore. He thought you might feel the same way. About vengeance."

Mary was silent for a moment. Her hands felt icy. She stared at the two photographs on her desk. The older one was like something from a history book, but the other one was all too real. She could see that same face watching Alex playfully as she slipped an arm about him, and she could see her smile at Steve Ryan as her hand closed about his. The loathing she felt twisted at her insides. She could drive a stake through Tracy's heart—she could do it gladly.

She pointed at Tracy. "What about her?"

Smith folded his brawny arms across his chest. The thin black hairs stood out against his white skin. "Destroy the master, and the slaves fall too. We think we can make a pretty good case against her in court, but we need to finish off the vampire first."

Mary stared at the old photo.

"Like I said, my client's had plenty of first-rate people working on this. We know exactly where she's hiding out. Ever heard of the Baumgartner mansion?"

"The one near Mount Hood?"

"Yeah. Looks something like a castle." Smith took another photo out. "It was built during the thirties, just after Timberline Lodge. Baumgartner liked the idea of an alpine castle, and he used the same stonecutters and artisans. We've got copies of the original plans. There's a secret passageway built into the castle and a hidden room at the top of this tower. We think that's where she'll be. She bought the place about eight years ago, paid cash for it. Going by the name of Madame Michelle Lombarde."

"So you're going there. To kill her."

Smith nodded. "Yep. Should be easy as long as we do our thing during the daylight. She doesn't suspect a thing, and she'll be helpless. Want to come along?" He grinned. "I could use some company."

"You're out of your mind."

"Come on, you know better than that. Are you coming or not?"

Mary stared at Tracy's face, then at the young man's. He looked even younger than Alex. "What was his name?"

"Uh . . ." Smith scratched at his chin. "Chris, I think."

Mary tapped at the table with the fingers of her right hand, her teeth clenched. "All right," she said. "I'll come."

Smith laughed. "Great—we leave tomorrow morning. I'll pick you up at nine. Where do you live?"

Mary shook her head. "No, I'll meet you. You tell me the time and place."

Smith frowned. "Okay. My office address is on the card. Be there at nine. I've got a four-wheel-drive Cherokee we can take." He reached for the photos.

"Could you—could you leave the pictures? The one of the . . . woman and the two of them."

He shrugged. "Sure. I've got extras." The fasteners on

65

his attaché case snapped shut noisily, and he stood up. "Very well, Miss Connely. I'll see you at nine tomorrow. Please be on time."

She was staring at the French woman's face. "Sure." She wiped at her eyes. "Close the door behind you, please." She didn't look at him.

"Miss Connely, believe me, I am very sorry about your brother." He said it with the gravity of an undertaker.

"Sure."

She heard him hesitate, then he closed the door. She raised her head and caught her lower lip between her teeth. The tears were running down her cheeks again. "Oh, Alex," she whispered. She wiped at her eyes, then put on her parka and took the photos. She took a deep breath.

The departmental secretary's desk was at the end of the hall. "Margaret, would you let my classes know I won't be in today? I don't feel very well. I'm going home."

The old woman looked concerned. She was one of the three people in Riley Hall whom Mary genuinely liked. "I'll do that. Is there anything else I can do?"

Unwilling to trust her voice, Mary shook her head. Once she was in the car she began to cry again.

She dipped her fingertips into the holy water, crossed herself, and walked down the center aisle between the rows of pews. The gray light outside left the church interior dim, and the blues, greens, reds, and yellows of the stained glass windows were subdued. Various saints, apostles, and Christ himself stood with conventionally

66

rapt expressions on their faces, circular halos of lead and clear glass framing their heads, while baroque-looking angels—plump cherubim or androgynous warrior archangels—watched reverently. In the eve the votive flame flickered under red glass.

When things were bothering her, she liked to come here. Even if it was only a second-rate imitation of a medieval cathedral, it was not a shopping mall, an office building, a school, or a doctor's office. The church was designed to calm the spirit, not to coerce or stimulate, and it did offer a kind of sanctuary. Today she remembered that demons and evil spirits could not cross its threshold.

She sat down and prayed briefly. Her parka unzipped, hands folded on her lap, she tried to meditate, but she was so tired she dozed instead. The big wooden doors at the back opened, and a raucous laugh echoed briefly through the church.

She stretched, and her long fingers gripped at her knees. As a child she had briefly feared demons. An old nun had told them if you dug down ten or twenty feet, you would reach the fire, the devils, and the damned of Hell. When she was a teenager she had made the mistake of letting her friends talk her into renting *The Exorcist*. The film had upset her, and she worried about it for a long time afterwards. Sister Margaret, one of the younger nuns at their high school, knew they were troubled, and she gave them a talking to, telling them that the movie moguls were trying to make money by playing on people's worst fears. The nature of the devil, of evil, was a mystery, but the Catholic faith was meant to be an affirmation of God and life, not a refuge from the devil. "Worry about evil men, not evil spirits," she had said, her dark eyes smoldering. "No devil can ever take away your free will or force you to do evil. Remember that God loves you, and that love is the most powerful force in the universe. It will endure long after everything else turns to dust."

Mary smiled. Sister Margaret's talk had certainly made her feel better, but what, really, had she known of evil then? It was only after Alex vanished that she began to wonder if God made sense. She had grieved for a long time, but finally she had decided that God could not be blamed for what Tracy did. Tracy was a person, and she was behind whatever had happened, not God. But then her father had dropped dead, and there was no one to blame, no one at all.

Her eyes were getting teary again. She had finally decided that you couldn't rationally figure out life, or God, or anything important. You believed or you didn't believe. And human love—her love for Alex and for her father—helped you believe.

So she had made it through her crises, but the boring, uninspired life she led was wearing her down. Literature and ideas had once been vital and alive, but now she was sick to death of them. Her relationships with her colleagues and her students were awful. She felt a few hundred years older than the eighteen-year-old freshmen girls, not a mere ten, and the faculty were all middle-aged and complacent in their mediocrity. Some had houses and families to occupy them, while the comfortably celibate priests were interested in nothing at all. Her only friend was Cathy Moore, a forty-eight-year-old nun who taught at Riley. Oh, and there was Fred, of course, but he was more of a spiritual advisor and surrogate father than a friend. There had been no men since

68

David, and that had ended a couple of years ago when she left Seattle.

Maybe she *should* get her hair cut and permed. She smiled, then remembered what had brought her here. There had to be some simpler explanation than vampires—that was craziness. All she needed to do to-night was tell Steve that Tracy was in league with Drac-ula's daughter.

She crossed her legs, tapped nervously at her thighs, then realized she hadn't had any exercise in days. No wonder she felt restless. The cathedral might calm the troubled spirit, but not the fidgety body which had been sitting idle after gorging on Chinese food. She hated ex-ercise for exercise's sake, the cult of running or laboring indoors over various fiendish machines, but she liked to walk or hike.

She drove to Mount Tabor and parked near the en-trance to the park. On clear summer weekends, the stal-wart youth of Portland claimed the parking lot at the top with their cars and blaring radios. School and rain kept them away today. The road curved about through the tall firs and passed an old reservoir which still held city drinking water, but she took a small path into the trees.

The rain had stopped, and a foggy haze still hung over everything. "Mount" Tabor was really a glorified hill right in the city, but it was quiet among the trees. You could imagine you were in a real forest until you saw the strip of road through the trunks or until you came to some moss-covered concrete steps set into the hillside. The walk to the top took half an hour and was steep going in parts.

Mary could tell she was out of shape. She stopped to catch her breath. The temperature was in the forties, but it was so damp she could still see the white mist of her breath. The bark chips on the trail were reddish brown and shined from the moisture. The leaves of a tall rhododendron were a dark glossy green, the plant heavy with swollen buds waiting for spring. She would have to come back when the flowers were in bloom. Her favorite time of year was the spring, especially those days when the sun moved in and out of the clouds. The yellow light would flood the pink blossoms and green leaves, the whole landscape suddenly luminescent.

She glanced at her feet, then started and stepped back. The yellow-brown form resembled a turd, but it contracted slightly as it moved forward. She made a kind of disdainful snort, then eased out her breath. "It's only a slug." You would think after all her years in the northwest she wouldn't find them so repulsive. She was glad she hadn't stepped on it.

She continued on, but with a wary eye on the path. The sound—intermittent, a mingling of sharp staccatos—grew louder as she rounded a turn, and she realized she had been hearing it for quite a while. A kind of murmur of wings moving, birds chattering, of general confusion, somewhere to the right. She had to leave the trail to search for the source. The sound gradually turned into a chorus of caws, and then up the hillside she saw the black shapes flitting about the dark green boughs of a giant fir. Some swooped about while others sat in the tree, but all shared in the general agitation.

Why would crows all gather together? Crows were carrion eaters. . . . The fear was so abrupt that the suddenness amplified it—sent it coursing through her body like an electric shock. Maybe taking this lonely path

70

hadn't been such a good idea. Something under that tree might have drawn the birds—something dead, rotting.

She forced herself to walk forward. Crows were so very black—their beaks, bodies, eyes, feet. As if they had been crafted out of the elemental darkness itself, a living metaphor for something. Perhaps for evil—for spirits and forces which did exist, the black things always there at the edge of your vision. Most of the time they remained hidden, but great nests of them existed, gatherings of evil where all the foul dark things came together and celebrated their power or chose their victims. Then the darkness would go forth and swallow up the hearts of men and women, and the people would torture and kill and do unspeakably cruel acts for their hidden masters. It had happened all throughout history. The evil truly swallowed them up, for they lost their humanity, their very souls. They were capable of any evil, any act, any . . .

Nothing—there was nothing under the tree—she was sure of it, but her fear would not go away. They were out there right now, the dark things which had destroyed Alex, the dark things which Tracy served. And now they were coming into her life—they were showing themselves again—they were hidden no more. She was caught up with these things, bound to them.

With a loud cry, a crow swooped down at her, its wings a dark blur of motion. She saw the shining black, malevolent eye and the beak. She turned and ran down the hill, her hiking boots sinking into the soft earth, the tree trunks and evergreen shrubs jouncing by.

When she came out of the trees and back onto the paved road, she slowed to a walk. She couldn't shake the fear, the sense of evil closing in on her. For once she

71

was glad to see her ugly old Ford. She took out her keys and got inside. Her hands trembled, and her breathing wouldn't slow down. All day she had tried to convince herself that Smith's story was preposterous, and she had almost succeeded. But not now. Just as she had always known Alex was dead, so now she knew about this. She didn't think, though, that Smith really understood what he was up against. She looked back at the park, but white mist hid the mountain top and the fir tree with the crows.

She stared through the windshield at Steve Ryan's house, then glanced briefly at her eyes in the rearview mirror. It was too dark to tell if they were red, but she must look awful. She had considered putting on rouge and lipstick but decided she was too old for that nonsense. She was also too old to feel this nervous. If she had a better idea what she was going to say, it wouldn't be so bad. Say anything, but don't, for God's sake, don't mention vampires.

She slid across the seat, opened the door, and got out. Five fifteen, and it was already getting dark. Soon the vampires could come out. A smile pulled at her lips, brief and mirthless. The porch light was on, the doorbell a tiny, yellow-orange circle of light. She pressed it, then put her hands in her pockets and wished again that the whole thing were over with.

He opened the door. "Hi. Come in."

He seemed bigger close up. "Thanks." She followed him, hands still in her pockets.

The living room looked like something you would see in an interior decorating magazine: thin oak strips, oiled

72

and unmarred, bordering an enormous oriental rug, the design intricate and multicolored; a dark leather sofa and a pale blue chair; white walls so clean and bright they almost hurt her eyes; real art on the walls, posters of a Renoir and of Ansel Adam's snowy Yosemite scene; a fireplace with the wrought-iron grate; and of course, an oak cabinet filled with fiendishly complicated looking stereo equipment, black-faced with quivering blue lights and bars, so many pieces she couldn't imagine what they were all for. Mozart was playing. He had to have a maid—there was no way he could keep it so spotless otherwise.

"Can I take your coat?" His face was calm, ordered, but not his eyes.

"Uh, no—I mean, I probably won't be here that long."

He gestured toward the sofa. "Have a seat. How about . . . would you like something to drink?"

"Uh . . . oh God, yes."

His smile went real for the first time. Straight black hair went halfway down his ears, and his sideburns curled down below the lobes. His forehead was broad and high, his hair beginning to recede on either side. His eyes had a faint slant; the pupils were brown. The black mustache was thick, with one or two gray hairs, and trimmed in a geometrically precise, straight line. His appearance and his clothes—dark blue wool trousers, a pale blue oxford cloth shirt with button-down collar, a red and blue striped tie—unsettled her. She could not remember the last time she had met anyone informally who dressed this way. Her acquaintances, male and female, all wore jeans or baggy cotton trousers. His clothes and his culture were alien, but forgetting the clothes, he was attractive enough, the kind of man she fantasized about in her weaker moments.

"I have wine or beer, or the makings of a mixed drink."

"Beer would be wonderful."

"Henry's dark or Budweiser?"

"The Henry's must be in the bottle, right? That's exactly what I want, and you don't need to bother with a glass."

He nodded, then left the room. He was in his stocking feet and walked with a slight limp. Why, she wondered, couldn't she learn to drink beer out of a glass like women were supposed to? And why couldn't she stop behaving like she was about fifteen? Men like him were never interested in women like her. That was the way the world worked. They had women like Tracy. She bit at her lip, tears filling her eyes. Fine—go hysterical again, that's all you need. She stared down at the carpet, following the pattern of red and navy on beige. Two brown wingtips sat, side by side, exactly parallel to the end of the couch, their pocked toes glistening faintly.

"Here you are."

"Thanks."

He sat down on the blue chair, crossed his legs and sipped at a glass of blush wine. Mary held the beer bottle against her stomach. With her old jeans, her low cut hiking shoes, her worn and soiled parka, and this beer bottle, she felt out of place.

"I remember you liking beer. You stayed up one night with Alex and me and nearly drank us both under the table."

She smiled. "I don't remember it quite that way."

"Did you ever get your Ph.D? English, wasn't it?"

"You've got quite a memory. No, but almost. My classwork and comps are finished, but my dissertation is going slowly. I'm teaching at Maryglenn. Did you . . . ? You were going to work for the power company."

"Yes. I'm still there. Unfortunately."

"I saw your picture in the paper last year when you won the Rainbow Triathlon."

"If you keep at it long enough, you get lucky eventually. That was how Alex and I met, you know. We kept running into each other—uh, sorry, that wasn't planned as a pun. You and your dad played poker with us another night."

She laughed. "You do remember everything. I'd forgotten that. Who won?"

"You did. You were one of the coolest poker players I've ever seen. It . . . it seems like such a long, long time ago."

"Yes, it does."

"I—I've been married and divorced since then."

She stared at him. "Oh. I didn't know." She never knew what to say. She shouldn't have been surprised. Men like him didn't stay single. The woman would have been beautiful, intelligent, and fit. Still, it hadn't worked, and he felt badly about it.

"How are your parents?"

"Mom's fine. I guess you wouldn't have heard about my Dad. He's been dead now for over four years, the summer after Alex."

He shook his head. "No, I hadn't heard. I'm sorry to hear it. I liked your father."

She shrugged. "It's been a long time now, but I still miss him. Alex, too."

"It must have been very hard for you."

She nodded, aware that she was near tears again. What was the matter with her? She wasn't the weepy type. She hadn't thought he'd be friendly, but that made it almost worse. She had to get the hard part over with. She took a quick swallow of beer, then set the bottle on the end table.

"There's a caster there," he said apologetically. "The wood stains easily."

She put the bottle on the cork circle, then picked up the manila envelope by her purse. "Thank you for letting me come over. Take a look at these two pictures." She gave him a snapshot of Tracy and Alex and the bigger photo of Tracy and Chris.

For a moment he seemed puzzled, as if he had forgotten Tracy, then he took the pictures and stared at them for a long time. He raised his eyes, but they were focused off into space. His face was pale, and he looked confused.

She took another drink of beer, then stared down at the bottle. Finally she said, "Well?"

"The resemblance is very close."

"Resemblance? You think that's all it is?"

"I don't know. She's blond in both these pictures with long hair, and . . . Sarah looked different, somehow. I suppose some time has gone by and . . . It may very well be the same person." He took a big swallow of wine, then tapped at the chair arm with his other hand. "You've never heard anything of Alex since . . . ?"

She shook her head. "Never. I think he's dead. I've thought so from the first. I think she killed him."

"Why? What possible motive would she have? Is she crazy?"

Mary shook her head.

76

"Then *why?*"

Mary opened her mouth, but nothing came out.

"And who's this other person in the picture?"

"His name was Chris, and they did find his body."

"How did you find out all of this?"

"A private investigator showed up at my office today and gave me the other picture. His name is Roland Smith, and he's licensed. I had him checked out."

"You hired a detective?" He sounded faintly disgusted.

"*Yes*—but not him. I hired a different one—a woman. My brother had disappeared, and then I saw the woman he had last been seen with, the woman he was supposed to have run away with. What else could I do?"

"And what did your private investigator find out about Sarah? She told me she works for a PR firm. They're in the phone book, and I called them today. They told me she was out sick. Has your investigator found out anything which would indicate she's dangerous or a criminal?"

"No. Not really."

"Have you told the police about your suspicions? Well, isn't it about time? Maybe they could get to the bottom of this."

She looked up and shook her head. "No—the police have to stay out of it."

His fingers kept tapping at his knee. He took a sip of wine and looked straight at her. "Mary, you need to tell me what's going on."

"I . . . I can't."

"Why not?"

She took a big swallow of beer but didn't notice the taste. "You would think I'm crazy."

The pockets under his eyes were dark, but she couldn't tell if it was only shadows or if it was from weariness. His eyes showed something of the powerful, contradictory feelings inside him. "I want to know."

"We think . . ." She laughed once. "I haven't even told you, and already it seems ridiculous. Look—here's Smith's card and . . ." She gave him the business card and the daguerreotype.

"Who the hell is this?"

"Smith says Tracy's in it with her, that they're allies."

"But this looks like it was taken a long time ago, or is this one of those dress-up photos?"

She shook her head. "No, it's from the 1860s."

"Christ! What are you talking about—what kind of nonsense is this?" His anger was out in the open now.

"I knew you wouldn't believe me, and I don't know if I believe it myself, but I'm certain Tracy is dangerous—very dangerous. She'll hurt you."

"You know that from a hundred-year-old photograph?"

"I know it from watching the two of you together. You look at her the same way Alex did, exactly the same. Don't those two pictures mean anything to you?"

He finished his wine, started to cross his legs, then winced.

"What's the matter?" she asked.

"Nothing. My leg is sore. You have no proof, you know that, don't you? Alex could be alive somewhere, and this other guy could be, too. And there's no real proof either that Sarah is Tracy."

"I know she's evil. I can see it. I can feel it. And do you think the way you met was just a lucky coincidence? Mrs. Hughes watched her waiting in her car for over an hour. Lots of people went by, but it was you she was waiting for."

That shook him. "Who's Mrs. Hughes?"

"The investigator, the woman I hired."

Steve moved about within the chair as if it were upholstered in nails. "I . . . and there's this photograph. Sarah's ally is well over a hundred years old, a hundred and fifty years old. What is she? A witch?"

Mary wouldn't look at him. "Not exactly."

A sharp laugh burst from him. "What does that mean? Am I getting warmer?"

Her face was hot, and she could feel the tears dribble weakly down her cheeks. She put the beer bottle on the caster and stood up. "I'd better go, I . . ." She didn't want him to see her cry.

He started toward her. "I'm sorry, I . . . I'm very tired, and I don't feel very well. I know you want to help, but . . ."

"I mean well enough, but I'm crazy, right?" She laughed once, then turned away. "I'd better go. Do what you want."

He slipped his hand about her arm. "Oh, sit down for a moment. Finish your beer. I'm sorry. I don't know what to think anymore. Believe me, I've been suckered by a woman before. I hate to think I'm stupid enough to let it happen again, but I probably am that stupid. Please sit down."

The tone of his voice and the gentleness of his touch held her more than the words. She sank onto the couch, took Kleenex out of her purse and dabbed at her eyes. "I'm tired myself. And I never cry like this."

"Kind of macho, aren't you?"

She shrugged. "I suppose so."

79

They were both quiet. He was back in the chair staring at the three pictures on the coffee table. Finally he handed back the two photos of Tracy. He nodded at the daguerreotype. "Could I . . . borrow this?"

"Showing it to Tracy would be both dangerous and stupid."

"I wouldn't do that."

They stared at each other. "Give me the picture," she said.

He stroked at his chin, his right foot bobbing up and down, then handed her the picture. "You really think that woman might be involved, her ghost or spirit?"

"Steve, I don't know exactly what to believe, but there is something sad and evil and mysterious in all this. Before today I didn't believe in ghosts or devils or evil spirits, but now I think I do. And I'm going to find out for sure."

A certain wariness crept back into his eyes. "What do you mean? Are you going to confront Sarah?"

"No." She pointed at the daguerreotype. *"Her.* Smith says he knows where she is, and he's going there."

"What the hell for?"

"To . . . to destroy her."

"Destroy her? Then she's still alive?"

"Not exactly."

Steve laughed. "All right, here we go again—I give up, what is she? Not exactly alive and not exactly a ghost, or a witch, or . . . I know—a *vampire."* He started to laugh again, but stopped when he saw the look on her face. She had been fiddling with the beer bottle and nearly dropped it. "Smith told you she's a vampire—and he's going to destroy her? Is Sarah supposed to be a vampire too?"

80

Mary shook her head.

"No, of course not—she's been up and around during the day. Sarah must just work for the vampire. Christ, Mary—Smith told you a story like that, and you actually believed him?"

Mary finished the last of the beer. "I told you I didn't know what to believe. I need to go now. Whether you believe it or not, be careful. I guess that's all I can ask of you."

Steve followed her to the door. "But you're going with him on this vampire hunting expedition?"

"It should settle things, one way or another."

"And when are you leaving?"

"Tomorrow morning."

"Tomorrow! You're joking. You're going somewhere with Smith to destroy a vampire tomorrow?"

"Yes."

"Have you thought . . . ? He may be crazy—he must be crazy. He's up to something."

"Mrs. Hughes said he's licensed, and he seemed quite sane. It's a chance I'll have to take."

"You can't go alone."

"Can't I?"

He shook his head. "And you think *I* won't listen to a warning? Sarah hasn't told me any crazy stories."

"I'd better go." She put her hand on the doorknob.

"Let me come with you."

Her hand went limp, slipped off the doorknob. "What?"

"You heard me. I'll come too."

She turned to face him. "I don't need anyone to take care of me, Steve. I'm a big girl now."

"Don't be an idiot." He bit at his lip. "I didn't mean

81

that. Listen, I'd like some answers, and so would you. Maybe we can get to the bottom of this. And it is only reasonable. Going off alone with a total stranger . . . At least you know me well enough to know I'm not some deranged sex maniac or anything. I *hope* you know me that well."

She laughed once. She had a sudden urge to hug him. It was so out of character, yet so insistent, it startled her. "I know that. All right, I would be glad to have someone else come along. Smith wants us at his office at nine o'clock."

"Let me copy the address." He took a pen out of his shirt pocket, a business card from his wallet, and jotted down Smith's address on the back of his card. "All right, I'll meet you there at nine."

She gave a weary sigh. "Thank you, Steve. Be careful, okay? Please." His eyes seemed almost feverish, and she wondered if he really was ill. She went through the door and headed for her car. The cold rain felt good on her face.

"At least that's over," she whispered, as she slid across the length of the car seat. Steve stood in the doorway, watching her. She wondered if he was seeing Tracy tonight and if he would show up in the morning. As she drove away, he raised one hand in a parting gesture.

Chapter 3

". . . Be careful, okay? Please."

She wasn't very big. Her hand hovered in the air before him, hesitant, poised, the fingers long and thin, the nails trimmed close.

She wore no makeup, and she looked tired. Three creases ran across her forehead in what he could already tell was a characteristic frown of concentration. A leather clasp held her red hair together in back. Her ears were long and white, the two tiny gold spheres centered in the lobes the only sign of personal ornamentation. Her clothes—navy parka, faded jeans, and scuffed hiking boots, gray turtleneck—were worn, colorless and totally lacking in style.

Her hand dropped, and he found himself looking away to avoid her gaze. Maybe he should stay home tonight. She turned and walked swiftly to her car. Her parka hid her hips, but he'd noticed she was slender, without much of a figure. He wondered if makeup and the right clothes would help, or if she would still be rather plain-looking. Probably not—only in the movies did women let down their hair, take off their glasses, and become gorgeous.

A passing car's tires hissed along the wet street, and the faint caw of a crow sounded somewhere in the distance. Why was she getting in on the right side of the car? The door must be broken. The engine sounded awful, probably needed new points and plugs. He raised his hand and forced a smile. She must be pretty dedicated to live the way she did. Obviously they didn't pay her anything.

When she was gone his smile faded away. Who the hell was he to be judging other people? Mary was intelligent with plenty of personality, and he remembered her being very funny. He had found her interesting at the time, but just not attractive enough. How different his life would be if he had gone after her instead of Brenda. Mary would never willfully deceive him the way Brenda had—he was certain of that. But Sarah . . . He had liked Mary back when he first met her—he liked her now—but because she didn't resemble a fashion model she was ineligible. Christ, he was stupid! Right now he could use a friend like her, just a friend.

He went back into the house and dialed the number on his card.

"Roland Smith Investigative Agency," said a woman's voice.

"Uh, does Mr. Smith do . . . divorce work?"

"This is just his answering service, but yes, I'm certain he does."

"I need to see him right away. Is he free tomorrow?"

"No, I'm afraid he'll be out of the office all day, but he could probably see you Thursday. I have his schedule, but you need to call during regular business hours to make an appointment."

"Is Mr. Smith licensed?"

"Oh, absolutely."

"Thank you."

He set down the receiver. Well, she wasn't completely crazy, anyway. He glanced at his watch. Sarah wasn't expecting him for another half hour. He poured himself a second glass of wine and sat on the sofa.

God, what a fucking awful mess. He took a big swallow of wine. Mary obviously meant well, but maybe this thing with her brother had driven her over the edge. What about those photos, though? Damnit, he wished she'd left them. He just couldn't be sure it was Sarah. And that old one . . . Good Christ, vampires! Someone was dingy as hell, either Mary or this Smith character. Why would he tell her something like that and scare her to death? It didn't make sense—none of this made sense.

He closed his eyes, conscious that his head hurt. And why had Sarah been waiting for him? Mary might be obsessed with Alex's death, and Sarah might just look like Tracy, and Smith might have wacko motives for inventing this vampire, but why was Sarah sitting there waiting for him? No one would steal just a coil wire— that was stupid. Sarah had been waiting for him, that much was true.

Maybe she was horny and that was how she picked up men. That made at least as much sense as her being in league with a vampire. He wished he had stayed out of this thing with Mary and Smith tomorrow. If Smith was up to something nasty, Steve was hardly the brave and cunning type to save the day. Why had he opened his big mouth and dealt himself into this stupid game? He would have to call in sick at work or make up some other excuse. Maybe his mere presence would keep Smith from trying anything.

He started to cross his legs and winced at the pain in his left knee. Time for more aspirin. He finished the wine, lay back and closed his eyes. He must be coming down with something. His joints ached, and he felt so tired. No wonder; he'd had three or four hours of sleep last night. Sarah's car was still parked on Second this morning, but by afternoon it was gone. He wondered if she really was sick or if she wanted the day off. Maybe she felt confused—like him.

Well, he would go to dinner and keep his eyes and ears open, but there were too many mysteries to know what to make of Sarah. If he didn't go, she would probably give up on him for good. She seemed nice enough, and that kiss she'd given him . . . Her body would be beautiful, so beautiful. He thought of pushing up that charcoal gray skirt and kissing the insides of her thighs.

It had been far too long, and he wasn't going to write her off yet. Mary had always struck him as solid and straightforward, but he hadn't seen her for four or five years. She was obviously upset. Maybe this was her way of meeting men. Sarah took coil wires, and Mary called you in a bar to warn you your life was in danger. He laughed. Unlike Mary, Sarah would never have to work at getting men.

He looked at his watch, then got up. His knee felt very stiff, and his right shoulder ached at the top of the deltoid. He wondered how he would ever do another triathlon when, more and more, just moving around hurt.

Oh, take some aspirin and quit whining.

By 6:30 he was walking up to Sarah's front door. A yellow light was on behind the white curtain in the front window. He rang the doorbell, then put his hands in his trenchcoat pocket and shivered. During the day it had grown much colder, and the weatherman was warning about freezing rain later tonight. His breath made a frosty white cloud illuminated by the porch light.

He rang the doorbell again, then tried knocking, then tried both knocking and yelling. Nothing. The door locked, the knob wouldn't move. "Shit," he muttered wearily. The sadness caught at his throat, and he thought again of betrayals. He shivered and wished he had worn his heavy wool overcoat.

Back in the car he asked himself how long he should wait for her. Maybe she got hung up at the grocery store. Maybe she was out picking up some other guy—sitting somewhere in her car with the coil wire in her pocket.

"Goddamnit," he whispered. "Don't take everything so personally."

If Mary hadn't meddled he might at least have had one night with Sarah, and that was better than masturbating over magazines like a high school kid. He started the car, then wrenched the stick into gear. Nothing had moved behind the white curtain. He nearly drove away, but then with a sigh he put the car in neutral and stepped on the parking brake. Small slips of paper and a pencil were in the glove compartment. He hesitated, then wrote:

Sarah, where were you? I'm starving to death! Please call me at 555-4685. I promise no one will bother us.

87

He signed it, then strode back to the house, opened the storm door and closed it on the note at eye level. She could hardly miss it there. Across the street a leafless tree rose over a small house, the branches and stems forming a black pattern against the gray-white sky. A dark shape hung at the end of one branch.

As he drove away he considered going swimming—a mile of laps never failed to relax him—but decided she might still call, and he did feel lousy. When he got home he went straight to the sofa. After collapsing, he whispered, "Here we are again." Maybe he should get a cat or dog, anything to make some noise and break the monotony. That would be cheaper than seeing a shrink. Things must be pretty bad for him to feel so down when he hardly knew the woman. He could try the bar scene again, but it made him feel so sleazy.

He turned on the TV, but he kept thinking about Mary and Sarah. An hour later he got up and fixed himself a sandwich. He started reading Martin's book on I.B.M.'s S.N.A. standards, then threw it across the room because he couldn't concentrate. Eventually he got up and put away the book.

About nine he got into the tub. The water was hot enough to turn his skin red. The heat penetrated, relaxing his muscles and dulling all the aches. He tried again to read, but now he felt sleepy. He lay in the water dozing. When the doorbell chimed, it took a couple of seconds to realize where he was. Abruptly he sat up.

"Who the hell can that be?"

Sarah didn't know where he lived. What if it were Mary with more news about vampires? He dried quickly, put on some pajama bottoms and a white terry cloth robe. The bell rang twice more. He strode through the living room and wrenched open the door.

Sarah stared warily at him. She looked terrible, her face pale with purplish circles under her eyes, her lips black in the dim light, but still her beauty showed through. The big dark wool coat hid her body, and her hands were in the pockets.

"Can I come in?" Usually only a formality, the words came out as a real question, almost a plea, as if she were powerless to move without his permission. Her voice sounded hoarse.

"Of course you can."

Her eyes closed, a faint smile showing on her broad mouth, then she stepped through the doorway and put her hand on his shoulder. "Oh, thank you. Thank you so much." Her hand dropped. "I wasn't sure you'd be glad to see me. I wouldn't blame you for being pissed."

He shrugged. "I did have an awful dinner."

"I really am sorry. Something came up."

"Come sit down."

"Your hair is all wet." Her fingertips touched his hair behind his ear, then slid down onto his skin. Her hand was freezing. "You'll catch cold. Did I get you out of the shower?"

"The tub actually." He walked over to the sofa, then turned slightly and knotted the robe belt. Sarah had sat at the end of the sofa, hands in her pockets, legs tucked under her, hidden beneath the dark coat. One hand came out and stroked at her hair. Her jaw tightened, and he saw the swallowing motion along the expanse of her throat. Her face was very pale, and her eyes looked wet.

"Is something wrong?" he asked.

She bit at her lower lip and shook her head. The tears started down her cheeks.

"Sarah . . . what is it?" He came over and put his hand on her shoulder. She leaned her face against his arm.

"I . . . I don't feel well. That's all."

"Are you sure?"

She nodded.

"Can I get you something? Food or a drink?"

"No. I . . . I can't eat a thing."

"I tried calling you at work today, but they said you were sick."

"I . . . it's the flu. I really don't feel very well. My throat hurts."

"You sound hoarse or something. Why didn't you call me?" He poured himself some brandy from a cut glass decanter and sat at the other end of the sofa.

She had let her head sag down onto the arm. "I . . . I had to go out unexpectedly. A friend of mine—a girlfriend—had an emergency. I didn't even have time to call. I wanted to. I didn't feel well, and I wanted to just stay home and be with you. But I couldn't say no. So I had to come over and tell you. I was afraid you'd be really angry."

He sipped the brandy, then sighed. "I did want to know what had happened, but you're officially forgiven." He wondered what she was wearing under the coat. Given that she was sick, he could probably forget any lovemaking tonight, but he did feel relieved at her explanation.

"Thank you." Her face was tipped almost on its side, and she hadn't moved.

"Did you get your car fixed?"

"Yes. You were right about the coi[...] new one in, and it started right up. T[...] very mysterious, that it made no se[...] wire. I told them that was just my lu[...]

He watched her face closely. "It w[...]

"Stranger things have happened to [...] and brushed again feebly at her hair. "I must look simply awful."

"No you don't," Steve said. "Not to me."

She ran her tongue over her lower lip, then leaned forward and gave his hand a squeeze. Her fingers were still icy. "You're sweet," she said.

"It must have turned pretty cold out there."

"Yes, it has. I'm freezing." Her eyes began to glisten again.

"Won't you tell me what's wrong?"

"I . . . not right now. I just want to sit with you like this and pretend everything is all right."

He frowned slightly, but she wouldn't meet his eyes. Both hands lay on her lap. They were bigger and stronger looking than Mary's, the long nails colored brilliant scarlet, the expanse below the knuckles smooth and white except for the faint shadow of the tendons. A half-inch of white gauze showed from under her left sleeve.

"Did you hurt your wrist?"

She gazed down at her hands, then tugged at the sleeve. "I burned myself. Ironing. That's what I get for bothering with hundred-percent cotton blouses."

"I have my shirts laundered."

She smiled. "How decadent."

Steve sipped the brandy. He watched her eyes wander restlessly, searching the room. "Are you sure you wouldn't like some brandy? It might warm you up."

k you. I don't think my stomach could han-

rah, are you in some kind of trouble?"

Her laugh was sharp and bitter. "I guess you could say that."

"I'd like to help you if I could."

She laughed again. "I'm afraid this time I've bitten off more than I could chew. Strong self-reliant Sarah has finally overreached herself."

"What are you talking about?"

"Nothing. I finally got what I wanted, is all."

He stared thoughtfully at her. Her eyes were animated, but her face was still unnaturally pale. "I'm not making much sense, am I? Tell me one thing, Steve—have you ever been afraid of dying, really afraid? I don't mean just worrying a little bit, but feeling—realizing with utter certainty—that you are going to die, that there is no escape, and that time really moves very fast. It's as if you're in a car headed for a cliff, and you can see it coming closer and closer, but there's nothing you can do—steering, brakes, nothing responds. You can't even open the doors. You are going over the cliff, and there's no escape."

Her eyes held him, the power there. "I have felt that way. Once . . . after Brenda left. When I was alone at night."

"Then you do understand! What would you do to escape? What would you give to live forever?"

Something in her face frightened him, and he wondered suddenly if she might have mental problems. That would explain a great deal. "I . . . I don't want to live forever—not at all." He took a big swallow of brandy.

"You don't?" She was surprised.

"*No*. Existence, mere existence, isn't that wonderful. I don't want to kill myself or anything, but I wouldn't want to live forever. It's not natural. I get tired enough of myself and my thoughts and stupidities, but to have to put up with them forever . . ." He laughed. "You can have it. Besides, my grandfather lived to be ninety-two, and it didn't look like much fun."

"But what if you didn't age?"

"I'd still get sick of myself. Your brain would age, your thoughts would age. I wouldn't want to be stuck with myself forever. I think I'd go nuts."

He was staring at the brandy, but when he looked up, something had happened to her face. She was already pale, but now her eyes were frightened, her lips parted slightly and twisted. For the first time her beauty was completely gone, her face a pasty, distorted white oval with hair sprouting from it, her dark coat hiding the rest of her, making her seem disembodied. The fear he felt must only be a faint echo of what had grasped her.

"Christ, Sarah." He slid over and took both her hands. They were still frigid. He squeezed hard. "Listen to me. *Listen.*" He put his right hand on her cheek. "*Sarah.*"

Her eyes finally focused on him. They had been somewhere very far away. "Oh, Steve, let's . . . let's talk about something else, anything else."

"I think we need to talk about what's wrong."

As they stared at each other, her grey eyes calmed. She shook her head. "No, not now—not tonight. I told you there was a . . . problem, but I can't talk about it to-night. I *can't.*"

He could see the fear starting again, throwing out its tendrils to pull them both in. "Hey, that's all right—it can wait."

The tears started running down her face. "Oh Steve, you really are so nice. I've never wanted to hurt anyone. You must believe me—whatever anyone tells you, I didn't want anyone *hurt*. I never, never, wanted that."

He drew her to him. He had his left arm around her, and she hid her face against his chest, her hand on his shoulder. Her body felt strangely still, and she remained somehow far away from him. He knew she was behaving very oddly, that she might be unbalanced, but it felt so good to hold someone again. Brenda would never let him comfort her.

"It's all right," he whispered, stroking her hair with his right hand.

One leg was still tucked under her, but below the long dark coat, a white ankle and foot showed, the toenails colored the same red as her fingernails. "Sarah . . . are you barefoot?"

She sat up abruptly and thrust both feet forward. "I guess I am." She laughed once, wiggling her toes. "I didn't even notice."

"Christ, your feet must be frozen solid."

"Yes, I guess they are." She laughed, then withdrew to the corner of the couch, drawing her feet up close to her, so that he could see both legs from the knee down. "You must think I'm really wacko, all right. I didn't feel well, and I knew I wanted to come see you. I'd taken my stockings off—pantyhose are so uncomfortable—and I forgot to put my shoes back on." She laughed again. "I've had such a headache. I didn't notice much else."

He stared at her legs. "Did you forget anything else?"

She laughed again. "No! At least I didn't forget my dress." She raised the edge of her coat, revealing a red knit material. She shook her head. "You must think I'm

94

an utter basket case." With a sigh she stretched out on the sofa, swinging her bare legs up onto his lap and letting her head fall back onto the sofa arm.

"I don't think that at all." He took her ankle with one hand, then began massaging her foot with the other hand. "God, your feet are like ice."

"I know. I've always had poor circulation in my feet. They take forever to warm up. Oh, don't stop. That feels so nice."

"Does it?"

Her legs and feet were so long and white, the red polish forming a tiny shell on each toe. Her legs had been shaved very close, and he could see the pores in her calves. He worked the palm of his hand into the curve of her foot.

"That does feel so good. Your hands are getting warmer."

"Are they?"

She opened her eyes and looked up at him. She ran her fingertips from his shoulder down along his arm. "Yes." She closed her eyes. "I'm sorry I went hysterical on you."

"That's okay."

"No it's not. We hardly know each other. You're getting the wrong impression about me."

"I thought it was supposed to be men who were afraid of crying and showing their feelings."

"Touché. Are you afraid of crying and showing your feelings?"

He swallowed. "Yes. I suppose I am."

"Probably because your ex used them as a club to beat you with." Her eyes were open again, but she looked drowsy.

95

He laughed once. "You got that right." He continued massaging her foot.

"This is the best I've felt all day."

"I wish . . . I wish you'd tell me what happened."

He felt both her leg and her foot stiffen, then she laughed. "No questions, remember? Not tonight."

"All right." His voice was faintly husky.

"Feet are funny, don't you think? I think my feet look silly."

"I don't."

She laughed. "Funny you should say that. They may look funny, but they're probably the most sensitive part of my body, especially there along the instep. They're not ticklish exactly, but I don't think stroking my nipples would be nearly so erotic as what you're doing."

He raised her foot and ran his tongue along the bottom from her heel up to her toes.

"Oh God," she whispered.

Holding her foot with his right hand, he kissed the sole, his lips and tongue making small circular motions. His other hand slid down her calf to her knee, then slipped under her dress. Her thigh was smooth and cool, and his fingertips touched the thick curly hair between her legs.

"Christ," he whispered. "You did forget something else."

Her eyes were closed. "I guess I did."

He probed with his fingers and felt her legs stiffen. She grabbed his arm with her hand. "Oh, Steve—that isn't doing my headache any good."

He set her foot down, but his left hand stayed where it was. Her calves were muscular for a woman, but her

96

thigh felt soft. He stroked her ankle gently with his right hand. "I suppose you'd like me to stop."

"I didn't say that. I'd hate to give you the flu, though."

"It would be worth it."

Her fingertip touched his cheek, traced a line down to his jaw. He took her hand with his, then kissed her palm. "God, you're so beautiful, Sarah."

"Am I?" she whispered.

"Yes. You're the most beautiful woman I've ever known."

She sat up and swung her legs down. He drew his hand away. "You're very nice, Steve." Her hand ran up along his leg, slipped under his robe and closed about the flannel pajama over his penis. He moaned, and she bent over and nuzzled with her lips at his neck just below the ear. Her mouth was cold, but he was too warm to care. He felt his pulse under her fingers. He turned his head and tried to find her lips, but she drew back and shook her head.

"I don't want to contaminate you."

"Christ, Sarah—I don't care about that. I want you."

She laughed. "And I want you, but we can do it without kissing. Mouths, anyway." Her hand continued stroking at him, but she bent her head and began kissing his chest. Her tongue licked his nipple. He buried both his hands in her long brown hair and held her to him. He couldn't ever remember wanting a woman so badly.

"Let's go to bed," he whispered.

She sat up. "All right. That would be more comfortable than the couch."

They both stood up. She unbuttoned her heavy dark coat, then lay it on the couch. The dress was a red knit that fit her snugly, emphasizing the curve of her hips.

White gauze had been wrapped several times about her left wrist. She unfastened the terrycloth belt at his waist, then slipped the robe off. Her big hands massaged his bare shoulders and chest.

"Couldn't I kiss you," he said.

"No. We want to keep you healthy. Are my hands still cold?"

"Yes, but I don't care."

"You'll have to warm me up." She took his hand, and he led her down the hallway to the bedroom. "You even make your bed. Don't you have any slobby habits at all? Here—unzip me."

She had turned, raising her hair with one hand so the white nape of her neck showed above the red dress. Steve pulled down the zipper, unfastened the black bra, then slid his hands around from behind and cupped her breasts while he kissed her shoulder. Her head went back and she murmured "oh." She moved her hips, and the dress fell to her feet.

He ran his right hand down along her belly. "I have condoms," he said.

Her head shook once. "That won't be necessary. It's all right."

"You're sure?"

"Yes. I took my own . . . precautions."

"Good." He kissed her shoulder, his fingers playing with her nipples.

She pulled his hands away, then she turned and slipped the bra off one shoulder, then the other. She brushed her hair out of her face with her left hand, and he saw a red brown stain on the gauze at her wrist. Blood, dried blood. A sudden queasy feeling passed through his genitals.

"What is it?" Her grey eyes were fixed on him.

"Your wrist—it looks like blood."

She stared at him, then finally laughed. "If I were going to slit my wrists, I would have done both of them. It's an ointment, a salve. It's brown."

"Oh." He felt embarrassed at his uneasiness. What did it matter anyway? The aureoles on her breasts were a faint pink, smaller than on Brenda.

Her eyes surveyed him, then she popped the snap on his pajamas. Her palms touched his chest, massaging him just below the nipples. He shuddered slightly. "My hands are cold, aren't they? I'm sorry." She kissed him on the chest, then on the belly. "I'm sorry they're cold, and my mouth, but I'm not a cold person, honestly I'm not." Her tongue flickered about his navel, traced a pattern along his skin, while she held him gently.

He groaned and clutched at her shoulders. "Sarah—oh God, oh God."

"You like that, do you?" She kissed him one last time, then stood up and drew aside the covers on the bed. "You don't need to wait one second longer." She lay down, slipping her feet under the covers and spreading her legs. "Come into me right now, my darling."

Steve put one hand on her knee. "Are you sure you're ready? I can wait if . . ."

"Yes, I'm sure. I'm not up for a full course meal tonight. I just want you in me, holding me."

The room was very quiet. The wind rattled the bedroom window. Steve could hear himself breathing, could hear his desire resonate in every breath he took. Sarah stared at him through half opened eyes, still and silent, her body utterly beautiful, and he felt almost that he loved her in spite of her strange behavior and any problems she might have. But that made him recall Mary, then Alex, and he realized he really didn't know much about Sarah. He hesitated, wishing he hadn't remembered, wishing that he didn't have to know the truth if it was going to be unpleasant.

She held up her right hand. Her palm had a faint orange flush, and her eyes were shiny again with tears. "Come to me, Steve—*please*. Take me—fuck me—love me."

He got on the bed, and she used her hand to guide him. He shuddered, then moaned, his back arching as he slipped into her. Her hands touched his sides, and his entire body felt aroused—his buttocks, his belly, and especially his sides where she held him.

"Oh, God—Sarah. I can't . . ." He felt as if he might go off any instant, which was hardly fair for her.

She thrust her hips upward and put her arms around him. "Don't wait—don't hold back—don't hold back!" She curled her legs about him while her arms clamped tight.

She was incredibly strong, stronger than any woman he'd ever held. He rocked wildly, then felt the awesome relief as his belly and genitals melted into her, flowed into her, his whole body suddenly exquisitely tender. A long shapeless cry flowed out of him, then his mouth closed about her shoulder.

Her arms clung to him, but then her fingers were in his hair, pulling his head back so she could kiss his throat. A kind of erotic shimmer fluttered along his neck. Suddenly she yanked hard at his hair, and he felt a sharp pain as if he had been stabbed in the throat.

He screamed in pain and ecstasy, tried to pull away, but her arms and legs gripped him, held him with terrible strength. Her mouth, too—it was fused to him. "Sarah!" He tried to raise himself up on his arms, but she wouldn't let go. The pain in his throat abated slightly, but now he was afraid. Her grasp was like metal: cold, hard and unyielding. He managed to roll over so she was on top of him, but he couldn't break free.

"Sarah!" he screamed. "Let go! Stop!"

He groaned and struggled, grabbed her hair with both hands and pulled as hard as he could, but nothing made any difference. This was like wrestling in high school when he had met someone heavier, stronger and meaner; they had you down and pinned to the mat in a minute or two, and all your efforts to break loose were futile. Black spots shimmered before him, and he felt the strength draining from his limbs. Vampires, he remembered, vampires bite you. He was afraid, but tired, very tired. He closed his eyes. Take care of yourself, she had said, someone had said, but he had to rest.

The room was still and quiet except for the murmur of the wind and rain. At last Sarah opened her mouth, releasing his throat. Some blood dribbled onto her lower lip, but she caught it with her tongue, then licked at the wounds on his neck. She shuddered, the tremor showing all along the white expanse of her back and hips. She let go of him and drew her legs up so she sat straddling him at the hips. With one hand she straightened his head, then touched him lightly on the jaw.

"Poor Steve," she whispered. "I think, though, that no one has ever wanted me quite so badly, my poor darling."

Her hands held his sides just above his waist, and she raised and lowered her hips, her eyes closed. *"Nothing."*

Her head twisted around, and she glared at the window. "You didn't tell me there would be nothing—nothing at all."

She got up off the bed, then grabbed Steve by the hair and pulled him up. His body was totally slack. "You didn't tell me he'd be nothing but dead meat—nothing but dead meat to *me.*" Her face twisted. "That's not quite right, Sarah. You're the dead meat—not him. Nothing but dead . . ."

She raised Steve higher, then hurled him off the bed onto the floor. His head made a noise as it struck the hardwood. She winced, then knelt down beside him and stroked his face.

"Oh, Steve, I'm sorry. I really am sorry. I . . . I can't even . . ." She stood, then bent over and picked him up, holding him as if he were a child, cradling him in her arms. She looked faintly comical standing there rocking a big naked man. She lay him on the bed, then pulled the covers over him.

"You must be cold. You can still feel cold and hot and desire and love. You're not dead yet, you're not like me, you poor darling. I stopped in time." She stroked his hair, then kissed him softly on the mouth. "But you will be. Soon."

She turned to the window. "You never told me what it would really be like. You knew I was a fool. I suppose it serves me right." She stroked Steve's face again, her fingertips brushing along his cheek. "I didn't even know myself what I was going to do to you until it happened. Your blood tasted wonderful, my darling. It was hot and came so quickly. You're not going to remember what happened. All of this is only a dream. You'll remember fucking me in a dream, and the dream was frightening, but you won't know why. You'll go with Mary tomorrow, and you'll forget I ever came to see you. You took your bath, and then you fell asleep. And you got this bump on your forehead when you slipped getting out of the tub. You need to be more careful."

She kissed him again, then turned his head. Along his neck near the collar bone were two small puncture marks, the skin about them blue-black. Her lips drew back to reveal her teeth. "Don't worry. I can wait."

She ripped the gauze off her wrist, made a fist and put it alongside his neck. The puncture marks in her wrist were the same. "See, we match, my darling. Betrayed by the one we loved." She laughed once, then touched him on the neck. "Wear a turtleneck tomorrow. Your throat may be tender, but you won't notice the marks."

She turned off the light by the bed. The darkness covered Steve's face, but light from the hallway flooded the foot of the bed. She walked to the window, drew up the blind, then yanked the frame upward. Cold wet air swept noisily into the room, caressed her naked torso and breathed between her legs. She picked up her bra, the bandage, and her dress, and put them on the bed, then walked into the hall.

Steve hadn't moved. His breathing was loud and faintly raspy. Sarah returned with her coat, then stuffed the bra, dress, and gauze into the big pockets. She opened the closet door and hung up the coat.

"We must keep everything neat. You won't see the coat, Steve, when you look in the closet." She turned to the window. "Happy now?"

With a flutter of wings the black bird landed on the sill. The head turned, its dark eye taking in the room.

Sarah stepped back. The whiteness of her body contrasted with the darkness all around her. She was tall and hard, her arms and legs slim and muscular. Her buttocks had the soft curve of a woman but were not at all flabby. She resembled a female Adonis sculpted from white marble, an embodiment of some ideal, but her eyes and her face were wrong. They were too frightened, too angry.

"See. I did just as you wanted, like I always have. Aren't I a good girl? You know, I think you were using me all along just like I used Steve and the others. You're a kind of liar, the queen of liars. And I wanted to be like you. Well, now I've begun. Aren't you proud of me?" She threw back her head and laughed, tears streaming down her face.

Something happened to her laugh. Her face twisted, then she clutched at her belly and cried out.

She fell hard to the floor, drew her knees upward, arms bent, her hands outstretched before her in two quivering white claws. Her pink tongue thrust grotesquely from her mouth, and a guttural croak of agony came out of her, deepened into something totally inhuman. Her arms and legs twitched, and a dark cloud seemed to coalesce about her. Her long beautiful white limbs wavered like something in a funhouse mirror, and her skin was shattered, black things erupting forth like boils. The darkness pulled and twisted at her form. She slowly shriveled into something small and black like burnt up embers.

When it was finished, a black bird stood on the floor. The crow fluttered up to the window sill beside the other bird which was three or four inches larger. The wind blew the wet cold air into the room, put a glimmer

104

of moisture on the hardwood floor. The bigger bird turned and flew away into the night, and the crow followed.

Steve groaned in his sleep, his limbs twitching. His face was deathly pale. He dreamt of Sarah.

Chapter 4

Mary watched Fred pour tea.

The plaid flannel shirt and the dark work pants seemed out of character. His white hair was parted sideways, and through gaps in the hair you could see the pinkish skin over his skull. His eyebrows were black and so were his glasses. Their frames were thick and square in a style which had been popular some twenty years before. Silence, quiet, hung about Fred. His voice was low and very soft. When you spoke with him, you were always aware of the pauses, of how words and thoughts came out of a void of silence. He handed Mary a blue and white cup of tea on a saucer which didn't match.

"Thanks," she said. She sipped the red-orange liquid. "It tastes wonderful."

"Good." Fred nodded, his smile tentative, a politeness only.

Mary sat back in the chair. The aged, oversized furniture, faded but comfortable, the hardwood floors and the radiator were what you expected of a rectory. "So," she said, "you haven't told me yet what particular form of insanity you think I'm suffering from."

Again the tentative smile, vanishing almost at once. "I've always considered you one of the sanest people I know."

"And fits of hysteria are also rare, right? I've never come pounding on your door before begging for sanctuary."

He shook his head, sipped his tea.

"Well, what do you think, then? Could there be a vampire lurking in the vicinity?"

He stared at her, the strained levity of her question dissolving before his gaze. "When you've been a priest as long as I have, you hear many strange stories. People come to you with them because you're a priest. Most of the time you can see at once that there is a rational explanation. The person may be simple-minded and excitable, or drugs are involved. Sometimes the person is clearly . . . disturbed. Obviously I don't think you fall into any of these categories."

He sipped at his tea, his brown eyes watching her through the thick lenses of his glasses. "There are things you can't explain, and occasionally, despite the rational explanation, you're still frightened. A friend of mine visited a family where the grandmother was obviously insane and in need of psychiatric care. Her family wanted him to do an exorcism, and he tries to explain that there were simpler explanations than demonic possession, that she should see a psychiatrist who could help her with therapy or medication. The woman was very excitable, and praying over her seemed to quiet her. My friend knew her affliction was surely a kind of insanity. All the same, the woman frightened him. One minute she would be perfectly normal and at ease, the next a terrible expression of evil would come over her, transforming her before his eyes. He managed to calm her, but he couldn't bring himself to visit the family again. He had nightmares about the woman for months afterwards."

"Uh . . ." Mary said. She put down the saucer and cup on the arm of the chair.

"I'm sorry—I'm a fool. That wasn't a very good story to tell you."

"At least you don't think I'm crazy."

He shook his head. "Of course I don't. That's nonsense."

Silence settled over the room again. Mary felt secure there. Both Fred and the house were reassuring. Little things like the tacky crucifix on the wall with the yellowed palm leaf folded beneath it were comforting.

"The whole business is certainly mysterious," he said. "I tend to agree with Steve, though. I don't like to think of you going off alone somewhere with this unknown detective. Perhaps it would be wisest to call the police."

She shook her head. "I can't—not yet. You may not think I'm insane, but they certainly would. I have a feeling too that Tracy would just disappear again, Smith would deny everything, and I'd never find out the truth."

Fred set down his cup and gave a longing look at the pack of cigarettes on the coffee table. "Go ahead and have one," she said.

He shook his head. "It's a filthy habit, and I know it bothers you."

"I owe you one tonight. Maybe it will help you think more clearly. Sherlock Holmes always smoked his pipe. Go ahead."

He shrugged, his lips pursing slightly. "Very well." He took a cigarette and lit it with an old fashioned silver lighter. "In the interests of penetrating this cloud of mystery, I'll allow myself just one." He drew in on the cigarette, coughed once, then exhaled. "Maybe I should come along too."

"Oh no—I didn't come here to drag you into this."

"It might be rather interesting, and after all, it's customary to bring along a priest. I've seen the old movies. Besides, I have a drawer full of crosses and other religious trinkets which have gone out of fashion. The consecrated host is also supposed to frighten vampires."

"Absolutely not. You can just forget about it."

The hint of a frown showed in his brow. "Why so certain?"

"Because . . . because I'd never forgive myself if anything happened to you."

"Don't you think I'd feel the same way?"

She shook her head. "No. That's not why I came here. There probably is some explanation for all of this, anyway. I've been working too hard for too long, so it's got me dingy. And Mr. Smith is very . . . strong and tough-looking. Steve might be able to handle him, but . . ."

Fred flicked the cigarette ash into the thick glass ashtray. "But definitely not a fifty-seven year old priest with cigarette-fouled lungs who tends toward sloth and corpulence. I understand, although I'm not flattered."

"I didn't say that!"

"No, you're much too polite and tactful. Well, the offer stands, remember that."

She sighed. "Oh, thank you, Fred, but you are the last person I'd ever want to drag into this business."

They both were quiet. Fred finished his cigarette and stubbed out the end. "More tea?"

"Does it have caffeine in it?"

"No."

"Sure, then. I can get it."

He stood up. "Let me." He filled her cup, poured what was left into his own cup, then sat down. "You've told me everything that's happened to you in the last twenty-four hours, but you haven't told me exactly what upset you enough to bring you here. You looked very frightened when you appeared at my doorstep. Why?"

Her eyes stared at him, then at the floor. The faded green carpet had a raised, escalloped pattern. "It seems so silly now. I . . . it's embarrassing."

"None of this sounds silly to me. It's all sinister and very disturbing."

"I . . ." The hand holding her cup began to shake. Annoyed, she set down the cup. "I told you about the crows at Mount Tabor. When I came home tonight there was a huge black bird sitting on the power pole by my house. I was almost to the door when I saw it. I . . . It scared me half to death. There was a crow at Steve's house, too. I remembered that when I saw the bird at my house. They're probably around all the time, and I just never noticed them. After today, though, they scare me." She laughed, but the sound was strained.

Fred finished his tea. "Lord, I don't blame you for being frightened. Crows are black sinister-looking creatures."

"The one at my house was enormous. I've never seen such a big crow."

Fred picked up the cigarette pack and examined it. "Maybe it wasn't a crow."

She felt suddenly cold inside. "What do you mean?"

He smiled. "I don't mean to suggest it was the devil incarnate, but it could have been a raven."

110

"A raven?"

"Yes, as in 'quoth the raven "nevermore." ' "

She laughed. "I haven't thought of that raven in a long time."

Fred read the cigarette package from the bottom half of his bifocals. "I had to memorize the poem when I was in the ninth grade. It took a very long time to forget. Pieces of verse came rapping, tapping upon my skull periodically like memories of the lost Lenore."

"I don't think I've ever seen a raven."

"You probably have in the mountains and mistook it for a crow. They're uncommon in the city. They're large evil looking birds with a peculiar cry, a kind of gargle, not the crow's caw. The peasants in the middle ages believed crows contained the dead souls of wicked nuns, ravens the souls of wicked priests."

Mary laughed, genuinely amused. "Fred, honestly! Where do you come up with these stories?"

With a sigh he set down the cigarettes. "Sister Immaculata, fifth grade. Actually that part I read in a book."

Mary laughed again, then glanced at her watch. 10:15. "It's getting late. I . . . I'd better be getting home."

Fred watched her carefully. "With some fiendish raven lurking about your dwelling? You're welcome to spend the night here—in the guest room, of course. The neighbors are certain to talk, but the bishop and I are friends."

She smiled, then bit at her lower lip. "You must be able to read my mind. I've been dreading leaving. I can joke about it with you now, but out there in the dark and the rain I was so scared."

He stood up. "That settles it. I wouldn't want to go

111

home by myself after the talk we've had. In fact, I'll sleep much better knowing someone else is in the rectory."

She kissed him on the cheek. "Fred, thank you. You're a nice person."

He smiled. "Thank you. Let me show you to your room." He grabbed the cigarette pack and put it in his shirt pocket, then headed for the stairs.

The guest room faced the street. The shade was only halfway down, and the yellow streetlight outside brightened the frosty glass. Fred found the light switch, and the window disappeared into the rest of the room. The bed had an old painted metal frame and a quilt, a braided rug of muted dark colors close by.

"The bathroom is just next door," Fred said.

"Thanks. I'm really tired. I think I'll go straight to bed."

"Do you have class tomorrow?"

"No, but I'm supposed to be at Smith's at nine."

Fred's dark eyebrows dipped below his glasses near his nose, and his mouth stretched taut.

Mary smiled. "You remind me of my father. He used to look something like that, only he was less restrained. He was actually rather ferocious."

Fred took out his cigarettes. "Your father was a very sensible man. I'm going to be up for a while. If you need anything just call me. I'll see you in the morning. I'll be saying mass at seven, and it lasts half an hour."

"Wake me up about six thirty, and I'll go to mass with you."

"Are you sure you wouldn't prefer the extra sleep? You look very tired."

She smiled again. "You're not supposed to try to talk

me out of going to mass! Knock on my door, though, and see if that doesn't get me up."

"All right, but if you don't stir, I won't try again."

"Make sure you wake me up by seven thirty or so. I do need to get home by eight." He nodded and turned, an unlit cigarette dangling from his mouth. She put her hand on his shoulder. "Fred, thank you. I really appreciate your listening to me."

He took the cigarette out of his mouth. "I'm glad you felt you could come to me. It would have been a rather lonely, boring evening otherwise. I hope this all works out all right. I don't like the sound of it. It worries me. You've never been a hysterical person, Mary. You're wise to be fearful of all this. Again, if you'd like me to come . . ."

She let her hand drop. Her jaw stiffened, and she shook her head resolutely.

"Well then, for God's sake, be careful."

She smiled at him, but his face was very serious. He put his cigarette back in his mouth and started down the hall. She closed the door, then sat on the bed with a weary sigh. She unlaced her hiking boots, slipped them off, then lay back. The bed was somewhat spongy, but the pillow had the lumpy feel of real feathers. It beat going home.

She'd had so many dreadful roommates, and her one brief romance had been so unsatisfying that mostly she was glad to live alone, but tonight it would have been nice to have someone. David and one of her roommates, Shari, had been whiners, always complaining about something to Mary, but never to the people whom they were mad at.

Fred was such a nice person. She'd known him for

113

over ten years. He'd taught the freshman literature class at Maryglenn her first year there, and she'd adopted him as a combination spiritual confessor and academic advisor. Many of the priests were pathetic nonentities, bland, but Father Fred Martin had real substance to him. She hadn't realized how good a teacher he was until she went to graduate school at the University of Washington. She'd never met his equal.

It seemed a shame he'd quit teaching, but he'd wanted to do something in the "real world" for a change. He decided to try being a parish priest. Saint Joseph's was in a poor neighborhood but drew liberal yuppie Catholics from all over Portland. Fred was a shy, very private kind of person, but his new job seemed to suit him. Although she no longer attended mass every Sunday, she did go to Saint Joseph's about once a month. She wasn't crazy about the music and the kiss of peace stuff (she knew Fred must feel the same way), but his sermons made the rest of the mass tolerable.

For Fred life remained fundamentally mysterious. She'd known he'd hear her out and not dismiss her story. However, in this case, she wished he'd come up with some neat simple explanation. If only the whole thing were some bizarre practical joke—although she'd want to murder whoever dreamed it up.

Vampires couldn't really exist. Smith must have had some reason for making up such a story. And crows were only birds, not wicked nuns reincarnated. She smiled. Tracy turning up had thrown her life off balance. No wonder she felt so vulnerable. And her life was wearisome. Teaching unmotivated students, reading awful themes, and working on her boring dissertation— that was all she ever did.

Yes, wearisome. She sat up and took off her socks. Would the dresser drawer contain a matronly old nightgown or some pajamas? No, only towels and bedding. She could sleep in her turtleneck and panties. She took off her jeans, draped them over a chair, then turned off the light. God, the sheets felt cold! And her bra was bothering her.

She sat up and pulled off her turtleneck. Her shoulders sprouted goosebumps. She could feel them even if she couldn't see them in the dark room. Sliding the bra around, she unfastened it, then threw it in the direction of the chair. Once she had the shirt back on, she pulled the covers over her, then lay on her side and drew her legs up.

The bed felt wonderful, but the room seemed . . . bright. She opened her eyes. Beneath the shade the window was a foggy yellow square of light. She should just go pull down the shade, but that would mean getting out of bed. Maybe later. She rolled onto her other side and closed her eyes. It wasn't so bad now.

Peeping toms usually weren't second-story men, but what about vampires? They could come right in. The scariest part of *Dracula* was when Harker looked out the window and saw the vampire crawling down the castle wall face first. Knowing Fred was close by helped, but she wished she hadn't thought of that. She had pulled out *Dracula* that afternoon and started rereading parts. Vampires couldn't enter a house unless you let them in. Even Dracula himself had to ask Harker to enter his castle freely and of his own will. As long as she or Fred didn't open the door or a window to them, they were safe. Besides, there were crucifixes in most all of the rooms.

She smiled. Superstitious nonsense! But if you were going to worry, you might as well use the same nonsense to reassure yourself. She turned over again.

The light from the window was still bright. She should get up, but she was so tired. The wind rattled the window, and she could hear rain striking the side of the house near the headboard. Nasty out there. So nice to be inside. Steve said something about freezing rain. She was walking now. What was he up to? She hoped he wasn't fucking Tracy. Her foot slipped—she was falling. Her body jerked convulsively, bringing her back awake, and she opened her eyes.

"Damn light." She turned over.

The thought about Steve had just seemed to pop into her head. She didn't like the word "fucking" and rarely used it. As a verb it had too many other connotations, while as profanity it was unoriginal and so widely used now as to be vapid. She wondered briefly if she would have trouble falling asleep.

Dear Mother God, she thought, this has been a troubling day. (Whenever she prayed, she gave God a female gender to remind herself that the deity was not Charleton Heston with a long white beard, but a formless spirit which also had a female side.) Help me and protect me and Fred and Steve from evil. Especially Steve. Tracy is so beautiful, and he's only a man.

Could she really blame Steve? Could she resist *him* if he suddenly offered himself to her? Before tonight she would have said yes without hesitation, but she had found him very appealing—and not merely in a Platonic way. It was all so foolish, all hormones and crazy feelings. You never wanted the people it made sense to want. You wanted the impossible.

The forest was almost dark, fog curling about shadowy trunks spotted with algae and moss. The trees must be a hundred feet tall, and the ferns at ground level were green now under sunlight. The window frame rattled, and she knew she had been dreaming. The sound of wind and rain came and went like the dream, leaving her in silence.

Later the woman appeared. At first she was brown and white like her photograph, but then her dress and eyes turned blue. Her face, her hair, were pale, only a faint cream to her skin, a hint of yellow in the hair pinned up in back. Her lips, however, were a brilliant garish red, the color something out of an early technicolor movie. She was very beautiful, but age had begun to undermine her looks, and something evil showed in her eyes and her mouth. The dress was a long formal gown which left her white shoulders bare, and she wore long gloves which came above the elbow.

"Parlons francais."

Je parle francais un peut, Mary thought, struggling to recall the words, *mais pas pour longtemps.* She hadn't done much with her French during graduate school.

"Connaissez-vous mon nom?"

Shouldn't that be *"savez-vous"?* No. It translated as "do you know my name" both ways, but connaitre was "to know" in the sense of being acquainted.

"Je suis Madame Rambouillet."

Mary was afraid, but she couldn't remember why. *"Qui?"* she said weakly.

"Madame Rambouillet. *La vampyre de Monsieur* Smith." Her lips opened slightly, and Mary could see the two sharp pointed teeth. *"Le sang est la vie, et je veux*

117

du sang. Votre sang. Ton sang, ma petite. Et le sang de ton frère."

Alex appeared beside her and smiled.

"Run, Alex!" May shouted. "Run!"

But it wasn't Alex—it was Steve. He was naked, and the woman put her hands on his bare chest. She had long white fingers, the red nails the same tasteless scarlet as her mouth. "You are mine," she whispered. *"Le mien."*

"No!" Mary screamed. "Run, Steve—run away."

The vampire laughed. She whispered to Steve as if he were her lover: *"Tu n'es pas digne qu'on t'enleve a ton esclavage maudit, imbécile!—de son empire si nos efforts te délivraient, tes baisers ressusciteraient le cadavre de ton vampire."*

He stared at Mary, his eyes confused. Dark hair covered his chest between the nipples, fell in a line down his belly. She could see the outline of the bands of muscle beneath his skin.

"Mary," he whispered.

She kissed him. His mouth and lips were warm and gentle. He stroked her naked back, then drew her to him. They rolled about the bed while the rain beat at the window. We shouldn't be doing this at the rectory, Mary thought, but she didn't care. Steve was so different from David, so strong and tender. What if Fred came in? And they really should close the shade.

"Arrêtes!" commanded the woman. *"Maintenant. C'est absolument interdit."* Her blue dress was Victorian all right, and next to her stood a man in black evening dress with white tie and tails. His face was greenish gray, the red seam of a scar running down his cheek.

118

"Moi aussi, je veux du sang—le sang de ton frère et ton sang, ma jolie fille."

"They want our blood—our *sang*," Mary whispered to Steve. She could see that he was frightened too. "He's a vampire like her, but I don't know his name. Anyway, this is only a dream."

Steve shook his head no and she drew him closer. She loved the feel of him alongside her, skin against skin. The bed was in a dark corner of the room. The two faces of the vampires pressed against the frosty glass, and now Tracy joined them. All three opened their mouths and hissed, white-faced cobras swaying softly, fangs and the pink curves of their tongues showing.

"Don't worry, they can't come in unless we let them in. We're safe here."

Madame Rambouillet's eyes were the worst. *"C'est futile de m'opposer. J'exige ma proie. C'est futile. Donnes moi ton sang. Ouvres la fenetre—maintenant."*

Steve looked at Mary. "She's right. It's useless. We'd better do as she says. Let them in."

"You're crazy! We're safe in here—leave the window alone."

"We'd better open it," he whispered.

Mary grabbed his arm. *"No."*

Madame Rambouillet was the only one left. *"C'est futile de m'opposer. Ouvres la fenêtre.* Open it—now."

Steve was halfway to the window. Mary held his arm with both hands and tried to pull him back. "No, Steve—oh God, come away from there! Come back to bed!" His eyes were confused, but he had stopped moving. He looked so lovely naked, and she was afraid of what the women would do to him.

Tracy appeared at the window, her big white breasts

wobbling slightly, the pink aureoles like another set of eyes. She leered at Mary. "Come on, Steve. Don't waste your time with her. Come to me."

He took a step forward, and Mary realized she was crying. "No—you can't! Not him! It's not fair."

Tracy laughed. She smiled at Steve and whispered, *"Je remplace, pour qui me voit nue et sans voiles, la lune, le soleil, le ciel et les étoiles."*

Wasn't that Madame Rambouillet, not Tracy? She was naked, and Steve was going to her. Mary reached out with her foot at the right moment and tripped him. His head struck the hardwood floor with a thud, then he lay quietly, half of him on the braided rug.

Mary clenched her fists. "I'll never let you in— never—never!"

Madame Rambouillet laughed. Her teeth showed and the sound wasn't human. *"C'est futile de m'opposer."* Her face wavered as if the glass between them had become a distorting lens. The color in her lips and eyes faded away to the brown of the daguerreotype, and then slowly she began to blacken and transform.

"No," Mary whispered. *"No."*

The black bird watched her through the glass, then swooped away with a strange cry. Mary stepped over Steve and stared through the window pane. The black thing flew about near the yellow streetlight.

"I'll never let you in!"

"C'est futile!" screamed the bird, fluttering before her. With a croak, it soared upward out of sight, then plunged downward. A crash, and broken glass showered over Mary. The bird's dark eyes glittered with triumph. Tracy and the man were behind her, mouths open, teeth bared, and Steve—he stood up and laughed, showing the

same sharp teeth, his flesh the same dead white. She tried to run, but they were too strong. They pulled her down onto the bed.

"C'est futile," the bird croaked one last time, then Madame Rambouillet's voice whispered softly. *"Et maintenant bevons du sang—ton sang, ma petite."*

Mary tried to scream, tried with all her might, but nothing would come out. The black things were in the room with her, and with the window broken all the others were coming, the night full of black shapes spiraling in toward the sharded hole.

"Du sang, du sang . . ." they whispered.

She fought with all her might toward the surface, and at last she jerked open her eyes. Her right hand held the metal pull at the bottom of the window. The room was cold, and yellow light shone through the foggy glass. She shuddered, then jerked her hand away from the window and stepped back. She had almost let them in.

"No," she whispered. "No, it was only a dream—a nightmare. Oh God, what a nightmare."

She raised her hand to pull down the shade once and for all, but something black fluttered past. She cried out and ran back to the bed. She couldn't bring herself to look back at the window, but she heard a bang as something struck the glass. She hadn't screamed since she was a child, but she screamed so loud it hurt her throat and her ears.

"Mary—what is it?" Fred's voice, and he rapped at the door.

She stuck one hand in her hair and willed herself to breath more slowly.

"Mary?" The door swung open, flooding the room with the light from the hall.

"Oh, Fred."

"Can I come in?"

"Oh, yes—*please.*"

He sat on the bed, and she grabbed his arm, burying her face against the flannel sleeve. "It's all right, Mary. You must have had a nightmare." His voice was so low and gentle it made her want to cry.

"No—no, it wasn't just a nightmare."

"Of course it was."

"No—*no.*" She sat up and looked at him. "Something was trying to get in here, something nasty. I woke up a minute ago, and I was over there at the window. I nearly opened it. I was going to pull down the shade when I saw it."

"You saw what?"

"A black bird—a raven."

He shook his head, hesitated, then touched her cheek. "You were dreaming."

"I know the difference between being asleep and being awake. Something was outside there. I know it. I know it."

Fred sighed. "Maybe . . . maybe I should go outside and have a look."

She gripped his arm with both hands. "God, no, Fred! I'm not sure what they are, but . . . We're safe inside, but you mustn't go outside! You can't!"

He shrugged. "I thought it might make you feel better."

She shook her head vigorously, then let go of him and lay back on the bed. "I'm scared, Fred. I'm really scared."

"It's all right now." She could see him staring at the window. "Whatever it was, it's gone."

They were both quiet. She could feel herself begin to relax, the urgency of her fear abating. "Fred, you've read *Dracula,* haven't you?"

"Years ago."

"Vampires can't come inside unless you let them in."

"Mary, it was only . . . only a bird, if even that."

She shook her head. "Don't you remember? Vampires can assume the shape of animals like the wolf or bat. Or a bird—it doesn't mention crows—but they can change their shape at will."

"Mary, it's night, and you've had a bad dream."

"The devil is supposed to be able to do the same thing, and many Catholics believe in the devil. I don't understand it, Fred, but something was out there. I'm sure of it."

He sighed, then put his hand on her shoulder. "Whatever it was, it's gone. I'll close the shade."

She sat up at once. "No—*don't.*"

He was halfway there. "I won't touch the window, but you'll have me terrified too about what's going to appear there."

She couldn't move. Her mouth was open.

"Dear God," she heard him whisper.

"Fred!"

"It's okay. I can't see anything, but . . . one of the panes is cracked. I don't remember . . ."

When the shade was down, she sagged back against the wall. The bed creaked as Fred sat down. "I don't think it will bother you anymore."

"I'm still scared. I'm so scared."

"Why don't you get up for a moment? Let's have some strong spirits—a drink."

"All right. I don't want to be alone. Not tonight."

123

"Neither do I. When we're finished I can rest in the chair here. Maybe that way we can get some sleep."

It seemed somewhat childish, but she wouldn't refuse his offer. "My pants are on the chair there, would you . . . ?" He handed them to her, then resolutely turned and looked the other way while she got up and put them on. "You're such a gentleman, Fred, but there's not really much to see."

"Don't put yourself down, Mary. I'll be the judge of that."

She snapped the button on her jeans, smoothed her hair back over her shoulders, and wiped at her eyes. "What time is it, anyway?"

"Twelve forty-five."

She followed him into the hall. "So late. But you weren't asleep."

"No. I've learned not to battle my insomnia. I was reading and I heard you scream. It was quite a sound."

"I can believe it."

He took out a bottle of Scotch, two tumblers, and poured them each an inch. Mary noticed that all the drapes were drawn. She coughed a good deal after the first swallow. He watched her carefully. "By the way, I'm coming with you tomorrow."

"Fred . . ." she began wearily.

"No more arguments. It's decided. You'll need all the help you can get."

She took a big swallow of Scotch. The house had the unnatural quiet and stillness of late night. Outside she could hear the wind and rain. "Thank you, Fred. Thank you."

Chapter 5

The moon rose slowly, its pocked face the same cold white as the mountain. Things were pursuing him through the forest, things which looked like women, but those were only their shells. Their eyes were holes; you glimpsed something dark and shriveled inside.

The moonlight had a bluish cast on the snow, and it was freezing. He would never be warm again. A howl rose above the soft steady moan of the wind. He glanced behind him. Sarah came out of the trees and dropped onto all fours. He turned and ran, but he knew he would never get away. The phone began ringing, and he wondered where it could be coming from.

He opened his eyes, swallowed, and realized his throat was very sore. He grabbed the phone by the bed. "Hello?"

"Steve?" A woman's voice.

"Yeah?"

"This is Mary. Mary Connely. Did I wake you up?"

"Yes."

"I'm sorry."

"That's okay. I must have forgotten to set my alarm. I'm glad you called."

"Steve, if . . . You don't really need to come today if you don't want to. A friend of mine, a priest, will be coming, so . . ."

He sat up quickly and winced at the pain in his head. "I'm coming."

"Are you sure? You don't . . ."

"Yes, I'm sure. What time is it, anyway?"

"Five after eight."

"I'll see you at nine, okay?"

A brief silence. "Okay."

He set the phone down and let his back slump against the headboard. His head and his throat hurt, and he was so tired. Why was he naked? He must have fallen asleep after he got out of the tub. He couldn't even remember going to bed. Maybe coffee would help his throat. He would have to get moving if he was going to be there by nine.

He pushed the covers aside and stood. Black diamonds danced before him, the pain almost like a blow. Whispers grew into a moan held on a single note, and the diamonds swelled into the shapes you saw when you closed your eyes, swirls of color, flecks of light. When he opened his eyes again he was staring at the window across from his bed. Rainy wind swept through the opening, and the floor glistened from the moisture.

Slowly he sat up. His left knee hurt. He had stood up too fast. "God, it's freezing in here." His robe was beside him, and with a frown, he grabbed it. He never left things lying around. He must have been unusually tired last night.

This time he got up very carefully, one hand on the

126

wall to support him. The pain in his head swelled, then gradually died down. He lowered his arm, dropped the robe on a chair, then limped over to the window and closed it. The cold breeze on his genitals made him shudder.

He looked wearily about the room, then went to the dresser. He took a black turtleneck out of the top drawer, jeans from the second one, and underwear and socks from the third. He wondered why he was shaking so. Cold, he was very cold. He put on the turtleneck, wincing as the collar slipped about his throat. He tugged at the sleeves, then folded down the neck carefully. After he finished dressing he went into the bathroom.

The face in the mirror was a stranger's. The eyes had a peculiar expression, blue black shadows forming pockets beneath them. He opened his mouth, but his teeth seemed crooked or twisted. Wrong—everything was wrong—something was changing him, some wasting force that would kill him slowly and painfully. The same force—not *him*—made the corners of the mouth rise into a grotesque smile which clashed with the terror in the eyes.

He turned and went into the kitchen trying to escape the fear that had him by the throat. For God's sake, what was the matter with him? He turned on the radio and put his hands on the window sill. The light hurt his eyes. Mozart, the music sounded like Mozart. He'd had bad dreams last night, something to do with Sarah, and he couldn't shake them. He didn't feel well, but it was only the flu—that must be it. You didn't just wake up with fatal illnesses like leukemia or AIDS. He certainly hadn't done anything to catch anything—had he? He frowned, but concentrating made his headache worse.

He opened the refrigerator. On the top shelf was a carton of milk and a glass container of apple juice. Nausea assailed him, coming in a great wave. He clamped his mouth shut, closed the refrigerator door, then sat down. The nausea and dizziness faded away. This was ridiculous—at this rate he would never get out of the house. All he wanted to do was go back to bed, but he had to go with Mary, he had to.

Finally he went to the sink and filled a glass with cold water. Swallowing hurt, but the icy water felt good on his throat. Someone somewhere seemed to be singing, a woman monotonously holding the same note, but when he concentrated the voice went away. The only sound was the music from the radio, and no one was singing.

He would need a heavy coat for Mount Hood. He went to the closet in his room. Next to his red ski parka was a dark heavy wool coat. He took out the parka, then put the hanger back by the dark coat. Since he still felt cold, he put on a rag wool sweater, then the parka.

He had the feeling he was forgetting something, something important. He hadn't shaved, and he always shaved, but he couldn't face it this morning. His eyes drifted around the living room, and the Martin S.N.A. book on the coffee table made him remember. *Work*—he needed to call them. It was a good hour past the 7:30 deadline.

He sat on the couch, dialed his own number, then told Marian he had the flu. She made sympathetic noises. He hung up the phone. "Stupid fuckers. Stupid boring goddamned worthless job, wasting your life . . . " Now he was raving. Everything was so hard this morning. He sighed, sank back into the couch and closed his eyes. If

128

only he could sleep for a while. Soon he heard the woman's voice again, the monotonous singing. His eyes jerked open, then he stood up.

Thirty-ninth was the fastest way to Powell Street. He had the heater on high, but he still didn't feel warm enough. The windshield wipers cut through the heavy rain. The sky was gray white, the sidewalks wet and gray brown, the firs a dark green close to black. The weatherman on the radio said it might snow later today.

God, he was sick of this weather. Three years ago he and Brenda had spent a week on Maui in March. The sky and sea had been so blue, the ocean water warm. Instead of bringing them back together, the trip had made it clear something was wrong between them. Maybe he should go again—go alone. Just leave Willamette Power and Peter and the stupid half-assed project. It would be warm there. He could lie on the beach and soak up the sun, let it heal him. Maybe he would meet some attractive woman in a bikini and fuck her all night long. But it was too late for that, too late for him.

Christ, what was wrong with him? This must all be because Sarah hadn't shown up, but no, that wasn't why he felt bad. Her body was so beautiful, her arms and legs so white and shapely, her breasts and—but that was only a dream. He'd better pay attention to his driving.

He turned left into the parking lot. The ugly square office building was next to a Seven Eleven. A real estate agency had the bottom floor, but a metal stairway led to the second floor. Smith would be up there.

Eight fifty-five, and he didn't see Mary's car. A couple of minutes later the old Ford swung into the lot. The engine still sounded terrible. Next to Mary was a man with white hair and glasses. Steve hadn't thought the priest would be so old.

He got out of the car, swayed slightly. The rain on his face was cold, but it made his head feel better. He walked over under the balcony out of the rain. A realtor in a suit and tie grinned from behind the glass, but Steve looked away, not wanting to encourage him.

Mary smiled weakly, then lowered her eyes. She still looked tired. Her face was pale, her long red hair pulled back, emphasizing the white curves of her ears. Under the gray sky the blue in her eyes was hard to see. She wore the same clothes as yesterday, dark parka and faded jeans.

The priest had on a black wool overcoat, a black suit with a Roman collar, the white bordering the black and a small square of white showing in front. His glasses had thick frames of black plastic, and the lenses shrank his eyes. His skin had a faintly pink tinge, the pallor common to Portlanders in late winter.

"Hi, Steve." Mary shook his hand. Her fingers felt small and slight. "This is Father Fred Martin."

The two men shook hands. "Glad to meet you, Father Martin."

"Call me Fred. This ecclesiastical garb is for Mr. Smith. I only dress this way when I wish to wield priestly clout."

Mary smiled. "You look very respectable. Mr. Smith should have no doubts about your vocation." She sighed. "Well, this is your last chance to be sensible and back out. Mine too. If anyone wants to leave . . ."

Fred shook his head. "We've been all through that."

Mary stared at Steve. He shook his head and looked

130

away. "Do you feel all right, Steve?" she asked. "You look like you might be . . . sick."

"I've got a headache and a little sore throat, nothing serious. I'm coming."

She slipped her right hand around Steve's arm, her left about the priest's. "Well, thank you. Thank you so much, both of you. Maybe Smith will change his mind when he sees all of us and admit it's a joke, and then we can all go have coffee together."

Fred shook his head. "It's no joke."

Steve felt very cold and somehow far away from all this, as if he were watching three pathetically small people across some vast distance. "No." His voice was hoarse.

Mary frowned. "What are we going to tell him about Steve? It makes sense that I'd ask a priest to come, but . . ."

"Just say I'm a friend."

Mary shrugged. "I suppose that's as good as anything."

Upstairs a shiny new brass plate on the second door said, Roland Smith, Private Investigator. The office inside was more imposing than the building, the walls and thick carpet soothing shades of blue. Behind a big oak desk sat a blond woman in a red dress.

"Could you tell Mr. Smith that Mary Connely is here to see him," Mary said.

"Mr. Smith called to say he'd be delayed, but you're to wait for him."

Mary shrugged. "Okay."

The three of them sat down. Fred began browsing through a copy of *People* magazine. Steve put his hands in his parka pockets and closed his eyes. The forest was near again, the snow on the trees bluish under moonlight. He opened his eyes. Mary was staring at him.

"Are you sure you feel well enough to come?"

"Yes."

Fred was interested in the magazine. Mary kept looking at her watch and crossing and uncrossing her legs. The wall clock said 9:35 when a man came through the door.

His black leather jacket emphasized his broad shoulders, the massive chest and arms. Steve knew he must be a body builder. Short guys like Smith frequently put on muscle to compensate for their size. Body builders spent more time working out than triathloners, but their stamina was low, their bodies stiff and inflexible. Swimming and running were boring, but at least you could do them outdoors. Spending two hours in a gym every day with other sweating hulks didn't appeal to Steve. Why bother with fitness, anyway? You got old and weak no matter what you did.

Smith smiled at Mary, but his mouth stretched into a taut line when they all stood up. "What the hell is this?"

"I brought some people with me."

"I can see that. What for?"

"This is Father Fred Martin. He thought he might be able to help."

"That's superstitious garbage."

The priest laughed. "My claims for the supernatural are somewhat less extreme than yours."

Smith was staring at Steve, his eyes a hard, cold blue. Even though he had black hair, the crewcut still made Steve think of Nazis. "Who's this guy?"

"A friend," Mary said.

Spontaneously, Steve put his hand on her shoulder and said, "Her boyfriend."

Mary stared at him, then turned again to Smith. Her ear and the side of her face were red. Smith watched Steve. "Your boyfriend, huh?"

Mary gave an abrupt nod. The priest seemed amused.

"I couldn't let her go alone," Steve said.

Smith shook his head. "Well, you can forget about coming—both of you."

"She's not going by herself." The priest's voice was quiet but resolute.

Smith opened his mouth, glared at them, then closed it. He spun about. "Let's discuss this in my office." He strode passed the receptionist. She smiled at him, then gazed severely at the others.

Smith sat down behind his desk, then the fingers of his right hand drummed on the surface. "I need to think for a moment." The room was silent except for the muted sound of the traffic on Powell. Finally he looked at Mary. "I can't believe you did this. What I told you was confidential. I suppose you showed them the photographs too? If my client was to find out you'd started spreading this story around . . ."

Steve's head hurt, and he had already decided he didn't like Smith. "Oh, cut the crap, and make up your mind what you're going to do."

Smith looked genuinely surprised. His nostrils flared, and he stood. Steve wished he'd kept his mouth shut. Smith would probably have little trouble beating him up. If only he had kept out of this whole miserable business.

"Why don't you both just calm down," Mary suggested.

The priest nodded. "That sounds like good advice."

Smith sat down and began tapping at the desk again. Finally he looked at them. His smile was not reassuring. "Okay, I guess they can come along, but I hope you understand there's some risk involved. This isn't any Hollywood vampire we're talking about. The woman's old and deadly."

"We understand," Steve said.

Smith stared at him, then at Mary. "Funny. I didn't know you had a boyfriend." He didn't try to hide his sarcasm.

"There's a lot you don't know about me, Mister."

Smith laughed. "That's for sure. I've got a couple things to take care of, then I'll be down. Wait for me in the car, the red Cherokee out front." He tossed the keys to Mary.

They didn't say anything until they were outside. "I thought he was going to hit you," Fred said.

Steve nodded. "I should have been more tactful, but he seems like such an arrogant little asshole. He probably has a black belt in karate or something."

"That was clever about being her boyfriend. It certainly seemed to throw him off balance."

"Yes," Mary said. Her face was still faintly flushed.

The Cherokee with its sharp square corners sat in the rain, the dark red color muted by the gray sky. Mary unlocked the front door.

"I'll sit in front," Fred said. "You and Steve can sit in back."

Steve let Mary in first, then got in and closed the door. The smell of cigarette smoke overpowered the vinyl odor. The red seats and carpet were spotlessly clean.

Steve wondered if Smith was as compulsively neat as he was.

"God, I hate that smell," Mary said. She winced, then looked at the priest. "Sorry, Fred."

"That's all right. At least we know Mr. Smith can't be all bad."

Mary massaged the palm of her left hand with her right thumb. Her fingers were long and slender, the nails cut short, not so powerful-looking as Sarah's hands. Her neck had lost its flush, the skin nearly white, and the tiny gold ball in the lobe made her ear seem small and delicate. "He's not trying to be sympathetic like he was yesterday."

Fred glanced at his watch. "He doesn't seem in any particular hurry. It's almost ten. Maybe I'll step out for a cigarette."

"Fred, it's pouring out there!"

Smith skipped down the stairs rapidly and got in the car. Mary handed him the keys. "Okay, this is it. Anybody wants out, now's the time. If you're the squeamish type, I recommend you leave right now. I'm gonna drive a wooden stake through this thing's heart. They're supposed to spout blood like a geyser and scream like hell. The lady here and my client have a reason for wanting this thing dead, but it's none of your business. I wouldn't stick around if you don't have to."

Neither Steve nor Fred said anything. "Okay, everyone does as I say and keeps out of my way. First one that gives me any crap gets the shit kicked out of him. I've got a black belt in tae kwon do. Clear enough?"

"Certainly," Fred said, but Smith was staring at Steve, who said nothing.

He felt very cold and somehow detached. Smith was

a fool playing with forces more powerful than he could imagine. Mary was stupid to be drawn in. There was something pathetic about her—her grief for her brother, her rigid narrow life, her loneliness. And the priest had even less reason to be here. Friendship and personal loyalty were empty abstractions not worth dying for. Maybe he was sexually attracted to Mary. She was probably the best he could do at his age. He should warn them away. Unlike him, they still had a choice. He opened his mouth to speak, but his head and his throat hurt so. Something warm touched his icy hand, and the heat surged up his arm like an electric shock.

"I said are you all right?"

The mists thinned, and he saw Mary staring at him. She had drawn away her hand. The Cherokee was at an intersection on Powell waiting for the light to change.

"Sure." He ran his tongue across his lips, felt the dry, ragged scraps of skin. "Just a little . . . dizzy."

Mary shook her head. "You shouldn't be here. You should be home in bed."

He shrugged. Home in bed. With Sarah. He thought of her body so long and white and beautiful, but then the fear again closed about his heart.

Mary waited for the light to change, then whispered, "Maybe he would take you home. We're off to a late start anyway."

If only he could go home, but it wasn't safe there, not after dark. He shook his head. "No, I'm okay."

"Are you angry with me?" she said softly.

"Angry?" He laughed. Why did he always choose women who would betray him? She had warned him about Sarah more than once. "I'm not angry at you—not at all."

136

"I thought . . ."

"You tried to warn me. I should have . . ." He had to get hold of himself. She wasn't supposed to know what had happened, and he couldn't exactly remember. He glanced at her hand, wishing she hadn't let go. Her touch had been so gentle. "Do you . . . do you know much about vampires?" He put both hands in his parka pockets.

Her eyes were gray, but with more blue. They were not like the gray sky or the mists all about them. *"Dracula* is one of the books I'm covering in my dissertation. Stoker got the vampire lore from Transylvanian sources."

"They kill people by drinking their blood, right?"

"Not exactly. The victims will appear to die, but they actually become vampires themselves."

"Really?" Steve forced a smile, then looked out the window.

"That's what happens to Lucy in the book. She bites little children. They have to kill her with the stake. Vampirism is like a disease, a plague."

"There's no cure?"

"Not once you're dead."

"Why not?"

"Because . . . there's no cure for death, and a vampire is a dead person, an animated corpse."

Smith laughed. "There's one cure—the wooden stake." He drew in on a cigarette he had just lit.

Mary frowned as the cloud of smoke drifted into the back. "I suppose it is a kind of cure. Lucy appeared very peaceful afterwards, as did even Dracula himself. But it's hardly a cure, not if it ends in death. The person is still gone forever."

Smith laughed again. "I guess for the vampire maybe the cure would be worse than the disease."

"Catholics don't believe in the finality of death, not in an absolute sense," Fred said. "There's the resurrection of the dead and life everlasting."

"Yeah, the old pie in the sky claptrap." Smith gave a kind of snort. "Everyone hanging around playing on their harps in their white robes."

The priest shook his head. "It needn't be quite so simpleminded. I admit the notion of an afterlife has problems. You can't exactly live with your immediate family anymore because there are now several generations present in both directions, backward and forward." He continued on with some other problems.

Steve closed his eyes. No cure. None. He heard Sarah whispering. He opened his eyes. Mary was watching him. "You're getting very far away again," she said.

"Sorry." He tried to smile. A disease, a plague. He looked out the window. They had passed the Gresham strip, the multitude of fast food joints, huge chain stores and gas stations. Words scrolled across a big electric sign with the ski conditions and weather at Timberline. Snowing and very cold.

"Tell me again," the priest said, "why it's superstitious nonsense to believe in God, but not in vampires."

"Listen, I've got damned good evidence this particular vampire exists. I didn't start out believing in them. You give me some proof God exists, I'll believe in him."

"What's the mechanism behind vampires if not God? In the stories they're creatures in league with Satan."

"There's no proof of that."

"Then what gives the vampire his power, his life?"

"How the hell should I know? What gives you your

life? Things are just the way they are. It doesn't prove nothing."

Steve stared at the firs, the tall dark trees rising high above the narrow two-lane road on either side. The rain was changing, a few flakes mixed in with the drops. The snow was slower, drifting languidly through the gray mist.

Mary wasn't listening to the two men talking. She seemed sad. She did have a kind of delicacy, the way her jaw curved into her ear, her slender throat, the shape of her hands. It wasn't weakness—no one could ever mistake her for being weak. She wore such drab, colorless clothing. The navy parka, the gray turtleneck faded and pilled at the collar, the jeans nearly worn through at the knees. Her hiking boots needed polishing; especially at the toes the leather was dry and rough. He wondered if she ever dressed up, or if her clothes reflected some feminist principle. More likely she was too busy and didn't have any money. And wasn't that better, really, than someone like Brenda who spent a fortune—of his money—on clothes and who constantly primped and fussed at herself?

The rain had become big wet flakes which melted when they hit the dark pavement, but along the side, the white covering was building up. He could feel himself drifting like the snow, floating down through the gray sky toward darkness.

"Mary." She turned to him. "I didn't make it clear earlier. I meant to thank you for warning me. I was upset last night, but you were right. You tried to ... I made you feel bad. I was being stubborn, foolish."

She stared intently at him. She lacked guile. That was the difference—with Brenda or Sarah you were never

139

really sure what they were up to. They always concealed something.

"I didn't want to drag you into this."

He laughed once, and it hurt his throat. "I was already in."

"I suppose you were. I didn't . . . It was none of my business, but I didn't want to see you hurt. Alex loved her so, but I never trusted her. I didn't say anything because I knew it would upset him, and it was only a feeling I had. I still don't understand what Tracy—how she's involved in all this. I wondered before Alex disappeared if I was being unfair, if I was only jealous because she was taking my brother away from me."

"You were right about her all along. Absolutely right."

Mary's brow broke into the three wrinkles characteristic of her frown. "Are you really so certain?"

Steve looked out at the snow again. His throat hurt, his head, and he was aware of the blood pulsing at his neck. "Yes."

"But . . ."

He laughed again. "I'm a terrible judge of women. I have a real talent for picking them. That's why I'm so sure about Sarah."

Mary shrugged. "She's very beautiful. When she walks through a room all the men will stare at her."

"Most of them will look, and that's all."

"She wanted you, Steve. She was waiting for you. You couldn't help it anymore than Alex could."

Steve felt anger stir beneath the fear and weariness. "Couldn't I? Is it all just a matter of hormones?"

"Of course not. There was more to Alex than that, and to you." She stared out the window at the snow. "Physical attraction is a funny thing. Perhaps it's just

140

there, or it isn't. I went with a man for a couple years. I wanted it to happen, and he tried, but it was never there." She gave an awkward laugh. "Chemistry, I mean. He wanted me to marry him, but I knew that wouldn't change a thing. It would have been formalizing the deceit between us."

"I don't think you could deceive anyone, not really, not over the long haul."

She stared at him, her eyes intense, her lips parted slightly. "I take that as a compliment."

"It was meant that way."

"Thank you. He made some fairly bitter accusations when we broke up. I thought he understood. I thought he knew how I felt and was willing to take things on those terms. It's funny. He was always so cerebral even when we . . . I don't think he loved me, not really. Not like Alex did with Tracy. Like I said, maybe it's either there or it isn't."

"Believe me, that doesn't always work either. I was crazy about Brenda, but it was obvious to everyone, even to me, that it could never last. Maybe what you're talking about doesn't always just happen. Maybe it takes time and . . . respect for the person. God knows, I'm sick to death of beautiful scheming women. You women are smarter than men. You don't automatically fall for someone with a beautiful body and nothing inside, someone vain and cruel and stupid. Yes, you're smarter than that." He realized his voice was hoarse and loud. Smith and the priest had stopped talking. "Sorry—I didn't mean to dump all of that on you. It just kind of slipped out. I don't feel very well, and . . ."

"It's all right. I . . . I'm sorry."

141

He shook his head. "Don't be. I did it to myself. You had nothing to do with it."

She raised her hand, and he could tell that she wanted to touch him. His own hands were still in his pockets. "It's never that simple, Steve. I . . ." She looked out the window. "God, look at it snow."

The flakes no longer melted on the pavement, but the cars ahead of them had cut black strips through the snow. The Cherokee interior gave things a reddish cast. Steve wondered if her face were flushed or if it were only the light.

"Women aren't always so rational, you know. They . . . I should let you rest. You look so tired."

"I like talking to you. It keeps the darkness from . . . it makes me feel better."

"What do you mean 'the darkness.' "

"Darkness? I don't know. It just . . . I'm not making much sense."

"Now what the hell is this?" Smith exclaimed. Ahead up the slope was a line of cars, their brake lights pairs of red eyes glaring through the falling snow. The Cherokee swerved slightly as he hit the brakes. They stopped behind a big station wagon with cross country skis on the top rack. "Goddamnit! It's nearly eleven already. I wanted this whole thing over by one or two. Wonder what's going on."

Steve closed his eyes and heard the priest say, "Perhaps there's been an accident."

"Fuck! That's all I need. Well, we're not going anywhere. I think I'll have a look." The car lurched as he put it in park, then the door slammed shut.

Mary laughed. "We were an hour late getting started, and now he's in a big hurry."

"I noticed that," Fred said. "All the same, I want to get away from the mountain before dark."

"God." He could hear the fear in Mary's voice. "So do I. I think . . . I think they know we're coming."

Yes, Steve thought, oh yes. He felt himself drift off into sleep. The door slammed again, and Smith was cursing. He tried not to listen. The things were still lurking in the trees, but the moonlight on the mountain and the snow was brilliant, nearly bright as day, only blue and glacial. Perhaps this was an asteroid, an ice planet far from the sun, and these alien predators were . . .

He didn't have to stay in the woods. He struggled toward the Cherokee, and Mary was there waiting for him. She pulled the gray turtleneck off, her face and red hair momentarily hidden. Her skin was white, and he could see the outline of her ribs. Her breasts were small, the nipples a faint pink.

This is a dream, he thought, but she does look this way. Her body is slim and beautiful, even if she doesn't have breasts and hips like Sarah. She isn't so strong, so hard, so cold. He ran his hand up along her flank. She felt soft and warm, and he was freezing. Her blue eyes stared into his. She kissed his knuckles, then her lips touched his, the kiss tentative. Her mouth was warm too.

"Oh, Steve," she whispered. She kissed him hard.

He tried to tell her this was not a good place, but she wouldn't let him warn her. She clung to him with her arms and hands and legs, she cried out, and then he saw Sarah in the closet, hiding in the shadows and watching, the dark coat wrapped about her naked form.

The dread closed again about his heart, and he realized what he was going to do. Mary's face was flushed, her eyes closed. He almost gagged, his tongue thrusting out, and then his mouth closed about her throat and was suddenly filled with the hot, wet taste of blood. Mary wailed, and he felt the life flowing out of her. Soon she was as cold and dead as he. He began to weep, but Sarah thought it was funny. She came out of the closet.

Something felt odd in his mouth. He touched his teeth, and they all began to slip out, scattering like tiny white pebbles across Mary's bloody throat. Only two teeth were left, big awkward things that didn't belong to him. They were like Sarah's. He wanted to vomit.

"She wasn't like us. Why did you make me kill her?"

Sarah's eyes burned with fury. "You're a fool."

"Steve—Steve." Mary was talking to him. Her face was bluish white like the pocked moon and the snow, shadows under her eyes, the blood on her neck black. Her teeth were ragged looking, broken and sharp. She was angry, and she was going to hurt him, to do something terrible. He wanted to scream, but somehow he could not—he was paralyzed, unable to move, to speak.

He opened his eyes and sat up. The Cherokee was moving again. The priest stared at him over the seat back, the brown eyes behind the thick glasses worried. His breath smelled of tobacco, and he had a small dark mole by his nose. Mary had her hands on Steve's arm. He let out his breath, swallowed with difficulty, and sank back into the seat. His throat felt worse, and he wished there was something to drink.

"You must have been having a nightmare."

He looked at her. The image of her naked was still vivid in his mind. He stared out the window at the falling snow. The wind was blowing now, screaming through the hundreds of trees. The tall massive shapes along the road seemed to have come alive, their shaggy boughs quaking. Ahead of them were two red tail lights. "What time is it?"

"One o'clock," the priest said.

"I slept that long? Why aren't we there?"

"Because of a fucking truck," Smith said. "It took them over an hour to clear the road. Our turnoff should be a mile ahead. We follow a paved road for about four miles, then there's a secret underground tunnel. That asshole—I don't think he's even got snow tires on—I'm going around him."

"On a curve?" Fred asked.

"I'm doing the driving. If you don't like it, you can get out and walk back. I'm in four-wheel drive with snow tires on all the wheels."

"But can you stop if . . . ?" Mary began.

"Just shut the fuck up, okay, Miss Connely?"

He stepped on the gas. They swept by the long battered shape of the station wagon, a big old Ford from '78 or '79. Steve caught a glimpse of the driver's worried face under a red and yellow ski hat.

"Oh God," Mary said.

They roared around the curve, saw the big square face of the truck, its yellow-white beams brilliant, then felt the low boom of its horn. Smith gunned the engine, careened into the right lane, but the road was curving again. On their right was a drop-off, firs beginning in a valley far below. Smith hit the brakes, and the Cherokee skidded out of control, sliding sideways. They hit the five-foot snow bank and came to an abrupt stop.

Suddenly it was very quiet. The engine had killed. All around them the big flakes tumbled slowly down, merging into the white landscape, burying them in the snow. The old Ford wagon went by.

"Jesus fucking Christ," Smith whispered.

Fred ran his fingers through his white hair. "He had absolutely nothing to do with it."

"Goddamnit, I told you to . . ."

Mary quickly leaned forward. "Will you please just shut your big mouth, Mr. Smith. You might have killed us all with your stupid, reckless driving. You don't pass a car on a curve when you're almost to your destination. That's just stupidity. None of us particularly wants to be here, but you did invite me, so you can treat us civilly, or we will leave you and walk back to that little store we just passed. If you want to continue to risk your life driving like a fool, you can do so alone."

Smith's face was flushed, his eyes incredulous. He opened his mouth, then closed it.

"Now would you like us to help you push the car out of the snow bank?"

Smith took out his cigarettes. "Yeah."

Fred reached for the door handle. "You steer, Mary, and let us three push."

Smith had thrust a cigarette between his lips. His hands shook as he lit it. He opened his door and got out. The howling wind swept into the car.

Fred smiled at Mary. "Well done."

She shook her head. "His type is usually better at bullying men than women."

Since his side of the car was in the snowbank, Steve slid across the seat, then got out behind Mary. He had to brace himself against the door. The white flakes turned gray black, then red and blue sparkled in the darkness, the cry of the wind melting into the women singing. Dimly he heard Mary's voice. Her face and the falling snow gradually came back into focus.

"I stood up too fast."

She shook her head, the three creases in her forehead. "You shouldn't be here—you're sick. You're as stupid as he is."

The comparison with Smith hurt. He turned away, but she grabbed his arm. "I'm sorry. Crashing into snow banks makes me irritable." She got into the driver's seat.

Smith exhaled a hot cloud of smoke which the storm quickly dissipated. He grinned at Steve. "That little lady's got balls. This shouldn't take much work. It's in four-wheel drive, and two of the wheels are free." He put the cigarette in his mouth and placed both hands on the back of the car. Steve and the priest joined him. "Okay," he yelled, the word distorted by the cigarette in his mouth.

The tire in the snow bank spun, but the other wheels grabbed. They all pushed while Mary drove the jeep back onto the road. She put it in park, then stepped out and let Smith back in front. Steve collapsed onto the seat. His head and throat throbbed, blood pulsing, feeding the pain. Despite the heavy rag wool sweater and down parka, he had to struggle not to shake. He must have a fever. Mary was looking at him, her eyes worried. He tried to smile.

Up the road, under the shelter of the firs, stood the red wood sign for a trailhead. "That's it," Smith said. "We take the first right after that sign." The Cherokee turned into the trees. It was darker, but the tall firs sheltered them somewhat from the wind and snow. "We follow this road for four miles, then ... What the hell?"

The Cherokee stopped. Steve leaned forward. A metal

gate barred the way, massive chains and a padlock securing one end. "Goddamnit, no one said nothing about no gate." He put the car into park. "Wait a minute." The door slammed shut, and they watched him walk to the gate.

"I'm glad I wore my galoshes," Fred said.

Mary shook her head. "This is craziness. I wonder if he really knows what he's doing."

Smith got back inside, blew on his hands, then rubbed them together. "I've got a hacksaw, but it won't work on that fucking chain or the lock. It'd take a special blade. We'd better walk."

Fred sighed. "I believe you said something about four miles."

"Yeah. There'll be a small shed on the right side. The tunnel to the house comes out there." He pulled the Cherokee over, then shut off the engine. "Let's go."

Steve could hear the wind moaning in the firs. He got out of the car and again had to lean against it while things grayed over. Gradually the twilight world between the trees came back into focus. The flakes fluttered slowly downward like tiny shreds of torn paper. He looked up. They made tiny icy pings as they touched his face. He pulled on his leather ski gloves, then took a wool hat out of the other pocket. Four miles wasn't so bad. He ran more than that all the time, but his knee already hurt and he felt so weak.

Smith had put on black leather gloves, but his shorn skull made Steve feel cold. He took a gym bag from the back of the car. "Here's lunch." He gave them each two big chocolate bars. "Be sure and eat them. There's plenty more. It's easy to get hypothermia in this kind of weather."

"Especially without a hat." Fred had put on his own black dress hat. Now he looked like a priest out of some old movie from the thirties.

Smith shrugged. His black leather jacket didn't look very warm. "Cold don't bother me." Holding the bag in his left hand, he went around the fence and started up the road.

Steve looked at the chocolate bars. Nausea flickered down along his throat. He put them in his pocket and followed the priest. Maybe walking would stop his shivering.

"Aren't you hungry?" Mary had caught up to him. Her right glove held half a chocolate bar.

"No."

The road wound uphill through the firs, their dark trunks blotched with green and white lichens. The flakes stung Steve's eyes and made it hard to see. Everything was gray and dark and cold, and he felt sick and dizzy. The pain in his knee grew steadily worse. He knew if he ever really stopped, he would never be able to get going again. His hands inside his parka pockets shook, and when he paused his legs would quiver, a shudder working its way up his back and locking his teeth together. The priest was in lousy shape, and Mary stayed with him at the rear. Steve had long legs but couldn't keep up with Smith—which was fine. He wanted to be alone. He didn't want to have to talk to anyone. It took all his strength just to keep walking.

They trudged along forever, and Steve ignored it when the sky darkened and the white forms of women curled, snakelike, about the trees. He concentrated on following Smith's black shape through the snowy void.

He was used to pushing on when his body cried out for him to stop.

Smith grew larger, blacker, and now several other black things materialized out of the snow. They threw themselves at Smith, howling and barking. "Oh, shut the fuck up!" Smith yelled. "Goddamnit. Oh, Goddamnit." The things kept on barking.

Gray lines formed a pattern against the universe of white. Steve tried to remember where he'd seen such a grid. Behind it, the dogs' black faces twisted in hate as they snarled and barked. A tall thin one threw itself at Smith again, and the lines of the pattern quivered.

"Goddamnit," Smith muttered, then yelled *"Shut up!"* at the dogs. At this, two more hurled themselves at the chain link fence.

Steve lifted his head and saw the snow-covered galvanized pipe running horizontally above his head, then the curling barbed wire. The snowflakes striking his eyes made him blink. Smith scowled as he walked by. Two of the dogs were big German shepherds, two were Doberman pinschers, the others he didn't recognize. They all had yellowish teeth, the insides of their mouths pink and wet. The pack of them would willingly kill a man, just rip him to pieces.

"Steve!" Mary called.

He turned, staggering slightly, and saw the others standing down the road together. His legs moved.

"Goddamnit, we must have walked right by it. Three-thirty already. Jesus—I can't believe it!"

The priest's face was flushed. Mary's orange ski hat was the only bright color Steve could see in the shadowy landscape dominated by the white of the snow and the dull dark browns and greens of the trees. "I can," the priest said.

Mary nodded. "Me too. I'm so tired. That has to have been more than four miles."

"It was. From the gate to the fence over there is four and half miles. We must have already passed the Goddamn shed. Let's go."

"Can't we rest for a moment?" Mary asked.

"No! We're running out of time. I sure as hell don't want to wander in there after the sun's gone down." He started walking.

"How are you doing?"

It took Steve a moment to realize she was talking to him. "Fine."

"Are you . . . ?"

The darkness snuffed out her face, a dull roar drowning out the barking dogs and the wind. A falling sensation, tumbling through the abyss, and then her face materializing again out of the gray.

"Oh God, Steve—are you all right?"

"His face feels hot," the priest murmured.

"Shit—this is all we need. Why the hell did he come along if . . . ?"

"Oh, be quiet—just be quiet." Her face hovered above him. "Can you get up?"

"I think so."

The priest held one of his arms, and she had the other. He swayed slightly as the darkness closed about him again. His skull swelled and throbbed, but they had a firm hold on him. He took a deep breath. "I'm all right. I was just dizzy."

The priest sighed. "At least it's downhill from here."

Smith turned his back to them and started walking. "Come on."

"Don't go too fast! You'll walk by the shed again." Mary smiled wickedly, then shook her head and looked at the priest. "Let's stay with him." They still held his arms.

"I'm all right." His throat was so sore the words came out funny.

"Sure you are. You look wonderful." Her nose was red, and the orange hat left only the bottoms of her ears exposed.

After a few moments they let go of him but stayed at his side. Smith was way ahead. He would wait for them to catch up, then eagerly start off again. The icy frost on his hair and eyebrows went with his angry visage. The snow would pile up on his head until he had to brush it off his short hair. The trees were a living presence all around them, silent and still. Snow hid the ferns, and the barren stalks of a blackberry bush thrust out like a tangle of thick gray hairs, a few shriveled berries hanging forlornly.

"Is it getting darker?" Steve whispered.

Mary glanced overhead. "Maybe it is. The sun is lower in the sky."

"It's not snowing quite so hard." The priest suddenly stopped and raised his arm. *"Look."* About twenty yards away, blending in with the trees was a small shack. "Smith—*Smith."*

"What!"

"There's something here."

When Smith saw the shed, he shook his head. "It was supposed to be closer to the road."

Underneath a cover of snow, the edge of the roof was

rotten-looking, thick yellow-green moss growing on the decayed wood. Overhead the limbs of the firs swayed softly. The wooden door was twisted in the frame, a black gap showing at the top, the padlock orange with rust.

"Can you pick the lock?" Mary asked.

Smith grinned. His teeth were white but crooked looking. "Step back a little." He raised his right leg, then screamed and kicked out. The rotted wood split at the hinges, and the door fell in. Smith opened the bag and took out a long chrome flashlight and a chocolate bar. "Anyone else hungry?" Mary and Fred nodded while Steve shook his head. Smith gave them each a bar, then turned on the flashlight and stepped inside.

"You ought to eat something," Mary said. "No wonder you passed out."

He shook his head. The shack had a musty smell but was warmer. In the middle of the floor was a big piece of plywood, the ends decayed and uneven. Smith got his fingers under the board, then raised it up and let it fall back against the wall. He shined the beam of light down. The hole was square-shaped, about eight feet deep, with a wooden ladder against one side. The floor was dirt, but the circular tunnel entrance looked like concrete pipe. Instinctively Steve backed away. He realized he was still trembling.

"Not very inviting," Fred said.

Smith shook his head. "No. I've got a couple more flashlights. It's about a fifteen-minute walk, then we'll get to a stone passageway. The owner after Baumgartner had the pipe laid in the late fifties, extending the passageway almost half a mile. Four-fifteen now, and it's not dark until after six. I think we may just get this done

153

after all." He gave Mary and the priest a flashlight, then climbed down the ladder. "Someone toss me my bag."

Steve was the last one down the ladder. His throat felt like someone was squeezing it. They were crowded together in the hole, and he could hear them all breathing. Everything seemed shimmery, probably because of his fever. The opening was a little under six feet high. Smith shined his light down the tunnel. A thin black trickle of water was in the center of the pipe, the walls covered with some dark moss or fungi.

Smith gave a harsh laugh. "I hope there aren't any fucking rats in there."

A muscle on the side of the priest's face twitched. "Did you really need to mention that?"

"They'd run out the other end if they heard us coming. Jesus, it's black in there. I never did like tunnels. It won't get easier—let's go." He stepped forward.

Steve could hear something breathing in the darkness, then the voices of the women. He closed his eyes, and Smith seemed to split into two images. One face was dead white with bright red blood pouring from the mouth and nose, the black leather jacket soaked with the blood. *"No!"* Steve screamed, and the tunnel amplified his voice, hurling the sound back at them even as the cry echoed off into the passage.

Smith pulled a square blue-black automatic out of his jacket pocket. The others all backed away from him. "Goddamnit! Don't do that, you stupid fucking bastard!"

Steve sagged against the dirt wall, his whole body shaking. Icy air came out of the tunnel, its open mouth spewing the stench of carrion, and the faces around him trembled and danced in the yellow-white of the flash-lights.

"Steve—Steve." Mary had hold of him. "What's wrong?"

"They're waiting for us—there in the tunnel."

"Who's waiting for us?"

"Them—the vampires—both of them."

Smith frowned. "Both of them? There's only supposed to be one."

"Oh."

"Listen, she can't come out until dark, and that's over an hour away. If there's anything alive down there, this little nine-millimeter buddy of mine will take care of it, okay?"

The priest shook his head. "You fire that thing in the tunnel, and we'll all be deaf."

"I don't plan on firing it, because I don't think anything's down there except maybe some rats, like I said. I think our friend here's just a wee bit chicken shit."

"It's you they want," Steve whispered.

Mary and the priest stared at Steve, but Smith nodded. "Sure. Me, I think it's you they want, and they can have your ass for all I care."

Mary rested her hand on Steve's shoulder. "Why don't you wait here? It's warm and sheltered."

"That," Smith said, "is one hell of a good idea."

Steve felt his eyes fill with tears. He wanted so much just to lie down and rest for a while. "No, I'm coming."

"But . . ."

Smith cut her off. "Okay, fine, but you keep your fucking mouth shut while we're in there, understand? No more yelling or whimpering or any of that shit, okay?" Steve nodded. In the dim light Smith's face

155

looked drawn and strained. "Let's go, then. Jesus, I hate tunnels." Holding the flashlight before him he started down the passageway.

Mary and the priest looked scared. Fred took off his hat and smiled wearily. "I'll go next."

Steve stood up and clenched his teeth. Mary grabbed his arm. "Steve."

He tried to smile. "It's okay." Stopping and starting made it worse. Her sympathy made it worse.

The blackness swallowed them. He had to stoop slightly to keep from hitting the top of the tunnel. The others wouldn't have that problem. Mary's light splashed yellow-white on the floor, then on the walls around them. He could hear all the footsteps, amplified, with a slight echo, and the labored breathing of the priest. Blackness everywhere, waiting for them, the world of light gone forever. This was the tomb, the grave. He was shaking again, and fear made the concrete walls waver and seem to close about him. He wondered briefly whether they could get him out if he collapsed again. Smith wouldn't even try.

Chapter 6

Mary was glad to be only five-foot-four inches tall. Walking on the curved pipe was awkward enough without having to stoop, as Steve did. Each foot wanted to be on the bottom where the dark water sat.

She wasn't particularly claustrophobic, but it was nasty sealed in like this, even the wall stained and slimy. Cold, too. She would have thought it would be warmer here under the earth, but the tunnel grew colder and colder. No one was really going to seal off the ends and smother them or flood the pipe with a torrent of water. And the concrete pipe was thick enough not to collapse. So why was it so frightening down here? She wished Smith hadn't mentioned rats.

Steve stopped walking. She put her hand on his shoulder. "Are you okay?" She felt him trembling.

"I . . . I think so. Is it much further?"

She opened her mouth, but Smith's voice reverberated back at them. "I hope not!"

Steve let out a ragged sigh. "Christ, I wish I could at least stand up right." He started forward.

She had known from the first glance at him this

morning that something was wrong. His face was so pale, his dark eyes weary yet agitated. He must have a fever now and probably chills. Why had he been so intent on coming along?

It would be nice to think it was for her, but they hardly knew one another. And what was wrong with *her*, anyway? She hadn't reacted to a man this way in a long time. She had thought she had finally outgrown it. She'd always found him attractive, but he had seemed distant and inaccessible. Men like him went for tall willowy blonds with husky voices and lots of makeup.

In the car he had seemed lonely, sad, and full of contempt for Tracy. That was real, she was sure of it. The way he had looked at her . . . He seemed interested, but for how long? Maybe when he was over the flu he'd go running after Tracy again. But she had been telling the truth when she said she had never felt this way about David, not after sleeping with him for over a year. Steve looked so sick. She wanted to take care of him—and to love him, to stroke his bare shoulders, his chest and his sides. Just once it would be nice to make love to a really attractive man, someone physically strong, even if . . .

"Jesus!" Smith's word careened off the concrete walls and swept past her.

Mary jerked to a stop, then caught up with Steve and shone the light past him.

"What is it?" she heard Fred say.

"I was right about the rats—big gray fuckers. They took off in the other direction. Let's get out of here— let's go. Jesus God, we must be near the end."

Steve's back quivered faintly and steadily. "Come on," Mary said softly.

158

He took one step, staggered slightly, and kept going. "I'm so cold," he murmured.

"It is cold down here, Steve. I'm freezing too."

Her breath formed a mist in the dim yellow light. A faint drip could be heard, growing louder. Mary shined her flashlight along the top of the pipe. Every few feet a seam formed a black line. Steve suddenly stopped. Before him water from a crack in the pipe came down in a thin stream.

"It's all right," she said. He began walking. Mary twisted sideways, not wanting the fetid water splashing on her.

Ahead of them was an opening. Someone bobbed a flashlight. When they stepped out into the square passageway Fred smiled at them and put his hat back on. His face was very pale.

"Dear God, I'm glad that's over."

"Yes," Mary said.

Steve slumped against the wall. Both Mary and the priest grabbed for him. "I'm all right." He sounded hoarse. "Now."

"Where's Smith?" Mary asked.

"He was in a hurry to get out of here. He said the stairway up to the house is only a couple hundred feet or so away."

"Let's go," Mary said.

They walked abreast, Steve in the middle, flashlights aimed at the ground. Dark slabs of stone formed the walls, ceiling and floor. At the end of the corridor, a steep stone staircase rose up the shaft to a stone landing, then another stairway rose in the opposite direction.

They came out into a chamber about ten feet wide and fifty feet long. The walls were of the same dark stone, but overhead were the last few feet of the joists, the massive beams supporting the wood of the first floor. On the outer wall, just below the joists, long slits opened in the stone, forming windows a foot high and three feet long. Through them came shafts of gray-white light, a few isolated snowflakes drifting down. Smith sat slumped against the wall smoking a cigarette.

Mary sighed. She knew how he felt. It was so good to be out from under the earth where you could see the light of the sky again.

"Welcome," he said, "to the basement—part of it, anyhow—of the romantic Baumgartner Chateau. That circular staircase there at the far end will lead us to Madame Rambouillet. We've got a good hour until sunset. This'll be a piece of cake now." He stood and tossed his cigarette butt aside.

Mary looked at Fred and Steve, then said, "Can't we rest for a moment?"

"There'll be plenty of time for that soon enough." He lit another cigarette, then picked up his bag.

They followed him, their footsteps on the stone echoing softly. The light from the windows had a pinkish yellow cast. She watched a flake swirl slowly toward her, vanishing on her cheek with a brief, icy sting. Fred took out a cigarette and gave her an apologetic look as he lit it up.

She smiled. "You've earned it. I almost wish I smoked." Steve looked exhausted, but his eyes wandered restlessly around the room. Mary slipped her hand under his arm. "I hope this is almost over."

He gave his head a shake. "It hasn't even started. I'm cold."

"You have a fever, don't you?"

"Yes."

"You shouldn't have . . . Why did you come, Steve?"

He stared straight ahead. "I . . . I don't know. I really don't know."

Smith stood before the circular stairway which wound up through a gap in the ceiling. "This goes all the way up to the top of the tower. There's a false wall along the whole south side, three feet of space between it and the real outer wall. There are two-way mirrors to the big bedrooms on the second and third floors. Baumgartner was a pervert, liked to watch the company balling. Guess he became quite an expert on the sex life of his guests. He used to invite movie stars up here all the time, especially the young starlets. There's a secret door at the back of the closet to the master bedroom which lets you behind the false wall. This has always been a big secret. Baumgartner worked with an architect he could trust and a very small, select building crew."

He started up the stairs, and Mary followed. "Come on," she heard Fred say gently to Steve.

"How do you know all this?" she asked Smith.

"I told you. Once we found out where she was, we got a full report on the chateau. They dug up the original architect's plans and even interviewed some old-timers. It took a lot of work."

The stairs were heavy oak planks which wound round a black metal post in a tight spiral. Mary had her right hand on the metal railing. The pungent smoke from Smith's cigarette hung in the air, and she could hear Fred puffing behind her. She passed through the opening. The long hallway on the main floor was much narrower than in the basement. A few small holes in the outer wall let in some light, but the dark stone was hard to illuminate.

"Didn't Baumgartner end up bankrupt?" she asked. She spoke softly. The place had a massive and sinister aura, the silence itself foreboding. Dimly she heard the wind outside.

"Yeah. He had to sell the place in fifty-two."

"And when was it built?"

"Late thirties, like I told you before. A year after Timberline Lodge. He did use a bunch of the same stonecutters and masons."

They were past the second floor, the narrow hall identical to the prior one. "And he really did spy on his guests?"

"He sure did. Maybe when we're done we can take a look through one of the bedroom mirrors."

Fred was breathing hard. "Could we please rest for a second? I'm sorry, but . . ."

"Sure." Smith was in good spirits. He leaned back against the rail and took out another cigarette. The orange light from his lighter flickered briefly across the dark stone all around them. "We got plenty of time."

The moan of the wind rose and fell softly. Mary wished this were over with. Dear God, protect us all. She wished she were somewhere warm and safe, like in bed with Steve, and that Tracy—or Sarah, or whoever she was—was gone forever. She had cast such a dark shadow over Mary's life. The trite metaphor didn't convey so evil an influence. If she really were somehow in league with a vampire . . . Mary wished she were dead—she deserved to die for what she had done to Alex. As for Steve . . . sick as he was, she doubted he

162

could have slept with Tracy last night. Perhaps he would be safe now.

The end of Smith's cigarette glowed red. "Ready?"

Fred sighed. "I suppose so. I didn't realize this would be quite so strenuous an endeavor."

Mary laughed. "Poor Fred. I know just how you feel."

"I haven't walked so much in years."

"How are you doing, Steve?"

"All right." His voice was hoarse, listless.

They climbed up and up. Mary's legs ached. When they went through the ceiling of the third floor, the space constricted, the outer wall curving tightly around the staircase.

"We're in the tower now," Smith said. "The false wall goes all the way up. There's another circular stairway inside the center of the tower, but it doesn't go to the top, up to what you might call the attic. That's where Rambouillet will be."

Mary hesitated. "How could your sources know that?"

"They know it." Smith sounded utterly confident.

"But how could they know such a thing?"

"Listen, Miss Connely, don't sweat it. You just let me worry about that."

Steve was right, she thought. He is a pompous little asshole. Fred was panting again, and Steve's breathing sounded hoarse and labored. The tower was darker than down below, the small holes in the outer wall fewer. Mary climbed past one, a bright oval which breathed frigid air on her. The light had changed. It must be clearing. If so, the cold would probably get far worse. She wiggled her toes in the thick wool socks. Not numb yet.

Above her the final opening was cut into the wood

planks between the thick joists. The stairway ended in a room with a twenty-foot circle for a floor. The stone walls rose about four feet above the floor, and all around the tower were windows about two feet wide and a foot tall. Overhead the dark wood tapered in a cone, the center a good twelve feet high. In the middle of the circle on a massive table sat a coffin of shiny black metal, the pink from the sky forming highlights along its length.

Mary stopped abruptly, fear shimmering along her spine and forcing a shudder. The coffin was proof that her worst fears were all true: she was caught in a vast web of evil.

"Dear God," Fred whispered.

Smith glanced at his watch, then strode to a window. Pinkish yellow light streamed from the openings on the west side. "Nice view," he said. "Still plenty of time." He walked over to the coffin and set down his bag.

Mary hadn't moved. Fred and Steve were beside her, the coffin between them and Smith. He used both hands to raise the lid. "Heavy bastard," he murmured. The black rectangle hid his torso, left his pale face floating in mid air. A strange smile pulled at the corners of his mouth. "She's here, all right. Have a look folks. You all wanted to come along."

Mary moved first. It was even colder up here than in the passageway. Her legs and hands were trembling. Smith leered at her. The top of the coffin faced west, its interior in shadow, the dimmest part of the tower. A white gown left the woman's arms and lower legs bare, and you could see the nipples and the darker pubic hair through the translucent fabric. Her feet flopped sideways at about a thirty-degree angle from the vertical, her long bony toes almost more like fingers. The thin

164

bare limbs and her narrow feet looked so cold, so vulnerable, the skin bluish white in the glacial air. Mary shuddered again. To be practically naked up here ... She should be frozen solid.

The woman's eyes were half open, her lips parted slightly. The long oval of the face lay on a pillow amidst a tangle of yellow white hair. She didn't look quite the same as in the daguerreotype, but she had been alive then. The only real color was in her lips, the rosy flush clashing with her icy complexion. She was very beautiful, but you could see that she was dead even though her eyes were somehow awake. Under the thin bluish lids, the fragments of gray-brown were conscious. She was watching them. And she was evil—nasty. Mary could well believe she fed on blood, on life. She might appear beautiful, but her body was only a shell—she was like a mosquito gorged with blood. Crush her, and you would leave only a smear of stolen blood. For a moment the sense of loathing overcame her fear.

"God," she whispered. "She's so horrible."

Fred's face was pale. "She looks like she's sleeping. Are you sure ... ?"

Mary shook her head emphatically. "Look at her eyes—she's not sleeping. She's dead, Fred—*dead*. Can't you see?"

"Oh Christ," Steve groaned.

Smith opened the bag and took out a long sharp wooden stake and a heavy mallet. "Miss Connely is right. She's very dead, but soon she'll be deader. I didn't think it would be quite so easy. Did you see the name?" He pointed the stake at the letters set into the black metal: RAMBOUILLET. He looked at Mary again, his lips still twisted into a smile. "Convinced I was telling

165

the truth? You and your pals shouldn't have any doubts now."

"She looks so cold," Fred whispered.

Smith shook his head. "She can't feel a thing. I guess that's not quite right." He laughed and raised the stake. "She'll feel this, all right. Who'd like to hold a flashlight for me? Not that I could really miss, anyhow." He was staring at Mary.

She flicked on her flashlight, shone it at the face—the eyes had changed—then on the chest. "Go ahead," she said.

Smith laughed again. "You've got guts, all right, lady—more than either of your friends."

"Just do it." She realized she hated that creature lying in the coffin. How many Alexes had it killed down through the years?

The ends of Smith's crooked teeth showed between his lips. He put the point of the stake on the sternum between her breasts, between the pink smears of the nipples visible through the white fabric. Up toward the collarbone you could see the lines where her ribs came together.

"Hold it steady now." Smith's voice was pitched oddly. "She won't hold still much longer." He raised the mallet over his head, then brought it down squarely on the stake.

Mary saw the white balls of the eyes protrude, the lips opening into a howl which bared the long sharp teeth; then the corpse's arms and legs jerked spasmodically. Cold dark blood splattered across her parka. Steve screamed once and collapsed, while Fred turned away. Smith struck again and again as the thing writhed and clawed, the long white limbs flailing about, its eyes full of hatred. Finally it lay still, the hate slowly fading from the dead eyes. Blood covered its chest, and Smith had more blood on him than Mary did.

He grinned at her, his eyes wild. "That wasn't so bad."

"God help us." Fred had knelt beside Steve. "Are you all right?"

Steve had clapped both hands over his chest, the blue ski gloves covering the red parka. "My chest *hurts,*" he whispered.

"Your boyfriend's really saved the day, Miss Connely."

"Shut up. Finish the job."

Smith raised his eyebrows. "You know about that?" Smiling again, he took an enormous knife from the bag.

"It's in *Dracula,*" she whispered, holding the light on the thing's white throat.

"You still want to watch?"

"Yes."

Fred gave her a strange look, then helped Steve up. "Come on, let's get away from here."

Mary saw the sharp steel edge slice through the white skin, opening a red seam. Smith's arms were very strong, and he grunted as he worked the blade. The thing might have made a final sound.

"So much for Madame Rambouillet."

Smith held up the severed head by its yellow white hair. The eyes were still open, but now all the life was gone—and the beauty. The face was ghastly. Mary shuddered and lowered the flashlight. The revulsion twisted at her insides, and she turned and walked away.

Steve had sat up, but his face was absolutely white.

167

"My throat hurts," he murmured. "It hurts." Fred looked almost afraid of her.

She went past them to a window, then dropped down on one knee to look out. They were on top of a hillside of snow covered firs, and across from them was the immense summit of Mount Hood, its icy ·ridges like blue white fire. It was clear now, absolutely clear, the sky a faded blue which turned pinkish yellow near the horizon. She could hear the soft moan of the wind in the distant trees below.

"I thought she might decompose," Smith said to no one in particular, "crumple to dust. Maybe she will later. So long, Madame Rambouillet. It's been fun." The coffin lid shut with a clump. "Mission accomplished, men—and lady. Still a few minutes before sunset, too."

Mary was aware of the tears in her eyes, but she didn't know whom they were for—Alex, that thing in the coffin, Steve, or perhaps for herself. For the strange exultation she had felt when Smith drove the stake through the vampire. She got up.

Smith lit a cigarette, then dug around in the bag and came up with a chocolate bar. He walked over by a window facing west, glanced out at the setting sun, then sat down. "I'm glad to have that over with." Out came a cloud of tobacco smoke. "Hey, I almost forgot—I came well prepared." He opened a leather-covered flask, then took a big swallow. "Jesus, that tastes good."

Mary watched him. He was so easy to dislike. That smug smile, that meticulously trimmed little black mustache, the shorn look above his red ears where his hair had been cut so short. And he was smiling at her, utterly satisfied with himself, as if he couldn't imagine she could possibly resist so magnificent a specimen of masculinity, his muscles and black leather.

"Come on, lady, have a swig."

She shook her head and looked out the window again.

"It'll do you good. Come on. It'll warm you up."

She wiped at her eyes, her fingertips covered by the rag wool gloves, then walked over to him. He grinned and handed her the flask. She took a swallow, then coughed. The strong liquid flamed down her throat like lava.

"What is this?"

"Bourbon. Straight bourbon."

She took another swallow. At least it warmed you. Smith still watched her, that faint, smirky smile twisting his lips. She walked over to Fred. Smith had frowned. The priest was standing, but Steve sat slumped against the dark stone wall, his face still dreadfully pale.

"Have some," she said.

Fred stared at Steve. "Give it to him first. He needs it."

Steve's eyes were feverish, and he looked only half awake. He shook his head.

Mary held out the flask. "Drink it, for God's sake—you look awful."

Steve's eyes were fixed on her. Finally he took the flask and drank. Immediately he began coughing, his right hand clutching at his belly.

Mary gave Fred the flask. They stared at each other. His mouth made a grim, straight line, and through the thick lenses his eyes were troubled. He took a big swallow, then handed her the flask. "Thank you." He still seemed wary of her.

She returned the flask to Smith. He was halfway

through his cigarette and the chocolate bar. "My client will be very pleased when he hears how this turned out."

"Your client?" Why did he seem amused?

"Yes. Finally he's avenged. For his son. Somehow I just didn't think it would be quite so easy. You know, you handle yourself pretty well."

She stared at him.

"Yeah. You sure have more balls than your boyfriend there." As usual, the word "boyfriend" was ironic.

Mary realized her face must be red. She wanted to slap him, but she turned and walked over to the window again.

Mount Hood had turned a vivid pink. The ridges and spurs of ice, the vast curves of the snowfields, were all enveloped in a rosy glow. Color was draining from the sky, seeping away into the vacuum of space. It looked like a scene from an astronomy book, some distant icy planet far from its sun. Portland, the college, her life as a teacher, her students—all that seemed light years away, a part of her life gone now forever.

Smith stood up. "Let's get out of here. We've got a long way to walk yet. There's a moon tonight, so we won't have no trouble following the road, but we better get started. I wanta get that fucking tunnel over with, too." He wiped off the bloody knife blade with a rag, then put both in the bag and zipped it shut.

Mary helped Fred get Steve up. "Can you walk okay?" she asked.

He nodded.

"Let's go then," Smith said. "Jesus, it is colder than a witch's tit up here."

Fred didn't move. Mary turned to him. "What is it?"

He stared at her without answering.

170

"Come on," Smith said.

Fred shook his head. "Not yet. There's something I have to do."

"What are you talking about?"

Fred walked slowly toward the coffin. "She would have been Catholic, once long ago. I need to pray for her. For her soul."

Smith laughed once. "Forget that crap. She's very dead."

Fred glared at him, then looked down at the black coffin. He used both hands to open it. He shuddered, then raised his eyes and began to speak. "Eternal rest grant unto her, oh Lord, and . . ."

"Shit," Smith murmured.

Mary walked toward Fred. She remembered the words from when her father had been buried. They lowered the coffin into the grave, threw down a spade of earth, and then you knew he was truly gone, gone forever—or at least for the long lonely years that remained of her life. Just like Alex. Grief rose up as it had on that day and seized her by the throat.

Fred took a white rosary out of his pocket and folded the corpse's hands over it. "May your soul rest in peace and may perpetual light shine upon you. May almighty God have mercy upon you . . . and upon all of us."

"Amen," Mary managed to say. She wiped at the tears with her gloved hand. Fred shut the coffin, then turned to her. She tried to say his name, but couldn't get it out. He put his arm around her, and they started for the stairway. She couldn't remember him ever holding her this way.

"Okay, let's get going." Smith was angry. "We don't

have time for this." Steve stared at them as if he were trying to resolve some puzzle.

Mary glanced out the window. The mountain was white again, all the color gone, and the sky had turned a pale violet. The peak looked farther away. The sun was down, night was coming swiftly, and it was already so cold, so terribly cold.

Chapter 7

They started down the stairway, round and round, ever downward, as if they were on a screw drilling deep into the earth. Toward the darkness of the tunnel, toward the tomb. Something was waiting for them there. His head and his chest and his throat and his knee ached, and he was so cold and tired of trembling. He would never be warm again. He would be left freezing in the earth like that dead thing in the coffin. None of them understood her suffering, her pain, but he had felt it even before Smith drove the stake into her.

He shuddered again, remembering the sensation of the cold hard wood sliding through his chest. It was as if he were some bug being impaled on a pin. And then what Smith did to her long lovely white throat . . . Such mutilation. Smith had reveled in it, enjoying her agony. Even Mary . . . He had seen the look in her eyes, the hatred. Only the priest had understood.

His chest hurt so. Could he be having a heart attack? But no, your average twenty-nine-year-old triathloner generally didn't have heart attacks. Nor did he feel a stake being driven into him or knives slicing open his throat. All along the stone wall echoed a kind of roaring he knew could not be real, no more than the red he saw when he closed his eyes or the bright colors swirling about the edge of his vision even as he fought to keep his eyes open. The fever, the fever made him . . .

An opening in the stone, a square of pinkish light, flickered briefly. He wasn't sure if he had blinked or if something black and winged had swept by.

Mary stopped suddenly, and he almost walked into her. "Did you see that?" she asked.

"What?"

"Something . . . something seemed to fly by."

He was glad to know he hadn't imagined it. "No. I didn't see anything."

The opening lit up her face, and he could see her pale blue gray eyes. "Good." She sighed, then started down again. "Thank God."

Steve wanted to say something, but his throat hurt too much. The pain wouldn't be so bad if he weren't so afraid. He couldn't stop being afraid, not since they had found the shack and the tunnel. He had known the tunnel was a gateway, but he couldn't turn back. Going through should be easier this time, but instead it was worse. Once the light was gone and they were in the dark stone passageway, the fear grew and grew until they reached the entrance to the concrete pipe. Even Smith looked worried, as if he suspected.

"The sooner we get going, the sooner we get to the other end." He shone the light on the concrete and grasped his bag firmly.

Steve groaned. "No. *No.*"

Mary touched him lightly on the arm. "Steve, it's all right."

Smith was glaring, but then he smiled. For an instant he was dead again, his face ashen, his leather jacket stiff with dried brownish blood. "I knew I could count on you. How the hell else do you suggest we get out of here if we don't use the tunnel? The dogs are still up there."

"You are a dead man," Steve whispered.

Startled, Smith dropped the bag. "What the fuck are you talking about, you crazy gutless bastard?"

Mary sighed wearily. "Oh, please don't start that." She still had hold of Steve's arm. "He's right, Steve. We have no other choice. It's the only way out."

The priest looked exhausted. "We have to stay together."

"Fred and I will be with you." Her voice was soft.

Smith grinned. "How sweet."

"Please keep your mouth shut," she said.

Smith went into the tunnel. Mary and the priest looked at each other. Their flashlights lit up the dark stones and their legs. "I'll go first," the priest said.

Mary gave Steve's arm a final squeeze. "I'll be right behind you."

Steve remembered as a boy standing on the high dive and freezing up, paralyzed by the distance to the water below.

"Come on." Mary's hand touched his back.

He stepped forward, stooping slightly so his head wouldn't hit the concrete. He sniffled once and realized his eyes were full of tears. If only his body would behave. He couldn't control it anymore. It quaked with a will of its own. Perhaps Hell would be like this, not a big open place with flames and heat, but a cold tiny hole, eternal darkness all about you.

175

A woman was singing again, but he couldn't make out the words. It might not be English. The others obviously didn't hear anything. They weren't deaf, so he must just be going crazy. A simple enough explanation. Perhaps it was a fever delirium, not insanity. The words were strangely beautiful, and his lips repeated them silently: fever delirium, fever delirium, fever delirium . . . One of the women distinctly whispered his name. Yes, he was going insane. That was all it was.

He saw the women before anyone else did. At first they were remote and tiny like something viewed through the wrong end of a telescope, and then he could see them in the darkness even as a cat would. The taller one he recognized at once. "Sarah." They both wore long white gowns made of thin silk which left their arms and feet bare. Steve felt colder just looking at them. Sarah was a few inches taller than the other woman, her light brown hair forming a tousled corona about her pale face. Her breasts and nipples, the curve of her hips, showed clearly under the fabric.

The shorter woman looked like a statue chiseled from milky marble centuries ago, her features clean and sharp. She had a few wrinkles about her eyes and mouth, her hair an ash blond color which made it hard to distinguish any white strands. Her eyebrows were high and darker, the eyes themselves fragments of blue-white ice, her long slender neck regal. Her skin had a faint bluish cast, all the life drained away. You could tell she was dead. Sarah, too. It wasn't quite so noticeable yet with Sarah, but it was still obvious. How could he have ever failed to . . . ?

"Jesus!" Smith cried out. The priest stopped for a moment, then walked slowly forward.

176

"Steve, what is it?" Mary's hand was on his back again.

The four of them came as close together as they could in the narrow tunnel. Steve didn't understand how he could see so much. The others were like wisps of mist between him and the two women. Sarah was in front of Madame Rambouillet, but he saw them both clearly. The concrete no longer seemed quite solid, and a harsh light flooded the tunnel, made the edges of things stand out with a preternatural sharpness.

"Tracy." Mary's voice resonated with fear and anger. The taller woman smiled at them, the expression utterly evil. Corruption had consumed her to the bone.

"He is yours," Madame Rambouillet whispered.

Steve felt the fear wash over him in great waves. Sarah's lips parted slightly, and she stepped forward.

An explosion, a boom, as if the earth itself had split apart. Steve clapped his hands to his ears. The noise seemed to echo inside his skull, swelling, not fading, refusing to die away. A red flower blossomed between Sarah's breasts, the tiny bloody leaves formed of flesh. She howled and fell back, her bare white legs and feet showing, then she seemed to fly up at them. Another boom echoed through the tunnel, the bullet careening off the concrete, but then Sarah had Smith by the throat, the gun clattering into the dark water at their feet.

The priest stepped back, nearly knocking Steve over, and all three of them retreated. Madame Rambouillet watched, a faint smile on her face. She made her way past Sarah and Smith, then bent to pick up Smith's bag. Sarah held Smith by the throat, smashing him back against the concrete, while he struggled vainly to pry

177

her hand free. The priest had shined his flashlight on them, and you could tell that his hand was shaking.

The smaller woman unzipped the bag. "So, you wished to kill the vampire, did you?" Her voice had a faint trace of a French accent, the Is pronounced like *ee,* the two syllables of "vampire" weighted equally. "You wished to rid the world of this curse." Her eyes gazed at Steve, then past him at Mary. "And you wished to avenge your brother. You were misled by this . . . insect here. What's wrong, Mr. Smith? Surely with all your muscles you cannot be restrained by a mere woman?"

She had taken out a wooden stake. She turned, and with a graceful, effortless motion, thrust it clean through Smith's belly just below his leather jacket. Sarah's hand held back any sound, but he gagged, his eyes protruding. Sarah gave a sharp laugh and let go of him. With a low groan he clutched at himself and slipped down along the curve of the pipe.

"Dear God," the priest whispered.

Smith's eyes were wide open and staring at them, his face white. "Jesus—help me—help me."

Madame Rambouillet had taken out the knife. The twelve-inch blade looked out of place held in her tiny white hand.

"I did not kill your brother, Miss Connely. Neither did the woman you know as Tracy. It was another vampire, a man, who did this thing. One of his tools, to be more precise. One who served him just as this Mr. Smith serves him. This brave detective, this fierce slayer of vampires—this pathetic vermin."

She was over Smith now, one bare foot in the dark water. Sarah had stepped back. "So you thought it would be so simple to kill me. You thought I was such a fool.

178

You are an imbecile. No mortal is clever enough to harm me. Did he promise you immortal life? Well, you are not going to live forever. You are going to die here and now. We will have your blood, but not in the manner which you might choose. You will die, and your body will rot in this dark place. The rats and other vermin will feed on your impressive muscles, for after all, they are nothing but meat, plentiful meat. Your bones will warn others who might think I am easy to destroy."

She grabbed his hand, then quickly and deftly cut his wrist to the bone before anyone could even move. The priest started, Smith howled feebly. The red blood gushed out below his palm. She let his hand drop, and he grabbed at his wrist with his other hand.

"For Christ sake—help me—*please.*"

Sarah laughed again. She knelt over him, then seized his arm and began to lap at the blood with her tongue. The gaping wound was like a mouth. Smith screamed, but you could tell that he was dying.

Madame Rambouillet raised her hand and pointed past them. "Go. There is a room on the second floor ready for you. Take the stairs, then go to the end of the hallway. Press on the right side of the panel, and you will enter the room through the secret passageway. Wait there for me. I promise that you will not be harmed. But now you know how I deal with my enemies." Her eyes shifted slightly, fixing on the priest. "Do not bother with your crosses, Father Martin. They will not frighten me. Now go."

"For God's sake," Smith moaned. "You can't leave—help me!"

Madame Rambouillet smiled. "No one can help you. He is already a dead man. Now *go.*"

179

Steve could see Sarah licking and sucking at Smith's wrist, could sense her pleasure as she tasted the warm living blood. She hardly seemed human any more, but her long white arm and her neck, the curve of her flank and thigh under the gown, were still so beautiful.

The priest turned, and Mary's flashlight briefly caught his face. His eyes were wide open behind the thick, glistening lenses, his mouth twisted. Steve knew exactly how he felt.

Mary made a kind of sob. "Let's get out of here—we can't help him."

They turned and walked away rapidly. Sarah laughed once. Smith began pleading again, but they couldn't make out the words.

Steve's head throbbed. A riot of sounds filled the tunnel—water dripping somewhere close by, the women laughing, Smith whimpering and moaning as Sarah devoured him, then the crunch of his bones under her sharp teeth, the priest gasping for breath, a dull rumble all around them like the earth humming. His blood had caught fire from the fever, his skull felt as if it might burst apart. Please, God, he thought—just get us out of this tunnel. Let me die above ground, in open air, and let my ashes be strewn so they'll soar with the winds—anything but being buried in this cold dark tomb—*anything.*

If Mary weren't in front of him, he could go faster. He thought of shoving her aside, then felt ashamed. The yellow beams of the flashlights danced wildly along the concrete walls. They must be near the end—they must be.

From behind, a mist suddenly swallowed them up in its damp icy blackness. Steve heard the priest yell. He wanted to cry out, but he couldn't breathe. He sank into the depths of the black lake water, the light of the moon gone now, his lungs screaming for air, but there was only the glacial water all around them. Then he burst free, and he was breathing again. Ahead, the dark mist swirled about in the yellow beams of light before sweeping onward.

The priest put one hand against the wall. "Good Lord—what was that?"

"Her," Mary whispered. She touched Steve. "Keep going—we're almost out of this."

Finally the lights showed the concrete narrowing to the circle where the pipe ended. Fred staggered out, then turned and sagged back against the stone wall. "Oh, thank God." His breath came in gasps. "So help me, I will quit smoking."

Mary was panting. "I don't have any excuse."

Fred stared back at the black hole. "We shouldn't . . . we shouldn't have run away."

Mary shook her head. "We couldn't do anything. The stake alone would have killed him, and they were too powerful."

Fred stared into the darkness. "We should have stayed with him. I've seen many people die. No one could do anything to save them, but they felt better because they weren't alone. It helps if . . . No one should die that way. No one." He glanced down at his hat, then put it on, his hands trembling.

"They wanted it that way. They would have driven us away." Anger warmed her voice. "They wanted him to die alone."

"Let's go," Steve said. "Let's get out of this place."

Mary nodded, and they started down the stone passageway. The big chamber in the basement was nearly dark, the light in the small windows a bluish purple. Steve felt some of the fear subside. At least he would die above ground, not in the underworld.

"I'm not going back there again," the priest said. "Not for anything."

Steve nodded. "That's right. Not for anything." His breath came out unevenly.

Mary's face was a pale oval in the dying light, even the fiery orange of her hat muted. "I wonder what she plans on doing with us."

"At least we can move around up here," the priest said.

Mary looked up at the windows. "Even if there were a way out, the dogs would get us. It's four miles back in the dark. And Smith had the keys." She shook her head, swallowed once, then looked at Steve. "You're so quiet. How are you?"

"I don't want to die like that." His voice was hoarse. He thought again of the tower, the stake tearing open his heart, the knife cutting a line of icy flame across his throat.

She took his arm and squeezed it tightly. They started up the spiral staircase, the yellow lights bobbing about on the beams overhead. Fear and adrenaline had kept Steve going in the tunnel, but now the weariness, the cold and pain were returning. When they reached the second floor, they started down the narrow hallway. The clumps of boots echoed, and through the scattered holes in the wall, the wind whispered frozen words at them. At the end of the corridor, to the side, stood a tall wide slab of wood. Mary hesitated, then pushed at the right side. The wood swung about, pivoting on its center.

They stepped into a large closet, the air permeated with the sweet smell of cedar. Mary opened one of the two doors. Steve had to duck to get under the clothes rod. The bedroom was larger than most living rooms and had two full-sized beds at the far end, the bedspreads and rug woven of a thick grey and burgundy wool. Two enormous windows, the dark stone arching in a smooth curve at the top, cast a cold violet light across the room. In the stone fireplace between the windows a fire burned, orange and yellow flames leaping and twisting about black logs.

Instinctively they went to the fire. The fireplace was big enough that they could stand together and share its warmth. Mary sighed, then peeled off her rag wool gloves, clenched and unclenched her fingers. They were red from the cold. Fred took off his hat. A few pops came from the fire, and a glowing ember shot like a meteor at them, landed on the dark stone sill and slowly died away. The priest pulled out a pack of cigarettes.

Steve was aware of the room growing darker. Women were whispering. He looked quickly at Mary, but she hadn't heard anything. He went to the window.

The summit of Mount Hood rose above everything, all white snow and blue-gray shadow, the sky behind it violet-black. A single bright star burned in the frigid emptiness. Winds stirred the snow, blurring the hard cold edge of the mountain. Mount Saint Helens had been gently rounded, the kind of politely symmetrical mountain a child would draw, while Rainier was a massive humped thing. Hood alone was pointed, sharp, something like a tooth, the jagged rear tooth of a dog. You could imagine some monstrous skull buried deep in the glacial snows, that single tooth thrusting forth, slashing at the sky itself. Steve shivered, turned, and collapsed into a big chair near the fire. His head and his knee felt better at once.

"Have a cigarette," Mary said.

"What? Oh." The priest's lighter flickered. "Thanks."

Mary unzipped her parka, glanced at Steve, then sat in the chair next to him. "Feel any better?"

He nodded. It was wonderful not to be walking, but he felt chilled again.

"You look cold. Your hands are still in your pockets."

He frowned, then slowly withdrew his hands. "The fire feels good."

The priest watched them. The hand holding the cigarette still had a slight quaver. His face was pale and weary, the black frames of his glasses only partially hiding the pouches under his eyes. "What do we do now?" he said softly.

"Nothing at all, Father Martin. Rest after what must have been an exhausting day."

The priest froze, while Mary stood up immediately. Madame Rambouillet was before the closet doors. A white robe, with frills at the chest and cuffs, covered her arms and shoulders, fell all the way to the floor. "You all look much better. The fire agrees with you, and the room is pleasant, is it not?"

The priest threw his cigarette into the fire, then stepped next to Mary.

Madame Rambouillet laughed. "How *gallante,* Father Martin, but if I wished to harm her, you could do nothing to stop me. You saw how ineffectual Mr. Smith's great muscles proved to be. The strength of a mortal can never match that of the undead. It would be simple for me to pick you up and hurl you through one of these windows. I suggest, therefore, that you relax yourselves and listen to me. Sit down. Sit next to your friend if it will make you more comfortable."

She walked toward them, stopping about ten feet from the fire. Mary and the priest sat on the small sofa. Madame Rambouillet stared at the flames, a small crease showing between her eyebrows. She was very beautiful, Steve thought, with the appearance of a woman near forty. The first full flush of her beauty might be gone, but the features—the strong thin nose and chin, the narrow lips—had a hard clean look, and she had a kind of authority you wouldn't find in a younger woman. Her pale blond hair was bound up in back, emphasizing her long slender neck. Her cheeks had more color than before, the bluish cast less noticeable. Perhaps it was only the warm light from the fire, or perhaps . . . Steve recalled suddenly that she was well over a hundred years old and that Smith's drained body lay dead in the underground tunnel.

"Realize that your lives are totally in my hands. Should I wish to destroy you, no power on earth could save you."

The room was silent except for the snapping of the fire and the faint cry of the wind. Why did I ever come? Steve wondered. His life was changed forever. He was bound to this woman.

"What about God?" Mary's voice had an edge of anger.

The vampire laughed. "I would not expect a miracle. He has seldom managed to frustrate me. No, only one man has frustrated me, another of my kind—Ruthven. It was he who destroyed your brother."

"*Ruthven?*" Mary whispered the word.

185

Madame Rambouillet smiled. "Ah, you know the name. It was familiar to many in the nineteenth century, not unlike *Dracula* today, but then we had neither cinema nor television, only an amusing opera. The original Ruthven, as you know, was a literary creation of Polidori, but this Ruthven is real enough. He adopted the name as a kind of jest. You are the first one to catch the joke in many years."

"You expect me to believe that this Ruthven, and not Tracy, killed Alex?"

Madame Rambouillet's smile wavered. Steve still felt sick and faintly dizzy. Things tended to blur and twist, but the vampire's face was abnormally sharp, as if he were looking at her through a tightly focused lens. Her eyes had a faint blue color, but were mostly gray.

"Use your intelligence. Tracy, as you call her, has only been a vampire for a little over twenty four hours. She held a respectable job, and you yourself saw her during the daylight. There is some truth in the lore about vampires. We are immobile during the day."

"Vampires are not the only ones who kill."

Madame Rambouillet shook her head. "You are strong and clever. I expected rather more of you. This is mere stupidity. Perhaps also, the jealousy." She glanced at Steve and smiled again.

Mary sat up stiffly. "What are you talking about?"

"You know very well. And I tell you again that you are letting your anger blind you. I do not expect you to like Suzanne—her name is Suzanne, not Tracy or Sarah—but you must not let your feelings overpower your reason. Suzanne has worked for me as long as you have known her. I had no reason to kill your brother. Ruthven did."

186

Mary's eyes were fixed on the woman. "Why?"

"Because Alex and Suzanne tried to destroy Ruthven and very nearly succeeded. He took his revenge, unfortunately, upon your brother. I was too late to save him."

"Why would Alex try to destroy him?"

"Because Suzanne asked for his help."

Mary's anger was out in the open again. "Then she did kill him."

Madame Rambouillet shook her head and unfolded her arms. "You are being obtuse. Keep silent for a moment. Ruthven and I despise each other. Our hatred dwarfs any feelings you mortals have. It has had over a hundred years to develop, to grow, to flourish. The undead do not love, in spite of what you may have heard. Ruthven is not some Byronic hero, a Heathcliff posturing at evil, and I am no romantic maiden. We are old, and we are dead, and we hate with a power and ferocity you can scarcely imagine. I would do anything to destroy Ruthven—*anything.*" As she spoke, her face blurred out of focus, her voice increasingly dissonant, and Steve thought she would transform into something else. Instead she clenched her fists, her eyes closed, then gave a hard, sharp laugh, the sound only remotely human.

"I show you only a glimpse of what I feel. Enough—this hatred is beyond your comprehension, but it is the central fact of my existence. I have pursued him across two continents. For many years there was a kind of false truce, but recently the battle resumed in earnest. Ruthven and I use tools because . . ." She laughed again. "This should amuse you. We cannot directly harm one another. A vampire cannot destroy a vampire. During the day we are immobile, paralyzed, and at night we are virtually indestructible. Can you harm an icy mist, a cold smoke? We are too strong, and even if we could be hurt, we can always dissolve ourselves and flee. This is why we use human agents. Only they can kill us. On your own you do not amount to much, but with our power and cunning behind you . . . I used Alex and Suzanne. Ruthven used Smith. And the three of you."

Mary's eyes were still fixed on her. "Why Alex? Why him?"

"Because he was young and strong. His athletic prowess was what brought him to my attention. It was not an endeavor for weaklings, as you should well understand—look at the two of you. Could you or the priest walk another few miles, or run, or fight with men or beasts? I think not."

Mary shook her head, her eyes filled with tears. "Oh God, I can't believe it."

Steve was so tired it seemed funny. People exercised to stay healthy, but he hadn't felt healthy for a long time. The whole thing had become a compulsive, losing struggle with pain and injury. He no longer enjoyed it, and he certainly didn't feel young and strong, not tonight.

"I suppose you chose Steve for the same reason," Mary said.

"Yes. We also wanted someone older this time. Your intrusion into the business with Mr. Ryan was unforeseen, but Ruthven had already decided to draw you in. He has a sense of irony. It would amuse him to turn one of my instruments against me. He must have also enjoyed the idea of using a woman. However, his sense of vengeance is rather all-encompassing. Even if you had

188

succeeded, he or Mr. Smith would have killed you shortly afterwards."

"Who was the woman in the tower?" the priest asked.

"No one that need concern you, a decoy, nothing more. She was a vampire. I had selected her for just such a purpose. Why should she suspect anything if I wished her to rest in my coffin in the tower? And Smith was more of a fool than I imagined. He didn't think to try to verify my identity. The fault is really that of Ruthven. He selected him for his muscular body, not for his brains. Of course, Ruthven has always had a weakness for sinewy youths."

"And Suzanne . . . She's a vampire now," Mary said. Madame Rambouillet nodded.

"You killed her yourself?"

"I gave her what she wanted, what I had promised. I gave her immortal life."

The two women stared at one another. Steve wondered how Mary could meet her eyes for so long. Mary shook her head. "You gave her death, only death."

The priest was frowning. "Only God can give immortal life."

Madame Rambouillet laughed. The sound had a jarring baritone quality. "Indeed? Then let him raise up Mr. Smith or her dead brother."

"What do you want from us?" Mary asked.

"Have you not guessed?" The priest went pale, and the vampire laughed again. "Relax, Father Martin. I can obtain nourishment from anyone. Your friend understands me better."

"You want us to kill Ruthven." Mary's voice was soft.

"Very good. May I call you Mary?" Mary frowned slightly, then nodded. *"Et tu comprends un peu francais,*

189

je crois?" Mary nodded again. *"Nous devons faire la causette.* It has been so long since I have spoken French with anyone of intelligence."

"You said yourself Fred and I are in terrible shape, and Steve's sick. We can't kill your Ruthven."

"I too have a sense of irony. It would amuse me greatly to see you destroy him. Also, I think Ruthven and I have relied too much on brawn. You are more intelligent, my dear, than either Suzanne or your brother. You may well succeed. And you have no choice but to try."

"No?" said the priest.

She shook her head. "There is no place where you can hide from me, and there is no way to protect yourselves. If you do not make the attempt, you will die, and not pleasantly, nothing so simple as having your blood drunk. I was fairly merciful with Smith, but it still took a while for him to die."

No one said anything. We're as good as dead already, Steve thought. He felt very cold, and he was trembling.

"How are we supposed to kill him?" Mary asked. "I don't know if . . ."

"No more wooden stakes. There is a simpler way." She gazed at the fireplace.

"How?" Steve asked. His throat hurt badly.

"You are going to burn him."

The priest stared at her. "What?"

"Not at night, of course. You would have no more luck trying to set him on fire than you would me. But during the day it will be simple. You will douse him with gasoline and light a match to him. He will burn like a great dead, dried-up log. A much faster, simpler

190

business than fooling with wooden stakes and knives."
She stared at the flames, a hint of revulsion in her eyes.

The priest shook his head. "This is impossible."

"Not in the least. Ruthven is on the coast, a four hour
drive from here. You may use the vehicle of Mr. Smith."
She took the car keys out of a pocket in her robe. "The
housekeeper will give you these in the morning. I shall
write out some instructions for you. You will spend the
night here, and tomorrow after breakfast, you will de-
part. The housekeeper will lock up the dogs and fetch
the car. You must finish your task before sunset. I trust
you will be warier than Mr. Smith. Ruthven has a mark
which makes him easy to recognize, a two-inch scar
along his left cheekbone. He fought a duel when he was
young and foolish. He is pale and thin, black haired, but
you will recognize him by the red seam of the scar. I
doubt he would think of a substitute, anyway. Oh, I shall
also leave for you two keys, one to his fence, the other
to his house. Ruthven has two or three companions
whom you will also burn. You will find them all in the
basement. They don't bother with coffins. It is the soil,
after all, which is important to us."

The priest shook his head again. "This is completely
insane."

"Remember the alternative, Father Martin—death, for
all three of you, and not a pleasant death, I assure you."
She stared at him, but he couldn't meet her eyes.
"Something worries you still, possibly something in
your pocket." The priest sat up stiffly, his eyes widening.
She laughed. "No, I do not exactly read minds, but your
emotions are rather transparent. Take the crucifix out of
your pocket if you wish. Go ahead."

His eyes fixed on her, he took a small silver cross

from his overcoat pocket. "Now hold it up as they do in the cinema." He extended his forearm toward her. Her smile flickered, but she took a step toward them, then another and another. She reached out to touch the cross, but he jerked it away. "Do you see, Father, why I say nothing on earth can save you should you disobey me? Garlic would be equally futile. These are fairy tales. Do you understand now?"

The priest bowed his head. "God help us."

"As I have said, I would not rely on him."

Steve let his head sag. Nothing could save them, nothing. They were all bound to this woman, this creature. The noose lay about their throats, and she could pull it tight whenever she wished. He remembered the red flower blossoming in Sarah's chest, but the gun hadn't slowed her in the least. These things really were immortal and indestructible.

"You will feel better after you eat. My housekeeper is a good cook. There is also an excellent cognac there on the desk. Help yourselves. And do try to get some rest. You have another long day ahead of you."

She stared at Steve, her eyes faintly amused, then walked toward the door. Her bare white feet made no sound, nor did her robe. She moved like a cold wind. At the doorway she stopped and turned. "Oh, you need not worry while you are here in my home. No one will harm you. Again, I shall leave for you certain instructions. Have you any questions?"

No one spoke. Steve was aware of his whole body trembling. The priest's face was grim. Mary had thrust her jaw forward, her lower lip taut, her mouth angry looking.

"Very well. Remember, your lives are in my hands."
She slipped through the doorway, a white silent shadow.

The priest's breath came out ragged. "Oh, Lord."

Mary stood up, walked to the fire and rubbed her hands together. Steve closed his eyes. We're all going to die, he thought. The only question is how. Either she'll kill us or the other vampire will. We haven't a chance. Somewhere a woman whispered his name. He opened his eyes.

Mary was holding two glasses. She gave the priest one. "Drink up. I doubt she would use anything so mundane as poison in the cognac. Besides, I just had a sip, and it tastes wonderful."

"Thanks." The priest took a big swallow.

She offered Steve the other glass. "Here." In the firelight he saw a few freckles about her nose. She had taken off her hat. Her face was red and wind burnt from the day outside, but her ears had been protected and were white looking.

He shook his head. Why did she bother when they were all going to die?

"Goddamnit, Steve—drink this!"

He jerked his head up.

"I know you don't feel well, but you can't just sit here like a—a cabbage, or something! You haven't had anything to eat or drink all day long. You've got to keep up your strength. You can't have the luxury of languishing—not here—not now. Drink it."

His eyes fixed on her, he drank. The liquid was fiery, but felt good on his dry throat. The shimmering at the edge of his vision abated, and staring at her face he could forget the darkness and Madame Rambouillet. He took another swallow. The cognac was very smooth, better than anything he had ever tasted. Mary was right. He couldn't just lie down and wait to die. Triathlons forced you to deal with pain, but this was different, a kind of psychic pain. Still, wallowing in self pity was no strategy.

"Thanks." He hesitated, an ironic smile pulling at his mouth. "I needed that."

She winced, then laughed. "You have a good ear for clichés. It would serve you right if I slapped you."

"You have it backwards. You were supposed to slap me first, before I said that."

"Things are easier in the movies." She poured some brandy for herself. "Crucifixes and garlic work just fine in the movies."

Chapter 8

The housekeeper was a small, slight woman in a black dress with white hair and dark eyes. She said little, and her words were colored by a heavy French accent. She was a very good cook. First came a leg of lamb with roast potatoes accompanied by a bottle of Bordeaux, then green salad and cheese, finally chocolate cake and coffee. The food, Mary reflected, was much better than at home. She wouldn't have thought she would have much appetite, but she and Fred were ravenous. Even Steve ate something.

They were in the formal dining room beneath two enormous chandeliers of cut crystal, the three of them taking up only a small part of the large table. The fine china, the oak floors and lacy tablecloth, the linen napkins and sterling silver setting—all of it seemed faintly unreal, like everything else which had happened in the last forty-eight hours.

Back in the bedroom, Fred put two more logs on the fire, used the poker to push them around, then sat down. Steve and Mary were together on the small sofa.

The priest sighed. "Well, the condemned man—the

condemned person—ate a hearty meal. It's odd how . . . even after the most horrible things, a good meal and a fire will make you feel better. I suppose it's not really being shallow. We should be thankful for that simple part of our natures which responds to such things. If we couldn't forget the kind of horror we saw today, its terribly immediacy, it would be hard to go on living. Poor Smith."

"We really couldn't have done anything, Fred. We couldn't have stopped them."

Fred massaged his left hand with his right. "I suppose not, but . . . What are we going to do tomorrow? I can't see more of this insanity."

Steve shrugged. "We don't seem to have much choice."

Mary felt her anger wake, stretch like a sleepy cat. "There are always choices. She isn't God, despite what she seems to think."

Fred took the crucifix out of his pocket. "You saw how much good this did. Nothing seems to frighten her, and nothing can harm her at night. I'm afraid Steve is right."

Mary tapped her foot nervously. "Maybe, but . . . one thing is obvious. We can't discuss anything 'subversive' until we leave this place tomorrow."

Fred stared into the fire. "She seemed to read my mind."

Mary gave her head a brusque shake. *"No.* She can't read minds, not truly. She said herself your feelings were obvious."

Fred looked up at her. "But do you believe what she said about finding us, about our not being able to hide?"

"I suppose so. Remember though, we must assume

she can hear our every word. That wouldn't take diabolical powers, just a hidden microphone. If Baumgartner was as perverse as Smith said, perhaps he had the rooms wired too."

She looked at them both, trying to show she was not ready to give up yet. She couldn't believe that evil was so strong. Surely God would not ... The vampire was not immortal; sooner or later she too would die, whether it took hundreds or even thousands of years. And if she had any weakness, an Achilles heel, she would not want it be known or even suspected.

Fred nodded. "You're right again, as usual." He had risen to pour himself more cognac. "I suppose we should get to sleep. As our hostess pointed out, we have a long day ahead of us." He sat. "There are only two beds here, but I don't much feel like splitting up and using another room."

"Christ," Steve murmured. *"No."*

His color was better than before, but he still looked pale. His dark eyes had a feverish cast, the lids puffy and weary-looking, dark shadows in the pockets. His black hair was tangled and unkempt, the start of a beard standing out against his pallor. The bulky red parka hid his shape. He hadn't taken it off all day long. Mary found the shaggy look more attractive than his usual meticulous grooming.

"You two can have the beds," Fred said. "I'm used to sleeping in chairs. I'm rather good at it."

Mary shook her head. "It's my turn tonight. You were in the chair all night long last night."

"As I've said, I've spent many a night snoring away in a chair. Half the time I can't sleep, so I get up, sit and read for a while until I fall asleep. However, tonight, despite all that has happened and this sinister setting, I think I will sleep. I haven't walked so much in years. I am very tired."

Mary sighed. "Me too."

Steve said nothing. He was looking afraid, withdrawing into himself again. When she had snapped at him before dinner, it seemed to drag him back into the world. He had looked better, and he had eaten and drunk something. She would have thought he was stronger. His vulnerability appealed to something maternal in her. Or was it merely maternal?

She raised her hands overhead and stretched. "I think I will lie down." She stood and went to the window.

Fred swallowed the last of his brandy. "I'll watch the fire for a while. It makes me sleepy."

Mary looked outside. The moon was up, the blue white light reflecting off the snow, dazzling. Mount Hood glowed white, and the sky was absolutely black, the stars hard sharp sparks with no twinkle. Again she thought of moonscapes, visions of worlds far from light and warmth and sunshine. It must be near zero out there, and the wind was blowing. She turned and looked at Steve. His eyes were fixed on her.

"You need to sleep, too," she said.

"I know, but I don't feel like moving."

She walked over to him and held out her hand. "Come on."

He grasped her hand, and she pulled, her arm straight. He stood, and she was aware again how tall and broad he was. He kept hold of her hand, blinked a couple times and swayed slightly like a tree about to be felled.

"Hey," she said.

His eyes came into focus on her. "Sorry. I get dizzy

when I stand up." His face was white and looked thinner, his cheekbones more pronounced.

"I'm not strong enough to keep you up."

"I would have let go. I wouldn't want to pull you down too."

She smiled. "Thanks." His fingers were big and strong, his hand hot. They stared at each other, and she felt a flush starting along her throat. "Come on." She led him to the bed. "Wait a second." He stood motionless while she pulled the covers aside, then he sat. "All right, now lie down." He swung his legs up onto the bed and sighed. She sat and began unlacing his hiking boot.

"What are you doing?"

"Getting your boots off you."

"You don't need to do that—really."

"You look too tired to move." She pulled a boot off.

"I'm glad I changed my socks this morning."

"Come on, you change your socks every morning, and I'll bet you keep them all in one drawer. They all match, and none have any holes in them."

He frowned slightly. "How did you know that?"

"Elementary. A slob can always recognize the compulsively neat. Your house last night was spotless, everything in place, and your clothes always look as if they came right out of the drawer. And I've never seen you unshaven or with messy hair until today. I remember that even from when you stayed with us. That's how I know you're not feeling so well."

"I am rather . . . compulsive, I suppose. Brenda used to comment about it." His face clouded over.

"Was she a slob?"

"No. She was compulsive in her own way. She certainly didn't dress like a slob. She spent a small fortune on clothes."

Mary laughed once. "Just like me."

"It can get tiresome being married to someone who always dresses like a fashion model. She couldn't . . . Thanks. They felt so heavy."

She set the other boot on the floor. "They are heavy, a few pounds apiece at least." She pulled the covers over his feet and legs, then sat beside him.

"I'm leaving everything on. I'm freezing."

"Madame Rambouillet doesn't seem to believe in central heating." She bent over to unlace her own boots, then pulled them off. "God, that does feel good. I'm with Fred—I haven't walked so much in ages." She took off her parka and tossed it over onto the end of the other bed. "I think he's asleep already. Neither of us got much rest last night." She noticed Steve staring at her, his eyes wary. "What's the matter?"

"Your cross," he whispered.

"Oh—this." She took it between thumb and forefinger, pulling the gold chain taut. "It's pretty, isn't it? My father gave it to me years ago, but I haven't worn it in a long time. I put it on this morning. It seemed appropriate, but I guess it won't help much with Madame Rambouillet."

His eyes blinked. "It's beautiful, but it hurts my eyes or something."

His face wasn't so pale as before, but he looked exhausted. She put her hand on his forehead, and momentarily something seemed to catch in her throat. "Oh, you feel so hot. You must have a high temperature." She hesitated, then moved her hand, her fingertips drifting down across his cheekbone, then along the length of his jaw to his chin. To her left, on the wall next to the bed, hung a full-length mirror, strategically placed, and she could see herself sitting next to Steve. She swallowed, then stared down at the floor.

His hand closed about her wrist, and his lips touched her palm. His mustache felt bristly, the skin of his lips ragged. He kissed her once, then again. He took her little finger in his mouth and withdrew it slowly. Her entire arm felt tingly, and she grasped at the covers with her other hand. David had never been half so gentle. Why now, when they couldn't possibly . . . ? "Oh Steve," she whispered, closing her eyes.

He clasped her hand against his chest. "I'm sorry. I . . ."

"Sorry? Don't be." She pulled her hand free, stroked him again and again along the cheek. She glanced back at Fred, but he hadn't moved. Steve's dark weary eyes watched her, his lips parted slightly. She touched his lower lip and felt the dry, torn fragments of skin.

He kissed her fingertips, then drew her hand away, again clasping it to his chest. "I can't kiss you," he said with great seriousness.

Mary felt a kind of ache again in her throat. "No?"

"I want to, but I can't."

"Why not?"

He closed his eyes. "I . . . my head hurts so when I try to remember, but I know there's a good reason." She stroked his cheek again. "Your hand feels so cool and so soft."

"Does it? You're afraid I'll catch the flu."

He was frowning, his eyes closed. "Maybe that's it."

Why did I drag him into this mess, Mary wondered,

but then she remembered that he'd already been dragged in and that she wouldn't have met him again otherwise.

He opened his eyes. "If we ever get out of all this alive, I'd like to see you again."

"I'd like that so much."

His breath came out in a wary sigh. "Good. Remember, you can't kiss me."

"What's a little flu? Anyway, I may not live long enough to come down with anything."

"Don't say that." He shook his head, then closed his eyes. "It hurts so when I try to remember. My head . . . my throat."

She ran her hand down along his face onto his neck. His eyes closed tightly, his mouth opening so that his teeth showed. "That hurts?" She curled her fingers under the black turtleneck and pulled it down. The puncture wounds had scabbed over, but the mouth-shaped bruises were a vivid bluish green. The shock was visceral, a kind of wrenching of her insides, the sudden horror you'd feel if you drew the bed covers aside and discovered a big roach. "Oh God." She jerked her hand away.

His eyes opened. "What is it?" He sat up.

She stared at him. "You don't know? You really don't know?" He shook his head. "Your neck—there are marks there. Bite marks." She pulled down the turtle-neck again, and he turned and stared at his throat in the mirror. She could tell that he hadn't known. "Oh, Christ." His eyes clamped shut, and a few tears seeped out. "I just don't remember."

"Tracy . . ." she whispered. "She did this to you. Last night. She must have come over after I left. You . . ." She told herself she had no reason to feel so hurt.

He lay down again, his eyes staring vacantly into space. Finally he looked at her. "You must think I'm a real fool."

She shook her head. "No."

"Well, I am a fool. You warned me. I can certainly pick them. I was so lonely. Do you know what that feels like?"

She nodded, tears filling her eyes.

"How could I be so stupid."

"She . . . she's very beautiful."

"I think . . . I almost remember." He shivered. "She tricked me—she betrayed me. Christ, I'm so goddamned stupid!"

"That's enough. Stop it." She put her hand on his cheek.

The fire had died down, and only one lamp was on near the sofa. His eyes were hot, the fever and anger burning inside him. She felt some of the tension ease out of him. "That's the reason why I mustn't kiss you."

She stared at him. "Maybe I'll take my chances." He was only a man, and Tracy or Suzanne—whoever she was—would be hard for any man to resist.

He shook his head. "You mustn't."

"Why not?"

"I . . . they want me. Both of them, but especially her. I've heard her calling. She's left her mark on me. I'll hurt you."

"As long as you're alive you can fight them."

"Can I?"

"Yes. If you want to. It's not over until we're dead."

"Are you sure?"

She drew one leg up onto the bed, bent over and put a hand on either side of his face. "Yes." They stared at

203

each other, then she leaned over and kissed him. Their lips and tongues moved slowly. His lips felt dry and rough. She slid one hand up into his hair, and his fingers clutched at the small of her back, then slipped under her turtleneck onto her bare skin. His hand felt big and hot. They opened their mouths wider. Finally she drew away, breathing hard. "You kiss very nicely," she said.

He smiled. "It makes my head hurt, but I don't care. You don't think ...? I really don't ever want to hurt you."

"They can't make you hurt me. Not really, not unless you want to."

"I don't. I like you, Mary. You're different from any woman I've ever met."

She shook her head, something catching again in her throat. "You hardly know me."

"I know you."

She sat up and looked over her right shoulder. Fred hadn't moved. She turned, saw herself and Steve reflected in the mirror. She sighed. "I wish we were somewhere, somewhere by ourselves."

His eyes opened slightly, then all the way, the black pupils like mouths screaming, and he dug his fingers into her leg. Her eyes flickered left again at the mirror—nothing—then right, her body swiveling about. Tracy—Suzanne—stood at the foot of the other bed, watching silently.

Because she didn't show up in the mirror, it was as if she had appeared out of nowhere. She wore the same white gown as in the tunnel, and her bare strong arms and her face had hardly more color than the silk. You could see the shape of her body, her hips and breasts,

204

through it. She would have been beautiful except for the expression in her eyes and the ragged wound where Smith had shot her. The sudden shock—being caught so by surprise—frightened Mary more than anything, but she told herself being afraid wouldn't help.

Suzanne looked different—she looked dead. It had been less obvious with Madame Rambouillet, probably because Mary had never seen her alive. The tension that all the small living muscles gave the face, the body, was gone. There was something slack and stiff about her expression, about the way she held herself. The difference was subtle, but quite obvious once you noticed. Gone too were the beat of the heart, the flutter in the hollow where the collar bones met, and the soft sound of air across the lips. Her stillness was uncanny. She could stand that way forever if she wished—she would never tire, her muscles never tremble. Only the dead were so quiet, so still. Steve's breathing was loud and rapid. You could tell he was sick and afraid.

"Let go of him," Suzanne whispered. Her voice sounded strangely hoarse. The lack of muscle tension again—this time in the larynx. Rage was there, but no edge or bite to the voice.

"Why should I?" Mary made the question as noncommittal as she could.

Suzanne's mouth pulled to the side. "Because, you silly little bitch, if you don't, I'll take you by the throat and crush the life from you."

"I thought . . . Madame Rambouillet said no one would harm us." Suzanne's eyes shifted, her hands forming fists. She doesn't like that, Mary thought.

Suzanne looked at Steve. "And you—how could you?"

Steve gave a sharp laugh. "Are you joking? You were using me all along. You knew about Brenda, and you knew about me. You played with me so you could draw me into the trap, just like you did with Alex."

"That's not true!"

"The hell it isn't! You had everything figured out. You knew just how to suck me in. All that crap about a former husband. Say the right things to me, pull on the old heart strings, stroke me a few times in the right places, and then you could lead me around by the nose. All that shit about being so lonely, having a problem."

The rage had faded from her dead eyes. "Steve . . . it's not true—I did care for you."

"Like you cared for Alex and the others?"

"You were different."

"Sure I was. You cared for me all right." Steve laughed again, something feverish and sad in the sound.

Mary shook his arm. "Stop it."

He yanked the turtleneck down. "You liked me so much you did this, I suppose?"

She stood up very straight. *"Yes. It's the greatest gift I could ever give you."*

Steve squeezed Mary's hand so hard she nearly cried out. "I don't want your gift—*keep it.*"

Suzanne shook her head. "It's too late for that. Soon we'll be together forever."

"No—take it back! I don't want it!" Mary felt him tremble.

Suzanne smiled. "I can't take it back. The marks on your throat are our bond. You are mine forever."

"No—no—it's not true. It's not." Steve shook his head wildly.

"You call that living forever?" Mary said. "You're not

206

alive at all—you're dead. Even I can see that. Whatever made you what you are is gone. She's dead, Steve, and the worst she can do is kill you too. That's no immortal life—it's a hollow imitation—a kind of animated nightmare that goes on and on, but it's hardly eternal. It will end—it will."

Suzanne's smile was gone, her face more rigid than before, fear showing in her eyes. "What are you saying? I will *live* forever. And so will he. Together—we will be together."

Mary smiled. "Just like Madame Rambouillet and her dear Ruthven?"

Suzanne hissed, then crouched low and made claws with her dead white fingers. She came at them like a snowy gust of wind. Mary grabbed for Steve and raised her other arm to block the blow. It never arrived. Suzanne was staring at her, motionless, her upper lip drawn back to bare her long canine teeth. Mary glanced at Steve, but he was puzzled too. She lowered her eyes and noticed her cross hanging there catching the yellow light from the solitary lamp. She took the end in her hand and lifted it slowly.

"This is what stopped you?"

Suzanne took half a step back. "I'll kill you, I swear I'll kill you." Her voice was guttural, nothing like the light melodic tone Mary had heard across the bar two nights ago. "Nothing will save you. I'll crush your neck. I'll squeeze it down to nothing, then I'll dig out your eyeballs, pop open your skull and smear your brains across the room. I'm going to kill you. I'm going to."

Mary glanced at Fred. The noise should have wakened him. Suzanne smiled. "He can't hear a thing. He can't stop me."

Mary held the cross and bit down hard on her lip. "I don't think you can," she said quietly.

"The hell I can't!" Suzanne made the claws again.

"I think . . . I think you're afraid of this."

"I'm not."

"You know that it's a symbol, that the person who wears it believes in God and Her love and in the true immortal life—not your ugly living death. It is a kind of nightmare, just as you are a kind of nightmare, but God's love is more powerful and mysterious than you and the others like you. I can die and be reborn, but you cannot. A corpse is a body with the soul gone, but your soul is trapped in that dead flesh, denied the true death that would make you live again. You wanted eternal life, but you've got eternal death instead. No wonder you're afraid of the cross. You're afraid of God and of life. You cling to your death you call life, but it will end almost before you know it. Perhaps God pities you. You're not even human anymore. You can't feel anything except hatred or fear."

"No—no. It's not true! You are the pathetic one with your talk of God and eternal life—there is nothing but this life! When it ends—and yours will be over very soon—then all is finished."

Mary couldn't bear to look at her any longer. "You are afraid. I thought I hated you, but . . ."

Suzanne's hands shook, her dead limbs quivering, but she couldn't come any closer. Finally she turned and walked over to a chair, a massive thing made of oak. She lifted it with one hand, then began to pull it apart. The arm rests were two-inches by six-inches and about two feet long. She broke one end off, then hefted the wood like a club.

"I can still smash your skull in!"

Mary watched in grim fascination. Suzanne's long white arm swung up and back, then blurred with motion. Other arms encircled Mary and pulled her down as the wood hurtled by. A hard sharp crack, then the mirror by the bed shattered into pieces. Steve held her tightly to him.

"Damn you!" Suzanne howled. She started tearing loose another piece of the chair.

Steve let go of Mary. "Run away," he whispered hoarsely.

"You can't run from *me*." Suzanne's face was twisted with hate.

She raised the other chair arm, but before she could throw it, Madame Rambouillet seized her wrist. "How dare you?"

"I will kill her!"

Madame Rambouillet wrenched the piece of wood away, then slapped her across the face. The force of the blow knocked her down. Mary winced, but Suzanne seemed more startled than hurt. She sat staring at the other vampire. She really can't feel anything, Mary thought.

"Get out of here—*now.*"

Suzanne stood slowly. "But . . ."

"Now." The word was all the more forceful because it was spoken so softly. The two women stared at each other. Suzanne was several inches taller, but she wilted before the other woman's gaze. "I will not have you interfering with my plans—*never.* You know I plan to use them against Ruthven, and you know I promised they would not be harmed."

Suzanne ran her tongue over her lips, then turned toward Mary. "She kissed him."

"What of it? Mortals are always kissing or pawing at one another. You are past that now."

The anger went out of Suzanne's face. "No." She shook her head, her eyes desperate.

"You are a fool. Would you be a slave again to the flesh? Your desires were useful to me once, but not now. You are one of the undead, not a mortal. Leave copulation and its amusing vagaries to them. We have more important matters to concern us. Now get out of here. *Go.*"

Suzanne stared at Mary. "And if I refuse?" she said.

Madame Rambouillet took a step back. Something in her eyes made Mary look away. "One day dead, and already you would challenge me?"

There was a long silence. Steve was holding Mary, and she could feel his labored breathing. His right hand was between her breasts, his left hand on her belly.

"Mary."

Madame Rambouillet was alone.

"I would speak with you. Don't worry, Mr. Ryan, I will not hurt her, and anyway, as I have told you before, you could not stop me."

Mary gently moved his hands aside. "It's all right." She sat up. Beside Madame Rambouillet was the broken chair. Fred was still sleeping peacefully. She turned to Steve. His eyes were weary and sick. She touched his cheek. "Go to sleep. I'll be all right. If she wanted to hurt us, she could have done it already, or she could just have left us to Suzanne."

"Exactly." Madame Rambouillet stood very straight.

210

The muscles in her face and her slender white throat looked as hard as metal.

Mary hesitated, then took off the cross. "What are you doing?" Steve asked, alarmed.

"That is not necessary," the vampire said.

Mary wasn't sure what Suzanne might do. "Keep it for me until I come back." She closed his hands about the cross.

"Are you sure?"

"Yes."

Mary stood up and followed the vampire. Fred was snoring faintly in the chair. "Wait a moment." Mary picked up a log and set it into the dying fire, then another. She blew hard, and the flames sprang up about the wood.

Madame Rambouillet went down the stairs, her white hand trailing lightly along the carved oaken bannister. The house seemed dim and cavernous, only a few small lamps turned on. Mary wondered how far she could trust the vampire, but, as Madame Rambouillet kept reminding her, she didn't have much choice.

The room next to the dining room was obviously the library. The bookshelves built into the walls were made of wood stained so dark it was almost black. The shelves filled with books went all the way to the ceiling. The fireplace was cold and black, the grate bare.

"Please sit down."

Mary pulled the chair out from the table and sat. One book lay open near the lamp, its pages brittle looking. She closed it and read the title: *Les Fleurs du Mal.* "Flowers of Evil," she whispered.

"You know Baudelaire?" Madame Rambouillet had

folded her arms. The fingers of her right hand were long and bony-looking.

Mary nodded.

"He had two vampire poems you know. His were sexual vampires, not the real thing, but his verse is always beautiful and insightful. *'Les Metamorphoses du Vampire'* was considered scandalous and banned. This is the other poem, *'Le Vampire.'* " She opened the book and pointed. "Here he wishes that poison or the dagger would free him from his vampire, but in poetic fashion these inanimate objects answer by calling him a fool:

Imbécile!—de son empire,
Si nos efforts te délivraient,
Tes baisers ressusciteraient
Le cadavre de ton vampire.

Can you translate it?"

Mary stared at her, then at the text. "Imbecile, from her empire, if our efforts would deliver you . . . your kisses would . . . resuscitate, revive, the cadaver of your vampire."

"Very good. *Tu connais bien le francais.* Charles was a true poet." She gave the name its French pronunciation, "Sharl." "He understood hatred, death, decay and sickness, as few mortals have. Especially death."

"You really did know him?"

"Yes."

Mary tried to recall when he would have died, probably the 1860s. "Was it different then, or . . . Do people really change much over time?"

"It was different. I was born in a small village. There was nothing mechanical or electric, and the woods

212

themselves were still wild and dark, filled with savage beasts. People do not change much, but there was less arrogance. Science and the machine had not yet become the new gods. Sickness and death could not be so easily denied, one could not so easily pretend one would live forever. There was not so much . . . ugliness."

"Ugliness?"

Madame Rambouillet's lips were pressed tightly together, only the corners rising slightly. "The hand of man soils everything now, kills everything. I who have seen other times, other places, know it for the blight it is. You breed like flies or other vermin. Amusing, is it not? The undead who live on the blood of the living are not so very different from the rest of you. You are like leeches on the hide of a giant beast, tiny black creatures stuck to its brown hide, slowly draining the earth of its lifeblood. Many of the leeches carry a pestilence, and none seem to understand that when they are finished, when the beast dies, they too will perish."

Mary felt a chill wriggle along her spine. This woman was eloquent, her vision difficult to dispute. "And you—do you understand?"

The vampire lowered her arms. Mary wished she would sit down. "I understand, I understand all. I know that even I shall not live forever, that all things that are born must die, that death is the final end of all things, the greatest power in the universe."

Mary's hands tightened about the ends of the chair arms. Madame Rambouillet's pale gray-blue eyes showed a faint mockery. "I heard your words to Suzanne. You seemed inspired, but you were only partly right. We may suffer under a kind of death, but there is no immortality, no God, no eternal life. Ultimately there is only death, but Suzanne and I can exist for many human lifetimes. Our bodies are not so ludicrously fragile as yours. Even as this world sickens and dies, we shall flourish, and we shall be well-nourished until that day when the last man and woman close their eyes forever." She smiled, and Mary turned away. "Do you really believe in God and that nonsense about eternal life?"

Mary swallowed once, then nodded.

"You have no doubts?"

"Of course I have doubts! Only the dead—or the undead—have no doubts."

Madame Rambouillet laughed in earnest. The sound made the nape of Mary's neck feel cold and prickly. Since the vampire didn't breathe and all the muscles were dead, the laughter was forced and strange sounding, ugly. "You are very clever, my dear. Very clever indeed, *ma petite*. Clever enough to value your own mind and to keep strict control over your life. Clever enough not be ensnared by a man and his wailing babes, or by the dream of great wealth. But perhaps not quite clever enough. You persist in the notion of an omnipotent deity who rewards His faithful followers."

"Her faithful followers," Mary said.

Madame Rambouillet laughed again. "Reversing the gender does not make this deity exist, but I do not wish to argue theology with you. We shall agree to disagree. Your vulnerability in another area is our concern here. I said you were clever enough not to be trapped by a man, but we both know that is not exactly true."

Mary felt the blood rush to her face. "I . . . What business is it of yours!"

"You look charming when you blush. That is one thing that has changed. When I was a girl, a blush—a

214

glance—meant everything. There was none of this wearisome intellectual baggage about relationships and commitment. There was no psychology, no endless discussions. A blush like yours would have been considered a kind of poetry. No man would have been able to resist you."

Mary felt the tears gather in her eyes. "Stop it."

The vampire turned and took a step away. "You are too sensitive. I am not mocking you, not really you. You are still young and a woman. I cannot expect you to behave differently."

"How kind of you."

"Touché! You can give as well as receive. Enough of this. You want this man, this Steve Ryan, and you could do worse. He is attractive, hardly so muscle-bound and stupid as Mr. Smith. His body looks lean and hard, and he will be sensitive to your needs, a good lover. He is a bit of a weakling and a whiner, but all the same . . . "

"Don't talk about him that way—don't talk about us."

Madame Rambouillet shook her head. "This coyness is foolish, but there is no need for me to elaborate any further. You have, however, one problem. He has Suzanne's mark on him, and because of that, he is a dead man. Even if you managed to get him away from her, he would die within a month or two at most."

Mary felt the fear again low in the belly, the same as when she had discovered the marks. "No—you're lying."

"You know me better than that, I hope, and you are also supposed to know something about vampires. He is doomed. Only one thing can save him."

Mary stood abruptly. "What? What are you talking about?"

"Sit down and don't excite yourself so. How was the

innocent and ludicrous Mina Harker saved from the evil Dracula?"

Mary sank back into the chair.

"Yes, if Suzanne is destroyed, then he will be free. Then he will live."

The tears slipped from Mary's eyes. She hardly knew him. Why should she feel so bad? She remembered Alex, then thought of her father's body dead and still, all that she loved gone out of him.

"Come, come—there is no need for your courage to fail you. I propose a simple trade. You dispose of Ruthven for me, and you shall have your man."

Mary's eyes widened. "What?"

"You heard me. If you would like, you can do the other job for me too. You've always wanted to kill Suzanne, haven't you?"

Mary shook her head. *"No."*

"If you ponder this for a while, you may discover that you deceive yourself. Be that as it may, I have human servants that work for me. She will be simple to dispose of."

"But . . ."

"She was a tool, but I grow weary of her. She lacks your strength and intelligence. She and Mr. Ryan were actually a good match, a pair of simpering weaklings. Unfortunately, this is frequently true with the beautiful."

"I don't believe you."

Madame Rambouillet folded her arms. "You have my word of honor. If you knew how I hated Ruthven, you would not doubt me. You deal with him, and I will take care of Suzanne."

"But . . . you said a vampire could not destroy a vampire."

"True, not directly, but she would be as easy to kill as that creature in the tower. Over time she would become strong and clever, but after one first becomes a vampire, there is a period of weakness. She is vulnerable as a newborn baby is vulnerable, and in her case the weakness will not pass quickly. She has foolish notions, romantic ones, and the reality of her condition has not met her expectations. She is . . . unbalanced, mentally unstable, as the psychologist might say. She is under stress." The vampire laughed. "In a few years we might have our hands full with her, but right now it will be *facile*— easy."

Mary was silent for a few seconds. Finally she looked up. "You really . . . ?"

"You have my promise. And remember, he is dead otherwise. His blood is tainted, he has a disease. Only I can cure him."

Mary sighed. "I'll do what I can."

"From Ryan and the priest I expect nothing. Only you have a chance of destroying Ruthven."

Mary nodded. She felt afraid again and cold. She wished she had kept on her coat and boots. The library was dark and empty, the books old and dead like the vampire, their pages made of the long-dead flesh of forests, their bindings the skins of dead animals, their contents the faint echoes of dead minds. "Can I go now? Please?" Her voice had a tremor.

Madame Rambouillet smiled. "Yes, you may go."

Mary stood, started for the door, then hesitated, wondering if she should walk right by the vampire. She swerved slightly, thought she was safe, then felt something strong and hard clamp onto her arm. Again the

217

fear, low and visceral, twisting at her insides as if something were crawling about her intestines.

"Remember one thing."

She had not been so close to the vampire before. The eyes had a dull flat sheen. There were no tears, nothing to glisten or reflect light, the surfaces dry and cold, and the face was so unnaturally still—no blinking, no little twitches or movements. Her stillness wanted to prolong itself, to melt into the true death. Something sculpted of ice or snow might be this cold, this still, but never any living thing. The silence between them fed Mary's fear, made it grow into a silent scream.

"You will not frighten me with crosses or verbal sophistries. If you betray me, I can put my hand about you this easily . . ."

Fingers curled about Mary's throat, the thumb and forefinger above the turtleneck, touching her skin. The touch also was like nothing human, far too cold, too strong, but not like metal either. The fingers were faintly damp with an odor like flowers starting to decay.

"And I can crush your throat easily, oh so easily, or . . ." The dead lips parted slightly.

She really is dead, Mary thought. She's not human, not at all—a reptile or an insect would be more human. Her body is only a shell with something dark and malevolent and formless inside. The woman—the beauty—once inside is gone. It is truly other—I and it. The thing leaned toward her, its eyes hungry.

Mary shuddered and closed her eyes. Her hands were trembling, but she knew there was no running away. Something touched her cheek lightly, and she heard a faint sound, the murmur of a kiss. When she opened her eyes the thing was still staring at her.

"Go now, *ma jolie petite.* Go to your sweetheart. *Vas.*"

The dead fingers slipped away from her throat. Mary turned and headed for the door. Don't run, she kept telling herself as she went slowly up the stairs. Don't give her—*it*—that satisfaction. She stepped into the bedroom, closed the door and locked it, even though she knew the lock was futile.

Both men were asleep, Fred slumped sideways. He was snoring, and Steve's breathing was labored and heavy. Both sounds were wonderfully reassuring. She pried open Steve's hand, took the cross and fastened the chain around her neck, her fingers trembling. She put on her coat, set more logs in the fire, then sat down on the sofa. Her arms were wrapped about her, but she was still shivering. Her feet felt especially cold.

She tried to weep quietly so she wouldn't wake Fred. She wanted to wash her neck, to scrub at her skin with some strong disinfectant, but she knew that wouldn't help. She felt soiled, dirtied deeply inside. The fear twisted about in her belly, and a sharp sob broke free.

Fred opened his eyes and sat up. "Mary?"

"I'm . . . Go back to sleep."

The tone of her voice made him stand. "What is it? What's happened?"

The tears filled her eyes, making it hard to see. She wondered if there was a stain like a mold showing on her throat or cheek, but that was ridiculous. "I'm . . . I'm all right."

He put his hand on her cheek. "The hell you are—what is it?"

"Oh Fred, she's so evil—so nasty." She put her hand over his, trying to blot out the stain with his warm and gentle touch.

Chapter 9

Steve was hiding where they couldn't see him.

In the living room the three women sat drinking coffee from blue-and-white china cups. Brenda's black hair had just been permed, the orderly disorder in the abundant curls a tribute to her hairdresser's skill. She wore a red sweater and matching flats. The fingers of her left hand toyed with a thick gold chain. Sarah had on proper business attire: power skirt and jacket of charcoal gray wool with a pale pink blouse, the V of the collar showing off her long throat and part of her chest. She slipped off the black shoes with spiked heels, and he saw the red of her toenails through the smoke-colored nylon. Mary still wore her hiking boots, jeans, and parka. She sat rather stiffly, her long straight red hair gathered behind her, and sipped her coffee while watching the other women over the rim of her cup.

"He's really not much as a man, I'm afraid." Brenda gave her head a tiny shake. "Rather pathetic, actually. He'll always be pestering you."

Sarah nodded. "And he makes too much noise. They

talk about women moaning and carrying on, but you should hear him!"

Brenda laughed. "That's exactly right! I always had to make sure the windows were closed in the summer. He's compulsively neat too, you know, and I guess that's the one time he lets himself go. Anyway, he really does make a lot of noise. It's very distracting."

"And of course he's much too fast," Sarah said. "Once he's inside you, off he goes, and then he starts falling asleep on top of you."

Brenda sighed wearily. "Really, I don't know how I ever put up with him for so long. He's like some big slobbery dog, good-natured perhaps, but hardly something you'd want to sleep with."

Mary bit at her lip. "He seems nice enough, but I guess you can never tell from looking at them."

Brenda finished her coffee. "Take my advice, dear, and find yourself someone else, someone who isn't quite so fit. He's forever running or swimming or bicycling, and then pulling some muscle. You'd think the continual exercise would slow him down, but somehow it seems to make him hornier. And he does smell bad, and you'll end up having to wash his stinky clothes. They always expect you to wash their clothes, and of course he wouldn't dream of wearing anything even the least bit dirty, so he's constantly changing into clean things."

Mary made a face. "I hate washing."

"Then I'm afraid he's not the man for you. He goes through two or three times as many clothes as any normal man. And he has a closet full of hundred percent cotton shirts which he must have ironed."

Steve almost cried out. That wasn't true!—many of

his shirts were wash and wear, and the cotton ones he had always sent to the laundry because he knew Brenda hated ironing.

Mary swallowed the last of her coffee and stood up. "Well, this has been very interesting. I . . ."

Sarah slipped her feet into her shoes and stood. She towered over Mary. She put her hand on her shoulder. "I know we've had our disagreements in the past, but Brenda and I felt you should know something about him. We girls have to stick together. 'Pathetic' really is the word that comes to mind for him. Someone as intelligent and self sufficient as you . . . Well, it would never work out."

Steve saw in Mary's face that it was hopeless. He could hold back no longer. He stepped into the room. "Wait, Mary—I . . ."

"You sneaky eavesdropping bastard," Brenda screamed, "get the fuck out of here!"

Steve hesitated. He would have thought her anger could no longer wound him, but he felt a familiar sorrow.

Brenda opened her mouth and bared her fangs. *"Go!"* she howled. Sarah raised her arm and pointed at the door, she too revealing her long sharp teeth.

"Mary, don't listen to them—they'll hurt you!"

Mary's brow wrinkled into the characteristic frown. Her mouth slowly relaxed into a smile, opening enough that he could see the fangs.

He felt the fear in his chest, his throat. "Oh, no—*no.*"

The women were all smiling at him—or was there only one woman?—and he saw the teeth and felt the pain in his throat.

"Get him!" someone shouted, and then he was running through the blizzard, snowflakes drifting about him, the color suddenly gone from the world. In the distance he heard them all howling and laughing, and he staggered forward although his knee was throbbing. The firs rose up around him, still and dark, and the mouths of tunnels must be avoided—those black holes would devour you and spill you down into their guts where Smith lay rotting. He was safe in the woods and the snow, but he was cold, so cold and lonely.

"Steve?" A woman's voice, soft now.

"Mary?"

"No." The snow swirled aside, and he saw Sarah standing by the firs. She wore the white gown, the silk so thin and translucent it would be like smoke, a cloudy nothingness, between his hands and her skin. The wound where Smith had shot her was gone, and she looked white and tall and lovely standing there, so incredibly, so perfectly beautiful. Her feet were bare, and the red toenails were the only color in the dream. Behind her Mount Hood rose in the distance, the winds stirring its glacial summit.

Tears glistened in her eyes. "Steve," she whispered.

He sagged back against a tree trunk.

"It's no use running. It's too late for that. Come to me. Come love me." She bent and pulled the gown up over her hips and chest, then over her head. The soft hollows of her armpits showed a faint shadow, and her nipples were pink.

Steve shook his head. "No."

"Come—please come."

She lay on the sheet with its pattern of green and brown, the green forming leaves of different sizes and shapes. *"Please."*

He shook his head again. "This is a dream—you're not real."

"Nothing is real."

"You lied to me."

"What does that matter? Women always lie to men. We did hit it off. You felt it too—that was real. You're very attractive. Come to me."

"You can't love me. You're dead. Mary said so."

Her eyes filled with tears. "But I do love you. She was wrong. She's a fool. I love you, Steve. I want you."

He licked his lips. What would it hurt in a dream, anyway? He could do anything he wanted to her in a dream.

"That's right. Anything you want. Touch me—kiss me—anywhere. Do anything. Beat me if you'd like."

He couldn't help staring at her body.

"Come on."

"No. You are dead. If I try to love you the flesh will fall off you, and you'll be nothing but bones."

"No. It won't happen that way."

"You'll hurt me again."

"I promise I won't, not this time."

He shook his head, tears filling his own eyes. "You can't love me."

"I can now. Here."

"Dreams aren't enough for me. I want someone real, someone warm and alive. You can't feel anything anymore."

Her cry was that of an animal, and he could see the white teeth in the black hole of her scream. The rest of the face shrank, and her body too, until she seemed all mouth—some embryonic, half formed thing with that gaping, hungry mouth rimmed with teeth, its insides

225

soft and pink and wet. His throat flamed with pain, and he could hardly breathe.

Her cry died away, and her words were a whisper inside his skull like his own thoughts. "You are bound to me—you are mine. You will be dead soon enough yourself. You will come when I command."

"Mary—help me!"

"She cannot help you now. See, she's sleeping like a baby, oh so peacefully."

Mary was lying on her side on the bed next to him, her red hair swept back, leaving her neck exposed. There on her throat and her cheek was something black. His vision zoomed in on her. The black stuff was alive, a thing which sent out tendrils through her skin, welding itself to the bone and reaching ever inward.

"What have you done to her?"

"Nothing—nothing at all." She laughed. "Madame Rambouillet has taken her under her wing, so to speak."

The mouth had shrunk, and Sarah was a beautiful woman again. Steve wondered if this really was a dream. Usually he always knew when he was dreaming, but now he wasn't so sure. He looked at the growth on Mary's face. It seemed larger. This had to be a dream.

"It isn't, you know. Not really."

"It must be."

"What would convince you that it is real?"

"I don't know."

"Forget all that now. Come to me. Do you like me naked or wearing just a little something? You seemed to like it last night when you found out I had nothing on underneath."

She was in her slip lying on his leather couch. The slip was pale gray with a floral pattern over her breasts.

226

She bent one leg. He could see the top of the smoke-colored stocking. Her other leg was bare and white, and she had nothing else on. "You do like this, don't you."

"Yes," he whispered. "You're very beautiful." But he knew this was a dream and that there would be no satisfaction, only a restless arousal.

"It doesn't have to end that way."

"It always does. I used to dream of Brenda, dream she loved me again. She would be naked, and I would be trying over and over to love her, but then I'd wake up and still be alone and frustrated."

"Oh, stop your talking for once and come here."

Why not, he wondered, but then he looked again at the other bed. The entire right side of Mary's face was black now, the growth thick and crusty. Her red hair was gone on that side.

"Jesus Christ," he whispered. Wake up now. This is the part where you wake up because you're so scared.

"Would you like the same thing to happen to you?"

He touched his neck, then saw himself lying on the bed, his face flushed and hot, and on his throat was something black. For a moment he wanted to scream, but then he realized he already knew about it. There must be a way to help Mary. What had she done earlier?

Steve . . .

If only she would stay out of his head. The cross—the cross was lying there on the bed, the chain about her neck.

The flesh fell off Sarah, just as he had foreseen, but underneath was something black and far more frightening than any skeleton. The mouth was howling at him, that newborn predator crying from the nest for food.

Wake up now—it's time to wake up, but the thing was

227

eating Mary's face off. He stood up and reached for the cross.

"No—you cannot!" shouted the voice inside his skull.

He set the cross on Mary's face, then put his hand over it. Women screamed, the wind crashing at the windows, trying to get in. Mary put her hand over his, and the black stuff blurred and turned into a gray smoke that drifted away. He lifted his hand and saw bare white skin, her ear and the curve of her jaw.

"Thank you," she whispered to him. "Oh, thank you."

"I did nothing. You're the one who made the cross mean something, you gave it power. You're stronger than any of these things, you and your faith."

She stroked his cheek. "Steve."

He bent and kissed her. Her mouth, her tongue, her breath were warm. Finally he drew away. "How do we get away from here? How do we ever find the time to love each other?"

Her face grew smaller and smaller. He knew she was saying something, but he couldn't hear. He tried to grab for the crucifix around her neck, but she was too far away. The thing with the mouth lay waiting in the darkness, the pink tongue writhing about within the cave of teeth.

"You were right," Sarah whispered. "It was *her* symbol, not yours. You think a cross will save an agnostic without the guts to deny God?" It began to laugh. "This didn't have to happen. We could have made love. I could have done anything you wanted. Now I'm going to kill you. I'm going to eat you alive, your muscles and flesh and organs, including your precious balls, then after I've sucked out the marrow, I'll even eat up all your bones. And you'll be alive the whole time."

228

Steve's throat burned, and the darkness settled about him. "Mary . . ."

"She can't save you now—no one can."

The fire at his throat, the pain, gave him the idea. He had been afraid for so long, but he remembered they didn't like fire. Madame Rambouillet had said so. A torch flamed in his hand, and he thrust the yellow fire at the mouth.

It screamed and scuttled back. He wondered how many legs it had. "That won't save you—it will burn out."

Anger was mixed now with his fear, anger at that thing, at being trapped and betrayed. Fire killed them. If he were to burn himself up, then he couldn't become one of them. He would be free. He would be dead for real. Perhaps there was a God and an afterlife.

"There's nothing, remember? You understood that in the night."

She would eat him alive otherwise. And he would become like her—the same *thing*.

"You wouldn't dare. You haven't got the guts."

He looked around and saw the red can of gasoline on the table. This was a dream, after all. He picked up the can, splashed gas all over his head, his parka and pants. The strong smell burned his nostrils.

"You wouldn't dare," but it didn't sound so sure now.

The priest had left his lighter on the arm of the chair. Steve picked it up, his hands shaking.

The thing began to laugh, and he heard Madame Rambouillet, Brenda, and Sarah speaking in unison: "You haven't got the guts, you're pathetic . . ."

He flicked the lighter and was instantly a torch, his whole body aflame. He screamed in agony and threw

229

himself at the thing. It tried to scuttle away, but he caught it in his fiery embrace. Now it was burning as they fell together into the blackness, the rush of air feeding the flames. He caught a glimpse of Mary's distant face, heard her scream his name, then his body twisted as he tumbled through the darkness. The thing writhed in his grasp as the fire consumed them both. Soon he would be nothing, and all would be dark. Then at last the pain would end.

He tried one last time to scream, but try as he might, nothing would come out.

"Steve—Steve," Mary called.

He opened his eyes. She stood over him, her face pale. Her hand was over his mouth. He tried to sit up.

"It's all right—it was a dream. It was only a dream. If you cry out you'll wake Fred." She drew her hand away, then stroked his face.

He could feel his heart beat, and the fear still hung over him. His arms and legs shook, and her face was out of focus. "Christ, Mary—the dream—"

"It's over now. Oh, you're so hot—you're burning up."

"That was the dream. I was on fire."

"You're not on fire, not really. You just have a fever."

He tried to keep from shaking. "I guess not. I'm freezing."

"Can you sit up? You can take some more aspirin."

He sat up very slowly. His head throbbed, and the room wouldn't keep still. He took the two tablets, then drank. The glass itself was cool under his fingers, and the water felt good on his dry, sore throat. He closed his eyes for a moment, then opened them and stared at Mary. "That was such a terrible dream." Her eyelids seemed puffy. "Have you been crying?"

Her mouth stiffened. "Yes. Earlier. I just fell asleep a few minutes ago." The side of her mouth twisted into half a smile. "Maybe it's better to stay awake in this house. I woke up just before you did. You were moaning and moving around. I had an awful nightmare myself."

"It couldn't have been as bad as mine. Christ. And it kept going on and on. Usually when you get scared enough, you wake up. That should have happened way earlier."

She took the glass from him, then reached down and squeezed his hand gently. "I finally did wake up," she said, "but after it had resolved itself." She noticed him staring closely at her. "What's the matter?"

"I . . . Your cheek and your neck . . . they're clear."

She sat up abruptly. The color went out of her face, and she touched her neck. "What do you mean?"

"Oh, in my dream, you had . . . black stuff on you."

She squeezed his hand, and he saw the fear now in her eyes, in the set of her mouth. "Tell me."

"It was on your cheek and your neck, and it grew like some fungus. I could see that it was . . . eating at you. Finally I remembered your cross. I put it over your face, and the stuff began to fade away. It turned into something like smoke."

She put her other hand over the cross, held it tightly to her. "I . . . I had the same dream. The thing was growing on me like a cancer or something, eating into my hair and my eye . . ." She clenched her teeth, then slowly eased her breath out through them. "You put the cross on me, and then I remembered what I had told Suzanne. I knew they could hurt me or kill me, but that as long as I believed in God and Her love they could never take my soul. And you touched me. You were so

231

brave, and your hand . . ." She began to cry, but she laughed and rubbed her eyes. "Then I woke up. Did you really dream the same thing?"

He nodded, some ill-defined fear dancing in the shadows.

"Maybe you did help me, then. What happened in your dream?"

Now he understood the fear. He kept his eyes fixed on her. "Sarah came after me again. She couldn't touch you, but she said you couldn't save me—nothing could save me."

The brief joy which had touched her face vanished. "I . . ."

"She said the cross was your symbol, not mine. She was going to eat me alive, but I fooled her. I poured gasoline all over me and set myself on fire, then I grabbed her. We were falling together, and I could hear you calling to me from way above. I was screaming and burning up. Probably we were falling toward Hell, but it wasn't really Hell, more darkness and nothingness. That's when you woke me up."

Unrestrained, the tears trickled down her pale, freckled skin. "Oh God, that's awful, so awful." She squeezed his hand again. "Just because part of the dream seemed . . . true, doesn't mean . . . I don't believe it—I just don't believe it. I'll help you any way I can—I . . . Don't give up, Steve. I know that if you give up, then you will be lost."

He stared at her. Her gold earring caught a speck of orange light from the lamp. She does have a kind of beauty, he thought. He put his other hand over hers. It felt so slim and cool under his hot heavy fingers. He

232

shook his head. "I won't. It's hard, though. It's very hard. I feel so damned sick and tired."

"I know. It will be morning soon. Things always look better in the morning."

Steve let his hand slip away. "Sarah—Suzanne—whoever the hell she is—was after me. She was calling me. I've heard her all night long. I don't think . . . I don't think that's exactly a dream."

Mary shook her head. "No. But you haven't gone to her, and it's almost morning. You . . . it sounds like you were winning in the dream when I woke you up."

"Winning?" He frowned, trying to remember. "She was surprised. She didn't think I'd do it. And when I grabbed her she was really surprised. She was screaming too." But it was hard to make a victory out of such a nightmare. He was beginning to feel afraid again. He closed his eyes. "I wish I could just sleep in peace. I'm so tired, but if I try to sleep—my dreams are so awful."

"Move over. Maybe there's safety in numbers. Anyway, I don't want to sleep again, not for a while. I'll be by you, and if you start moaning or jerking or anything, I'll wake you."

He stared at her, his eyes blinking. The darkness at the edge of his vision had a tendency to sprout colors and begin dancing. "Are you sure? It seems . . ."

"Don't you know you're never supposed to refuse a woman who wants to get into bed with you? I think it was Zorba the Greek who said that was the one sin God would not forgive."

He smiled. "Okay." He moved over and slid down onto his back.

She put her pillow next to his, then lay down and pulled the covers over them. She turned onto her side and held his arm loosely with both hands, her toes brushing against his leg. "How romantic. We certainly couldn't have more clothes on. Even with wool socks my feet still feel cold."

He sighed wearily. It was so easy to start shivering. He hadn't had a fever like this in years. He wouldn't be much help tomorrow. What was the use? They might as well leave him here to die. His body jerked impulsively, and then he was trembling again.

"What is it?" she said.

"Nothing. I'm just scared, I guess. No, not I guess—I am scared. I don't want to . . . to be . . ."

"Don't think about that. Think about something else. Think about . . . think about my hand stroking your face."

He felt the tips of her fingers trace a line along his jaw. "Your hand feels so cool."

"Good. Think about that. Think about . . . about how much I . . . like you, and . . ." Her voice wavered. "Do you like Chinese food?"

"What?"

"Do you like Chinese food?"

"Yes. Very much."

"That's a relief. Think about being in Portland and going out to dinner with me to a Chinese restaurant. For you, I might even wear a skirt. Do you like hot dishes, Szechuan and Hunan?"

"Yeah."

"Good—so do I. We can get all fired up. Think of the two of us eating dinner. No vampires—they're gone, dead, past history. It's just you and I alone. And all that hot food, those incendiary red peppers. Just relax, that's right. Maybe we can play footsy under the table. Don't

234

worry about anything. I'll be right here watching you. I like watching you . . . so much. I . . ."

He was aware of her fingers stroking his face, then the restaurant faded away, but now her presence permeated the darkness.

"Sleep, my darling. Sleep," was the last thing he heard her whisper.

Part Two

Deux guerriers ont couru l'un sur l'autre; leurs
        armes
Ont éclaboussé l'air de lueurs et de sang.
Ces jeux, ces cliquetis du fer sont les vacarmes
D'une jeunesse en proie à l'amour vagissant.

Les glaives sont brisés! come notre jeunesse,
Ma chère! Mais les dents, les ongles acérés,
Vengent bientôt l'épée et la dague traîtresse.
—O fureurs des coeurs mûrs par l'amour ulcérés!

Dans le ravin hanté des chat-pards et des onces
Nos héros, s'étreignant méchamment, ont roulé,
Et leur peau fleurira l'aridité des ronces.

—Ce gouffre, c'est l'enfer, de nos amis peuplé!
Roulons-y sans remords, amazone inhumaine,
Afin d'éterniser l'ardeur de notre haine!

"Duelleum"

Two warriors charged each other; their weapons
Splashed the air with light and blood.
These games, these clangs of iron, are the din
Of youth fallen prey to wailing love.

The swords are broken! like our youth,
My dear! But our teeth, our sharp nails,
Soon avenge the sword and the flawed dagger.
—Oh fury of mature hearts ulcerated by love!

In the ravine haunted by ocelots and snow
        leopards,
Our heros, embracing wickedly, have rolled about,
And their bloody skin will flower the dried
        brambles.

—This abyss is hell, peopled with our friends!
Let us wrestle here without remorse, inhuman
    Amazon,
To eternalize the fire of our hate!

                                        "War"

Chapter 10

Mary sighed and opened her eyes. Gray-blue light had filled the room, and the morning seemed a kind of miracle. *Fiat lux*—let there be light, and after such darkness she could well believe that God was light. Steve lay motionless on his side, his breathing quiet now, his mouth opened slightly. His lower lip was cracked and had split, then scabbed in the middle. His face had a gaunt look, both eyes in shadow. One hand still rested on her arm.

She moved away, then kissed his knuckles. The blue veins formed a pattern along the back of his hand, the black hairs thickening toward his wrist.

She closed her eyes, wishing again they were somewhere else, alone together, and without all these clothes. It would be so nice to draw close to him, to feel skin against skin. That was the best part about sex, feeling a man's naked body along your body, especially his stomach. No one had touched her in so long, not even a kiss. David had never really been comfortable with the whole business, always self-conscious and cerebral, and somehow cold even as he told her he loved her.

Was she being a romantic fool to think it would be better this time? If there ever was a "this time." She remembered again where they were and what she would see if she pulled aside his black turtleneck.

Dear God, she thought, be kind to us. Perhaps it would never work, but she wanted the chance to find out. She was sick to death of living like some scholarly monk, and she had never felt this way about David, never wanted him so badly. The chemistry was definitely there this time. Let us have our chance. She kissed his knuckles again. You should understand, God, mother of all things. You made us to love one another. The Pope may not think lust is divine, but we know better.

Thinking had wakened her and made her remember. "He has a disease." Madame Rambouillet's cold beautiful face, her dead eyes, in the dim light of the library. She bit at her lower lip, glanced again at Steve, then got quietly out of bed. The muscles of her legs protested every movement.

Fred had pulled a chair over to a window and sat staring out at the morning, cigarette in hand. Mary paused before the fireplace and put out her hands to warm them. Two big logs burned vigorously.

"Morning," Fred said. His black suit looked wrinkled.

"Good morning. You must have started this fire. It's wonderful."

"I think I finally woke up because I was very cold. It must be below zero out there this morning."

Mary walked over to the window and put her hand on his shoulder. "I'm so stiff. It hurts to move around."

He made a noise between a laugh and a snort. "I

242

didn't think I was going to be able to get out of my chair. Everything from the waist down hurts."

"This room looks so different this morning with all the light." The two arched windows on either side of the fireplace were at least six feet tall, framed in stone.

"It is a definite improvement. The mountain looks awfully cold, though." The blue sky was absolutely clear, the edges of the mountain, the slabs of ice, sharp and clean. "Every so often you can see the wind blowing the snow around up near the top."

"It was cold and strange last night under the moonlight," she said. "I don't think I'll ever feel quite the same about Mount Hood."

The two of them stared silently out the window. Finally the priest said, "I suppose we'd better get going."

As if on cue, someone rapped lightly at the door. Fred stubbed out his cigarette and stood up. "I'll get it." Mary was right behind him. He turned the round brass knob.

In the doorway was Madame Rambouillet's servant and behind her was a giant. Actually, Mary reflected, he was only about six and a half feet tall, but he must weigh well over three hundred pounds. His long hair and full beard were black shot with gray, his tiny blue eyes out of place in the broad, fat face. His nose was twisted to the side, and his teeth were brown. Fred took half a step back, and Mary grasped his arm just above the elbow.

"It is eight-thirty," the woman said. *"Madame* asked of me that I wake you. John has locked up the dogs and brought the car. I will have your breakfast ready shortly."

Mary and Fred looked at each other. *"Merci beaucoup,"* Fred said. "We'll be right down."

The woman nodded, then turned. Fred closed the door. "Impressive, wasn't he?"

Mary nodded. "She probably brought him along to let us know we had better behave. No altering the plans for the day or doing anything rash like searching the house."

"I wouldn't want to argue with him."

Mary shook her head. "Me neither. I'll see if I can get Steve up. I wish we could let him sleep. He was so sick last night, and he was having bad dreams."

"A skeptic might argue that that was caused by the unsettling events of the day and that our hostess had nothing to do with it."

Mary stared at him. He looked weary already. "Are you a skeptic?"

"Not in the least."

Steve sat on the edge of the bed while Mary put on his boots. His face was very pale, but he said he felt better. All the same, he let Mary and Fred help him downstairs.

By day the dining room was almost cheerful. A row of tall windows let in the dazzling yellow-white light reflected off the snow. They were served ham and eggs with toasted french bread and dark strong coffee. Mary and Fred were ravenous again, but Steve ate hardly anything. Afterwards the cook brought them a map and Madame Rambouillet's instructions.

John led them through the living room to the massive front doors. His left shoulder dipped lower than his right, his walk slightly out of balance. Outside, the freezing air was a shock to the lungs, and they could hear dogs barking somewhere close by. The fresh white snow covered everything between the house and the firs twenty yards away. The Cherokee was parked in front, its crimson paint dazzling in the bright sunlight, crusted snow still on its roof.

Mary paused by the car door, her breath forming a steamy cloud. The dark shape of the house rose before her with its strange, solitary tower. She thought of the headless woman up there, a stake through her heart, and Smith somewhere nearby, underground, still in darkness, total darkness now. She shivered, and the brilliant sunlight and the white snow suddenly seemed feeble. She realized how close by night was, dark and powerful, casting its shadow even now across the daylight. Perhaps the stones of the house had been cut from that same darkness, crafted out of shadow.

Baumgartner might have thought of himself as a modern-day knight with an alpine castle, but he was nothing more than a petty little voyeur. The house was a monument not to his glory, but to his perversion, and now it had been given totally over to evil. Even if Madame Rambouillet and her servants were driven away, something malevolent would remain. Evil permeated those stones, a part of their substance now, and it would never come out—no more than the blood which stained Lady Macbeth's hands.

She opened the car door. Inside, on the backseat, sat a red gas can and the blue nylon bag Smith had been carrying in the tunnel. Mary wanted to have Fred throw the bag away, but they might need something in it.

The Cherokee was still in four-wheel drive. Mary swung it around and followed the tracks in the snow back toward the fence. Fred waded out to open the gate,

245

his galoshes sinking deep into the snow. The narrow road ran downhill through the firs, their dark green boughs topped with white. Yesterday in the blizzard, the world had seemed a confined maze of gray and white, but everything had opened up under the bright blue sky. They turned onto the main road. The snow was packed hard, the icy highlights glistening.

Fred looked in back. "Steve's asleep. He . . . he doesn't look very good."

"I wish we could get him to a doctor, but no one could do anything for him. Not really. I told you last night what she said."

The sun was blindingly bright on all the snow, and Mary wished she had dark glasses. She was getting a headache.

"Mary, are we really going to the coast to try to destroy this Ruthven?"

"I am. I have to."

"Well, you know I can't let you go alone. I . . . it all seems somewhat futile."

She could hear the fear and pain in his voice. "Oh Fred, you don't have to come."

"As I keep telling you, you must have a priest along. It's positively required for these types of adventures."

"Madame Rambouillet wasn't like anything in a book or movie. I told you . . . she's not human. No actress could ever portray a real vampire. It takes more than white makeup and fake fangs."

"The cross certainly didn't frighten her, not in the least."

"It worked on Suzanne."

"I wonder why."

"She hasn't been dead long enough to be like Madame Rambouillet. Maybe she does feel something for Steve, but she's changing. She's not finished."

They were silent again. There were no other cars headed down, but on the other side, several vehicles with thin cross country skis or the thicker downhill skis passed them. "Actually," Fred said, "neither of us has much of a choice. You heard what she told us. There's no place we can hide. She'll hunt us down and kill us."

"I feel like Dorothy in the *Wizard of Oz*. Remember?" She smiled. "She was supposed to kill the Wicked Witch of the East."

"I doubt a pail of water will work."

"No. I wonder why she hates Ruthven so. She truly hates him. That's the one thing we can be certain of."

"But if we manage to destroy him, would she really let us go free?"

Mary frowned. Her head had begun to ache in earnest. "She promised me if I killed Ruthven that Steve . . . Are you sure he's asleep?"

Fred turned again. "Yes. He's out."

"Like I told you, she said she'd dispose of Suzanne. She gave her word, but I don't trust her, not really. Oh, she probably would kill Suzanne, but only because she's tired of her and because she likes killing. She might even let us go back to Portland, but we'd always know that she was out there, that she or one of her kind might decide to come after us. I don't think . . . I don't think I could go on living in Portland knowing she was close."

"I know," Fred said. "In all the stories, nothing good ever happens to those who bargain with the devil. He always wins." He sighed. "Could I have a cigarette?"

"Yes."

"As I said, it all seems futile. Well, anyway, we have

to kill Ruthven first. I suppose we should focus on that problem before worrying about what happens next." He drew in on the cigarette. "Just what I was trained for in the seminary. A lot of good I've turned out to be."

She glanced at him. He was staring straight ahead, the brim of his black hat coming almost to the black glasses. "What's that supposed to mean?"

"I haven't been much help. I knew I had aged and that my lungs were in bad shape, but I didn't realize just how sedentary I had become. My whole body hurts today. And I've never been so frightened in my life. When we saw them in that tunnel . . . Dear God, I was scared."

"So was I, but I'm awfully glad you are here. That's macho stuff, Fred, thinking you're supposed to be muscle-bound and unafraid. I didn't want you with me because I thought you were John Wayne." He remained silent. "Well?"

She heard him release his breath and smelled cigarette smoke. "We shouldn't have left Smith alone in the tunnel."

"What could we have done? He was dying."

"That's why I should have stayed. Priests are supposed to comfort the dying."

"You couldn't have done anything—it wouldn't have mattered."

"No? Are you trying to tell me that you would want to die alone with those two things feeding on you, leering at you while your life drained away?"

She felt her eyes fill with tears. "No. I suppose not." They passed the Zigzag ranger station which meant they were nearly out of the Mount Hood National Forest. "You're only human, Fred, which is why I'm so glad to have you here. You've certainly been a comfort to me.

I . . . Anyone would be afraid of them—anyone. They're terrifying. Human evil is bad enough, but they're far worse."

He was quiet for a while, then stubbed out his cigarette in the ashtray below the radio. "It's rather ironic. I was raised on stories about the devil and demons. As a child, they were very real to me, and when I was in the seminary, the devil was still treated as theological doctrine. When he went out of fashion in the sixties, it was a relief. Human evil was powerful and inexplicable enough, and it was manifest all around us. The devil seemed a scapegoat, an obvious rationalization to justify our sinful natures. I was glad to be rid of the old horned fellow, but now . . ."

"Maybe vampires aren't human any longer, but they began that way," she said. "Something corrupted them, some choice they made, and started them toward what they've become. Suzanne worked for Madame Rambouillet for years—of her own free will—I know it. Maybe she wanted power or immortal life, but she made her choice. They are in a kind of hell, trapped in those dead bodies."

"It does resemble eternal damnation," he said.

"It's more like purgatory. Madame Rambouillet understood that she wouldn't live forever."

"Vampirism may fit in their case, but what of the victims?" He glanced at the back seat. "What have they ever done?"

Mary shook her head. "I don't know. I just don't know. None of the explanations for why evil exists ever made me feel any better. It's more mysterious than God."

Fred held his cigarettes in his left hand and jiggled

249

the pack repeatedly. "Things were simpler when I was a lad. The good fathers had an explanation for everything. The universe was a most orderly place. You see that same order reflected in the old movies. Crosses are sure protection, and in the end, virtue triumphs and evil is vanquished. I can't see any way out of this. Destroying Ruthven can't be so simple as she suggested, but we have no choice except to try."

"That's right. I can't just let him die, Fred. I can't."

Fred was silent for a moment. "I left Smith, but I won't leave him or you. I swear I won't."

Mary felt her eyes grow teary again. She was so tired, and it did seem futile. "Thank you."

Packed snow covered the roads all the way into Gresham. Normally that was less than an hour's drive, but it took them twice as long. Interstate 84 was fairly clear of snow, and they drove west, then took the Highway 26 tunnel through the west hills of Portland. Traffic was light the next few miles, the freeway still clear, and they made good time passing Beaverton and Hillsboro. When they got off onto Highway 6, which cut through the Coast Range to Tillamook, snow reappeared on the road. By then it was one o'clock, and they stopped at a small drive-in to pick up some hamburgers. Steve was still sleeping in back.

"That's the best thing for him," Mary said. "The dreams shouldn't be so bad during the day."

Fred drove while Mary ate her hamburger and read through Madame Rambouillet's note. They were to go south from Tillamook about forty miles, then turn right past a certain billboard. A gravel road led to a house protected by a high fence and armed guards, but Madame Rambouillet said the guards would be "dealt with." The keys to the gate and the house had been put on Smith's key ring. In the cellar they would find Ruthven. All the vampires were to be burnt. They could immobilize the others by placing a cross or the host on the wood covering their graves, but not Ruthven. He should be burnt first—before sunset.

Madame Rambouillet must have used an old-fashioned fountain pen. The fluid look of the ink didn't come from a ballpoint or a marker. Her script was small and neat, the tails of the Gs and Ys done with an elaborate flourish.

"My Ruthven you will not fail to recognize. I told you of the red scar which runs over his left eyebrow and cheek, a red seam some two inches long. His hair is black, but may show some white depending on when he has last fed. He has high cheekbones and an aquiline nose, his eyes of a very pale gray. I told you he was no Heathcliff, but he does have the dark and stormy countenance of a romantic hero. His eyes have great power, and his scar seems to burn red at times. His sentiments, however, have nothing of the romantic inclination."

The note ended with: "Remember our discussion concerning Mr. Ryan. Bonne chance, *ma petite.*"

Mary remembered the vampire's icy lips touching her, *"ma jolie petite"* coming out of the darkness. She stared at the snow, blinding white under the sun, but the fear came anyway, sharp and visceral.

The road wound upwards into the Coast Range. Thin gray clouds gradually drifted across the patch of sky showing between the trees. The air was heavy, damp and cold. She turned up the heater a notch.

Ahead they saw a wall of gray-white mist, its tendrils reaching for the dark trees and shutting out the last blue in the sky. Fred turned on the lights and slowed down. The two yellow shafts shone through the fog, and they saw wisps of gray nothing curl and twist slowly.

"Shit," Mary murmured, glancing at her watch.

"What time is it?"

"Nearly two. We only have about four hours left."

"Maybe we should stay in Tillamook tonight and try again tomorrow."

"In her notes she warns against that. I . . . Ruthven probably knows we're coming." Even though she knew it was true, the words were hard to say.

"What do you mean?" Fred sounded scared.

"She knew we were coming. Their hatred somehow binds them, and they have their spies, human and otherwise. Maybe the crows I saw . . . In the stories they can change shape. At your house, that thing that broke the window—it must have been her. Of course it was her."

"No." Fred shook his head. "No."

"It had to be. And Ruthven must be as clever as she is. We mustn't give him any extra time. She said she would deal with the guards. Oh God, we've got to get there—we have to."

"We have four hours. We'll make it."

But the fog grew thicker still, and the road curved constantly. They were down to about thirty, and even that seemed fast. "Be careful, Fred. We want to get there in one piece." She yawned. "I'm so tired."

"Sleep for a while."

A sign formed in the mist, then swept past: Tillamook, 63 miles. Her father used to take them to the coast every summer for a week, and they would always stop in Tillamook for ice cream at the dairy. Those days seemed so remote in time and space that they couldn't possibly be real, only a kind of fairy tale. These mountains were so different in the summer with warm yellow light on them. Then green dominated; you sensed the life of the vegetation growing all around you, the marvelous fertility of the Northwest. Now the impression was not of life, but of death and decay—browns, blacks and grays, fungi and lichen covering a rotting world.

She wondered if she would ever see this forest again in the summer, or see the blue green sea and feel hot sand underfoot. Was this the last day of her life? Alex had been here in summer just before he disappeared.

She closed her eyes and began to pray silently, not so much words as fragments of thoughts, the feelings stronger than any words, and in it were Fred and Steve and Alex.

The prayer faded away into a dream. The ocean was bottle green, the yellow-white sunlight shimmering on the waters. She walked onto the dark band of wet sand and waited for the foaming white surf to cover her bare feet. She laughed at the cold, then stared down at her feet. Her toes were splayed apart, and she wiggled them slightly, working her feet deep into the wet sand. The surf rushed her again, lingered, then drew back, leaving a surface of water that seeped into the sand. The wet sand reflected the blue of the sky.

Steve took her hand and stared out at the ocean. He had his shirt off, and he was tanned, his body lean and hard. A band of muscle ran down along his neck to his collar bone. Two reddish dimples of scar tissue were all that remained of the bite marks.

How I love you, Mary thought, and then the dream whirled elsewhere, but the sense of well-being remained. It was still with her when she opened her eyes

253

and saw the white fog enclosing the car. A few isolated snowflakes floated wearily down. She squeezed shut her eyes, wanting the dream back, but it was too late. She sat up and glanced at her watch. 3:30 already.

"Feeling better?" Fred stared ahead into the fog.

"Yes. I had such . . . How are you doing?"

"Okay." He sounded weary, and she could see the tension in the way he held the wheel.

"We must be getting close to Tillamook."

"I think so, but everything looks the same."

Mary looked over the seat. Steve's half-opened eyes focused on her. In her dream he hadn't been so pale and thin. "Mary?" He sat up very slowly. "What is this? Where are we?"

"We're in the Coast Range on the way to Tillamook. To Ruthven's."

He let his breath out slowly. "Ruthven's. Like she told us." A sign went by that said: Portland, 55 Miles. He turned his head, winced slightly, then put his hand on his throat. "Oh, well. I was hoping it was a dream or something. Wait a minute. If we're going to Tillamook, why did that sign say Portland, fifty-five miles?"

She had just seen the sign, but she had to struggle to remember. It was as if someone had used an eraser to wipe away the memory.

"Sign?" Fred said.

"He's right." Mary closed her eyes and tried to calm herself. "Stop the car, Fred. Turn us around. We're going the wrong way."

"That's impossible." Despite the conviction in his voice, he pulled over and stopped. "I wouldn't do that, Mary—you know I wouldn't. I promised I wouldn't run away again."

254

"I know that, Fred, and I believe you. He's right, though. I saw the sign too and simply ignored it. They're playing tricks on our minds. I shouldn't have gone to sleep. I don't think it would have happened if I was awake too. Turn around, Fred. There's room here."

"That's impossible!" He took off his hat and ran his hand through his white hair. "You don't just accidentally turn around in this kind of fog. Don't you trust me?"

"Of course I do, but you can be tricked, and so can I. We didn't even notice the sign. Go on. We're running out of time."

Fred turned the wheel sharply, then accelerated in the other direction. "It's impossible." His jaw was thrust forward.

"We should see the sign soon."

"Here it comes," Steve said.

Fred slowed the car as they passed the sign, then stopped. It was only about fifteen feet back, but the fog was so thick they could barely make out the white letters against the green background: Portland, 55 Miles.

Mary watched Fred's face redden, the muscles in his jaw tense. She felt afraid again. What was the use? Maybe they should just go back to Portland. An hour and a half, and they had gained practically nothing.

"Goddamn it to hell," Fred muttered. She hadn't heard him curse before.

"Never mind, Fred. We'd better get moving. We haven't much time."

He started the car forward. Mary wondered what they would do if they didn't make it to the house by sunset. Would Ruthven come after them tonight?

"So much for my vows of vigilance and bravery," the priest said.

Mary sighed. "Don't, Fred. It doesn't help anything."

"I must have wanted to run. Otherwise it wouldn't have been so easy for them."

"We all want to run. I should have stayed awake."

"I really don't remember when it happened. I just don't remember."

"Just stop it, Fred—okay? Kicking yourself doesn't help anything."

She watched the snowflakes splatter against the windshield. They drifted slowly down, struck the glass, and then the wiper arm brushed them away. The fog was thicker and darker, the forest lost in its white mists. The universe had contracted, had shrunk down to this small shell enclosed in shadow.

That's the way we are, Mary thought, trapped inside a shell. Normally you could see outside yourself and know there was a larger universe full of beauty and power, but not now. They were trapped inside themselves just like the vampires. Wasn't that really the way it was? You could never truly see with another's eyes or know what they felt. Everyone was an isolated spark of life surrounded by infinite mists and nothingness. The fear manifest itself as a tightness in her chest, and she felt light headed.

"You know," Steve said, "turning the car around at least makes some kind of sense, your unconscious trying to protect you, but in my case it was more stupidity. I don't remember anything about what happened with Sarah. Mary had warned me, but I must have let her in anyway."

"Will you both just stop it!" Mary rubbed angrily at her eyes. She looked out the window and fought to control her breathing.

They were all quiet for a long time, then she heard Steve move and his hand closed about her right shoulder. "I'm sorry. You're so strong that we—I . . . I've had a good sleep, and I feel better. I can watch with Father Martin if you want to rest."

She shook her head.

"I know it's hard when I'm dressed like this, but I really wish you'd call me Fred, especially after all we've been through. Even the older ladies in the parish have finally started calling me Fred. Whenever I hear 'Father Martin,' I think of Spencer Tracy or Bing Crosby in a Roman collar, and then I feel inadequate."

Steve laughed. "All right, I will—Fred."

Higher up the snow was deeper, and Fred kept their speed down around thirty. After a while, Mary took the wheel again. Steve had offered to drive, but Mary told him to rest. She knew he was sick, and neither she nor Fred were physically very strong. They might need to rely on him. They reached Tillamook around 4:30 and headed south.

The snow was gone, but the fog was thicker than ever. Mary remembered green fields stretching off to the fir covered hills, cattle grazing, but now she couldn't see beyond the edge of the road. Green fence posts and barbed wire formed in the fog, a black and white cow, a car, a mailbox and house, then swept by, and something else would materialize. A cold steady drizzle fell. They came to a clearcut, only ghostly silver stumps left, and Mary thought of Madame Rambouillet saying mankind was a blight upon the world. Fred and Steve had been talking, getting to know each other, but now they were silent.

"Is it darker?" Steve asked.

257

Mary bit at her lip. "Yes. What time is it?"

Fred raised his left hand. "Five-ten. About an hour to go."

"Where's the damned sign? If we miss it . . ." She was so tired of hearing the engine roar, tired of staring tensely into the fog. Something was different—the sound of the rain had changed and the shine of the hood. She touched the brakes and felt the car quaver slightly. "Oh, fine—I think we've got freezing rain now."

"You had better slow down," Fred said.

"I don't know. I think I'd rather die in a car wreck than . . . Oh, I'm sorry."

"The same thought had crossed my mind." Fred's voice was tense, the pitch higher.

"Is it colder too?" Steve asked.

"Yes." She turned the heater up. "You sound chilled, Steve. There's more aspirin in my purse. It's a little early, but . . ."

He laughed. "Overdosing on aspirin is the least of my worries right now."

Mary smiled. "I could use some myself. My head aches so."

Fred bent over and pulled a can out of a paper bag. "Ah, why don't we make this a communal partaking since this corporeal frame is still painful from our expedition yesterday. We can wash down the sacred tablets with the final can of orange soda."

Mary made a face. "Orange soda? I would have chosen something else for my last meal. I always wanted to try Dom Perignon champagne."

Steve drank, then leaned forward and handed her the orange can. "It's overrated and overpriced."

"Still, I'll bet it's better than this."

"I've never tried it either," Fred said.

"If we get out of this alive, we can split a bottle three ways, my treat," Steve said.

The road dipped and curved off to the left, the car surrounded again by the dark shapes of firs. A yellow sign like a square sun appeared in the mists: Joan's Beach Crafts, 2 Miles. Mary hit the brakes, the car wavered, and she pumped the pedal. "That's it—that's the one." She had slowed down to twenty, then clenched her teeth, and took the turnoff into the trees.

The gravel road was barely wide enough for one car, and the tree trunks seemed close together, almost touching, as if they were hairs on the back of some great dusky animal. The sky had vanished, the mist closing about them. The yellow beams from the headlights seemed insignificant, and Mary thought how utterly and impenetrably black these woods would be when night fell.

"It's really not sunset yet?" she murmured.

"No," Fred said. "We have a good forty minutes."

"It's so dark."

The road rose steeply. Mary was glad for the four-wheel drive. All around them the trunks began to sway, and they could hear the wind moan overhead where the boughs of the trees interwove like fingers. The forest was alive, every tree trembling in unison, sharing some primal fear. Rain splattered the windshield, stopped, came again, while the wind cried out in rage, then faded to a whisper.

The sound of the rain on the car had a metallic clatter, and the trees wavered and changed before their eyes, the needles suddenly glistening under the headlights. As they went higher still, the ice coat thickened.

"It's a good thing this is a gravel road," Steve said. "You'd never make it up a hill like this if it was smooth and covered with ice."

The road leveled suddenly, the path opening up, and the lights shone on the ice covered fence, the pattern formed by the wire all sparkly. Beyond the fence was nothing but white mist.

Fred opened his door. "I'll get the gate."

Mary pulled the ring and the other keys off, leaving the Cherokee key in the ignition. "Here. It's the red key."

He walked toward the fence, his coat and hat absolutely black in the dying light. He unlocked the padlock, then swung open a ten-foot section of fence. The jagged lines of barbed wire along the top were also covered with ice. He slammed the car door shut. "It is so cold and wet out there."

Mary drove through the gate. A small building materialized to the right, a big glass window in front, the door hanging open. "I wonder," Mary said, "if the guards . . ."

Fred looked in Smith's bag. "I'd better check." He pulled out a flashlight.

Steve opened his door. "I'll come with you."

Mary noticed Steve lean against the car. She wondered if he would be able to stand, but then he walked over to the guardhouse. He and Fred stopped at the doorway, the yellow-white beam of the flashlight swinging around. Neither man moved for a moment, and Mary thought about getting out. Before she could, they started back.

Steve sagged wearily into the back seat. "Christ," he murmured. "Jesus Christ."

Fred was pale, his mouth drawn back. "She took care

of them all right. Their throats were cut, blood every-where."

Mary licked her lips. "What time is it?"

"About five thirty-five," Fred said.

"That gives us about half an hour. I hope your watch keeps good time."

The Cherokee jounced slowly and rhythmically as she followed the road. An enormous rhododendron appeared out of the fog, the long green leaves and swollen buds thick with ice. Further back were isolated firs rising into the mists. The road was suddenly smooth, the tires quiet. The headlights lit up the big front porch and the stairs, but most of the house remained hidden in the fog. Mary put the car into park, then shut off the engine.

After hours of driving, the quiet was a blessing. They could hear the wind in the nearby trees. Mary turned off the headlights, and the misty twilight swallowed them up.

"Let's go," she said. "There isn't much time. I'll carry the gas can."

"I can carry it," Steve said.

"You take care of yourself. Fred, you take Smith's bag."

The pavement underfoot was slippery. Again she was glad for her hiking boots. The long walk in the blizzard yesterday would have been impossible without them. The wind buffeted her, and she felt the icy sting on her face of tiny frozen crystals.

Fred aimed the light at the stairs, then up onto the porch. The place hadn't been painted in years. The wooden pillars supporting the porch roof were streaked black and white, and the porch itself looked blotchy; dark spots showed on the planks. The big windows of the house were black squares, and the dark wooden door had a knocker in the middle.

"Be careful on the stairs," Fred said. "The wood looks rotten."

Mary and Steve went first while Fred held the light for them. She took Steve's arm and stayed to the right where the wood looked better. He was wobbly. There was something tentative to his step.

"Careful—it's icy," she said.

The light shook, then fell away, leaving them in shadow. "Shit," Fred mumbled. Mary turned and saw him hunched over on his knees. She set down the gas can, then went down the steps.

"Are you all right?" She took his arm and helped him up. The flashlight cast white light under the stairs where it had fallen.

"Yes. What's a little abuse to the patella at this point?" He picked up the gym bag.

"Go on. I'll get the light. My shoes are better." After retrieving it, she went up the stairs again. The flashlight made Fred and Steve look unnaturally white, their fear obvious. The door knocker was a gargoyle face with protruding eyes and a pointed tongue thrust forward, the bronze weathered to a blotchy, uneven green.

"I don't want to touch that thing," Mary said.

The thick lenses of Fred's glasses looked foggy. "We can forego the knocking."

Mary shined the light on the lock. "You've still got the keys, Fred."

He unlocked the doorknob first, then a second lock about a foot up. "The door may be an antique, but this is a modern deadbolt." He gave the door a push and it swung open.

262

Mary smelled something musty and putrescent. She and Fred stared at each other. "Let's go," she said. She handed him the flashlight. He stepped inside. She picked up the gas can.

Steve had clenched his teeth, and it was light enough for her to see his eyes. She took his arm. He was trembling. "Are you all right?"

"No."

"What is it? Are you sick?"

He shook his head. "They're in there, all of them, and they're afraid and angry, especially him. This is a very bad place, worse even than the chateau."

"Mary?" Fred stood in the open doorway.

Her fingers tightened on Steve's arm. "Come on," she said, but his body seemed rigid and immobile.

"Promise me . . . promise me . . ." His voice was strained and hoarse, barely recognizable. ". . . you won't let me become like her—you'll kill me too, burn me, if you have to. Promise me."

Her eyes filled with tears. "I can't promise that. Come on—we have to hurry. There's no time."

He hesitated, then stumbled forward. "My throat hurts," he whispered.

Her hand tightened about the handle of the gas can, and she bit her lip hard. There was no time for sorrow, hysteria or love, no time. She went into the house.

Chapter II

The inside of the house was colder and damper than outside. Fred swept the flashlight around the living room. Cobwebs were thick in the corners, dust covered everything, and the furniture was torn and dirty.

"Someone's almost as good a housekeeper as I am," Mary said. "I didn't think anyone could ever beat my cobwebs."

Steve put his hands in his parka pocket, but that didn't keep them from shaking. He had never felt so cold, and everything hurt. He stared down at the floor and tried to swallow. Maybe he was hallucinating, but it seemed as if he could almost see in the dark. The flooring had the fine tight grain of oak. Below in the cellar were the others, their fear obvious, impossible to ignore. Ruthven was angry, his rage like a blue white flame. Their thoughts blended into a kind of music, the voices not human, bestial and primitive. He wished he didn't have to listen, but there was no way to shut it off.

He started across the room. "This way," he said. Fred shone the flashlight ahead of him, but he didn't need it. Light only made his head hurt worse.

The stairway to the basement was at the end of the hallway. He put his foot on the top board, staying to the right away from the rotten side. Halfway down was a broken board. The white light jumped and danced on the stairs, and he raised his eyes to avoid it. The darkness wavered, and he saw a red orb hovering over black waters, sinking slowly. The coming of night both terrified and excited him.

"Dear God, what a stench," Fred mumbled.

Steve stopped at the bottom of the stairs, frowning. He couldn't smell anything. The dirt floor pulsed slightly, as if the earth were breathing, and he sensed the living presences in the shadowy pockets. Their fear and their voices were increasingly difficult to ignore.

He was aware of Mary close by, but he couldn't quite see her anymore. "Steve," she whispered. *"Steve."* Her hand tightened about his arm.

"Am I really awake? I didn't think you could dream while you were awake."

"You're awake. Stay with us—*please.*"

"I'll try," he whispered. The tiny gold posts on her earlobes seemed to glow in the dark, and he thought how nice it would be to kiss her throat and her breasts, to make love to her. She wasn't like Sarah or Brenda, she was nicer than either of them. How good to caress her skin with his lips and sink his teeth into her throat, how good to fill his mouth with fresh hot blood and warm himself with her life.

"Jesus." Turning away, he shut his eyes as tightly as he could, but he still saw her dead face with the blood trickling down her neck. He felt her terror as she tried to escape, her small slight body pinned beneath him. Why had she ever trusted him?

265

"Steve." Something touched his face. "Come back to us—we need you—we need your help."

She had pulled off her wool glove, and light came out of her hand. It made his throat feel better. The room twisted, then steadied, and he remembered where he was and what they were doing. "Hurry—please hurry," he said. She stared at him, and now he could see her strength, a kind of aura about her face. That was why Ruthven feared and hated her.

"Fred, get out the hosts. We'll use them to contain the others while we deal with Ruthven. I wonder how many vampires there are. There are so many holes."

"Five," Steve said, "including Ruthven. "Two women and two men, only one isn't a woman. She's only a girl."

The priest stared at him. "How can you know that?"

Steve wondered how they could be deaf to such screaming and howling. "I know."

Mary pulled his right hand out of his parka pocket and gripped it firmly. "Show us. You take the gas can, Fred."

The yellow-white light jounced along the hard brown earth. Steve went to the beautiful woman in the black gown. She was the oldest after Ruthven and had been with him the longest.

A white radiance like a strobe or lightning flash suddenly lit up the room. Blinded, Steve clapped a hand over his eyes.

"What's wrong?" Mary asked.

"That light—I can't see."

"What light? What's he talking about?" Fred said.

"Never mind. Pour some gas on that plywood, then put the host on it."

Steve blinked and lowered his hand. The priest

266

sloshed gas onto the wood, then set the host down very carefully. "Forgive us, Lord," he whispered.

Steve stared at the round white host, attracted and repelled. It wasn't so dazzlingly bright now, but still gave off a warm white light quite different from the flashlight. He could sense the thing writhing under the wood, cringing and screaming.

Mary squeezed his hand. "Where are the others?"

The two men had died young, still in their twenties. They were well muscled. Last was a girl who had only been thirteen. "She's more of a child than a woman," Steve whispered. "She was innocent and didn't deserve this. Ruthven did it himself. Part of her wants to be free, but the sick part is growing stronger. It hates us, and she could kill us just as easily as any of the others. The host hurts them. The light blinds them, and they understand what they've become, all that they've lost. She misses . . ."

Mary squeezed his hand. "That's enough. Take us to Ruthven."

"He's at the end there. He's like Madame Rambouillet, but even older."

Mary tugged at his hand, and he let her lead him toward the far wall. Behind them, the four hosts on the wood cast warm half-globes of light. Steve was shaking worse than ever, and his throat felt as if someone had pounded in a couple of nails. He could almost feel the blood oozing from the wounds.

Every step became harder. Ruthven was like none of the others. He seemed more angry than afraid, perhaps because he knew they could not destroy him. His ancient corpse lay rotting in its grave, and Steve smelled the stench all at once, as if some putrid black flower had

267

suddenly burst open. Things crawled about Ruthven in that hole, small black vermin sharing in his darkness—slugs, beetles, other insects. Somehow they all fed upon each other, passing death amongst themselves, and even the vermin were tiny sparks of consciousness, fragments of damnation.

"Can you lift the board, Steve?"

He shook his head. "Please—don't make me. You must feel him, don't you? It's not just craziness, is it?"

Mary stared at him. "No. It's not. I feel him, all right. Come on, Fred. Let's do this. Our time must be nearly up."

"There's about ten minutes," Steve said. "For Christ sake—*hurry.*"

Mary and the priest bent over the hole, and then the rotting board came up and over, landing with a loud clump.

"Dear God!" Fred said. "Look at him. And he stinks so."

"Don't look at his eyes," Mary said. "Give me that gas can."

Steve wouldn't look in the hole, but somehow the eyes still found him. The face was yellow-white, waxen, not like living flesh and muscle. Something slimy and nasty had been molded about that skull and those damned eyes, some strange substance neither dead nor alive. The eyes were gray like water on a cloudy day or like clouds themselves, and they weren't human either. Their shape was wrong, their expression.

"My God," Fred murmured. "Do you see those bugs and things crawling around in there? *Lord.*"

"I see them. Give me the matches, Fred."

The priest took a small box of matches out of his

overcoat pocket. Mary opened the box. Fred's hand made the yellow-white light tremble. He and Mary looked pale and spectral. Steve knew they were afraid, but he couldn't feel their fear as he could the vampires'. She managed to get out a match, then struck it three times.

"Shit." She made a sharp, strained laugh. "Let me try another one." The rasp of the match head against the box was tiny, ludicrously feeble in the darkness beneath the house. She struck the match twice more. "I have a feeling . . ." She couldn't finish speaking. She tried three more matches, then made ready to throw the box away, but restrained herself.

"Mary—what are we going to do!" Raw fear sounded in the priest's voice.

She bit at her lip, stared at Steve, but there was so much noise and movement that he couldn't think. Ruthven was laughing. He found them all funny.

"Your lighter, Fred—quick, get it out."

The priest's breath came out in a quick "huh," and he fumbled in his overcoat pocket. "You're a brilliant lady. In twenty years of smoking, it's never failed me, and I put lighter fluid in it just the day before yesterday."

The lighter was the old-fashioned, square silver kind. The priest flicked the tiny wheel with his thumb, and they saw the yellow sparks which vanished immediately. The priest stared at Mary, his eyes wide open and his mouth pulled back. He clicked the lighter four more times then hurled it down and grabbed Mary's arm. "Let's go—let's get out of here!"

Mary shook her head. "No."

"He's waking up—even I can tell that! We've got five minutes—we can be in the car by then."

269

Mary clenched her teeth. *"No."* She grabbed Fred by the shoulder. "Stop it, Fred—I need your help *now."*

"I don't want to die down here—it's better outside. The smell . . . Please, can't we just get out of here?"

Mary drew in her lower lip, bit at it. "Madame Rambouillet thought she was so clever. I wonder if she knew. Maybe Smith . . ." Her eyes widened, and she dropped down onto her knee and put both hands into the bag. She was up in a second, the stake in one hand, the mallet in the other. "We can still try the other way. Smith was well prepared. Fred, I don't know if I'm strong enough, physically strong enough, to . . ."

The priest shook his head. "I can't—I just can't."

Mary looked at Steve. Even though her face was out of the light he could see her eyes. The fear he felt was worse then anything that had ever come before. Hands seemed to slip into his belly and yank playfully at his guts.

"Steve, you're stronger than either of us. We don't have much time. You could do it almost in one blow."

Ruthven was afraid now. He had thought they were beaten, but doubt crept into that waxy face, a tremor pulling at the dead mouth. You will suffer for all eternity if you do this thing, I swear it. You are one of us. You are mine.

"Steve—*please."* She was squeezing his hand again.

"Can it be true?" he whispered. "Can I be damned already?"

"No! You're still alive—you can fight them until you're dead!"

He closed his eyes, and suddenly he remembered Sarah naked on the bed and him sliding into her, embracing her, emptying himself into her, even as her

270

fangs pierced his throat. He moaned. "I let her into my house—you warned me, but I let her in anyway."

"You made a mistake—you're only human. I don't care about that. It doesn't matter! You can still fight them. You can prove you're not one of them. You can save us."

He tried to forget about all the howling and screaming, but the shimmering, the colors, were harder to ignore. "Give it to me—the stake."

She put it into his left hand and closed his fingers about it with her own. "You know I'd do it if I could, but it would take too long. We have so little time."

"Yes," he whispered.

The voices of the damned must shriek this way in Hell, and Satan himself could not be uglier than this thing cursing and threatening him. He turned, but Mary held his arm.

"Oh, Steve, I know it's impossible, but I do think I love you. Honest to God I do. Whatever happens to us—oh, I just wanted you to know."

The ache he felt in his chest was not pain. He wanted so badly to hug her, to love her, but that could never be. He stepped into the hole, and his left leg gave out, the knee buckling. The face was before him now, impossible to avoid. Whether its rage or fear was stronger he could not tell. He must do this quickly—one hard sharp blow. He held out the stake with his left hand, raised the mallet high with his right. Ruthven was telling him how he was weak and sick, mentally and physically unable to do this thing. Sarah thought he was weak too—that was why she had chosen him.

His arm swung forward, and somehow he hit the stake dead center, the full weight of his extended arm and the mallet driving the wood through **Ruthven's** chest. The two screams sounded at once and broke the stillness of the dark place. Steve felt pure agony, as if a spear had been thrust clean through him, piercing the muscle of his heart. He clapped both hands over his chest and fell sideways.

"Get him out of there—help me!" Mary screamed.

Ruthven's shriek never died away. It clawed for his skull, threatening to tear it open. Nothing but pain, the universe all darkness and pain and shrieking.

"Oh, Steve," Mary whispered.

Something drew him sideways up out of the black pool of pain and death. Did he tell her he was sorry? He had failed her and Fred. Ruthven was not dead, but Steve could no longer bear the torture. He swam toward one of the globes of white light, then let himself sink away into its peace and silence.

Chapter 12

Mary put her hand on Steve's throat and felt his pulse under her fingertips. "He's alive. Oh God, I wish this was all over with."

Fred's hat had fallen off. He looked old, tired, and afraid. "What do you mean?"

Mary shined the flashlight in the bag and took out the knife. The blade was twelve inches long, very sharp, with dried brown blood on it—Smith's blood. She remembered him wiping it clean after using it on the vampire in the tower. "We have to cut the head off."

"Oh Lord," Fred moaned.

She stood up and hesitated before the grave. When the stake struck Ruthven, he had come alive, but now he lay still again, his white face and hands almost glowing. He wore black, and the earth was dark, so that the head and hands already seemed like pieces that had been cut off. There were things crawling around down there. Mary knew if she waited any longer she would never be able to move. Snakes might not really be able to paralyze birds with their gaze, but this thing was far more powerful than any serpent.

She gave the light to Fred. "Hold this."

She jumped into the hole, knelt, and drew the blade across his throat. A line of red opened above the Adam's apple. His lips parted, a bloody foam on them, and the scar over his eye was the same color as the blood. She coughed once, something hot and bitter rising in her throat, then swallowed. Her hand jerked the knife back forth, opening a big gap in the dead flesh, then the knife caught on something hard. She couldn't cut through it. In high school she had had to dissect a formaldehyde soaked frog, long dead, and this flesh was equally lifeless.

"Oh, Fred—I can't . . ."

He was down in the hole beside her, handing her the light. "Give me that." He took the knife in his right hand, his eyes wide open behind the thick lenses, and then he shoved the blade back into the wound across the throat. He clenched his teeth as he put his weight onto the knife, trying to cut through the neck vertebrae. Blood bubbled over the back of the blade as it sank deeper. Fred's breath made clouds of steamy vapor.

Ruthven's jaw jerked open, revealing the great yellow fangs, his black tongue arching as blood poured from his mouth. He made a hissing, gurgling noise, and the smell made Mary want to vomit. Fred hesitated, then pressed hard again. The blood blackened, seemed to smoke, and the face turned the color of ashes.

For an instant Mary thought he was dying. A terrible joy filled her, but then she realized that Ruthven was dissolving before their eyes. First his flesh became mist, and they saw the white of his skull, tendrils of smoke drifting out of the dark eye sockets, then it too melted away.

A cold wind swept through the darkness, swirling aside the smoke and leaving them on their knees in the empty grave. Fred let the knife drop. Mary took his hand and squeezed. Both their hands were bloody. "Too late," she whispered.

Fred opened his mouth but couldn't speak. They stood.

A howl shattered the silence—"Let us out!"—and then all of the vampires were screaming to be freed, the wooden boards jumping from the blows of fists or feet.

Fred licked his lips and put his arm around Mary. She felt him trembling.

"Silence!" The voice was that of a reedy tenor, and it rang out like a bizarre parody of God proclaiming the last judgment. The others were immediately quiet.

Mary turned slowly, the flashlight in hand. The voice had come from behind her. Ruthven stood with his arms folded, his gray eyes triumphant. The wounds in his chest and throat had vanished, but the scar over his left eye was still red. He was very tall with long arms and fingers. Perhaps because she had seen his flesh melt away, she was aware of the skull under the skin.

"You have failed," he said. "You came close—too close—but you have failed, and now you are mine. You will suffer for what you have done, suffer in ways you would not have thought possible. You will wish you had let her kill you or that you had taken your own lives."

Mary knew he was talking to her alone. Her mouth was dry, and she felt the fear in the center of her chest. It was nearly as tangible as the vampire, a hand squeezing her heart with bony fingers.

"Get out of my grave. It is not ready for you. Yet."

They obeyed. He spoke with an English accent, a

275

touch of refinement which didn't fit his appearance. Mary tried to think what they might do, but she was too frightened. She couldn't take her eyes away from him. He stepped toward them, and Fred grabbed her arm, held it tightly, as if to keep himself from turning and running.

"So my dearest Madame Rambouillet sent you, Miss Connely. Did she tell you that she sent your brother and that delightful harlot of hers once before? Your brother also drove a stake through me. Would you like to know how he died? My Charlotte thrust the same stake through his heart. I have a quaint little boneyard in the woods where I put annoying people after I have disposed of them. Your brother's remains are there, Mary. You don't mind if I call you Mary, do you? Your corpse will soon be there, Father Martin. I regret that it cannot, by any stretch of the imagination, be called consecrated ground. You, my dear Mary, will not be with your brother and the good father. You will remain here with me forever."

Mary couldn't turn away her eyes, but she managed to lower the light. She wished he would hurry. Anything was better than this fear.

"Take off your coat, Mary. Take off your coat and stay a while." Ruthven laughed, and although his voice sounded almost human, the laughter did not. It was forced and guttural—dead.

Mary heard the soft ragged sound of her parka zipper as she pulled it down. Fred opened his mouth, then took a host out of his pocket.

Ruthven laughed again. "No thank you, I'm not hungry right this instant. Besides, the flesh of your dead god does not appeal to me." His white hand lunged,

276

grasped the priest's black garments below his chin and pulled him closer. With his other hand he took the host, put it in his mouth, and chewed reflectively. Turning his head, he spat out the fragments, then laughed again. Mary wanted to cover her ears. She could see Fred struggling not to scream.

Ruthven extended his arm, hurling the priest across the room. Mary swung the flashlight, and the beam caught Fred as he struck the stone wall. He fell in a black heap, his body twisted, his face down. Mary took a step forward, but something held her, then whirled her about. The flashlight hit the dirt, leaving her for a second in darkness, then came on again. Ruthven's face was in the shadow, but she could see the eyes and the twisted smile of the mouth. His fingers squeezed her arm so hard she knew she would be bruised, but she wouldn't cry out.

"You aren't going anywhere, Mary. Now it's just the two of us, just you and I. We are going to have a little chat, and then I am going to feast on you. Before the night is over, we shall lie together, you and I, in my grave."

Her sorrow for Fred helped take the edge off her fear. "Is he dead? Let me go to him."

"I'm not sure. He's rather fragile at his age. It doesn't matter. I want him dead. Accommodations are rather limited here, and with his background . . . I'm afraid it would never work out, a priestly vampire." He laughed again.

Mary stared at the ground, tears blurring her vision. At least the flashlight was still casting light at her feet. She could see her shadow stretched out across the dirt floor and onto the wall, but Ruthven cast no shadow. He must be wearing black clothes, but the darkness about him was strangely formless. Both he and his clothes didn't quite seem real.

"You like the light, do you? Perhaps I should turn it off now."

"No!" It slipped out before she could stop herself.

"Really, you are too old for such childish fears. Soon you will be afraid, not of the dark, but of the light. It will hurt your eyes even as it hurts mine. You will dwell here with me and my companions in the blessed eternal darkness."

"No." She began to cry.

"Now, now, don't cry." Suddenly he grabbed her other arm and shook her hard. "Get hold of yourself—the night is young. The entertainment is just beginning. I did not think you would yield so easily. I expected better from you."

She swallowed once, focusing on an ember of anger that had flared briefly. "Let us watch—let us out!" screamed a woman's voice, and more cries came from the holes where the others lay confined.

"I told you to be silent!" Ruthven shouted. "You can join me whenever you wish. No magical wafer can imprison me. You are too old to behave like children. Show some courage and set yourself free, or you'll just have to enjoy things as best you can from down in there. Can't you taste her fear? It's almost better than blood. It gives even blood a warmer, sweeter taste, my Mary—as you will soon understand. Perhaps there is some simple biochemical explanation like adrenaline and an increased metabolic rate. Sexual arousal also affects the taste. Now then, you were going to take off your coat and make yourself comfortable."

He released her, and she collapsed, sat on the cold wet earth supporting herself with one hand. A few feet away Steve lay on his side. She wondered if he were dead yet. Her eyes sought out the bright yellow circle of the flashlight.

The hands grabbed her again and hoisted her up. For an instant her boots kicked at the air, then she was on her feet again, swaying, Ruthven leering at her. "Really, I had no idea you were so weary, but I must ask you to remain standing. It's only polite. Now take off your coat."

She ran her tongue over her lower lip, but her tongue felt like dry wool. It took both her hands to work the zipper. Ruthven slipped the parka off her right shoulder, then her left, always keeping one shoulder in his grip. For a moment he was still. Mary could barely see his face in the dim light. His incessant talking in his whiny British tenor was grating, but the silence was worse.

"What a charming crucifix."

Mary lowered her eyes and caught the faint gleam of metal.

"And what a shame it doesn't frighten me. It's such a convenient weapon in fiction. The literary heroes and heroines who fight Dracula and his kin are such ineffectual idiots. If all it takes is a cross to keep us at bay, how can they ever become our victims? All they would need to do is have a cross tattooed across their necks. Then they could never be harmed." He laughed again.

His left hand closed about her throat, and she remembered Madame Rambouillet, the smell of her, the polluting touch of her dead flesh. He was the same, exactly the same. His other hand slipped under the cross, grabbed the collar of the turtleneck, then yanked violently. For an instant the hand at her throat was crushing her windpipe, choking her, and the little light left exploded into colors and swirls.

She would have fainted, but he was holding her shoulders. Something cold lay between her breasts, the metal of the cross. He had ripped away the front of her shirt. The room wouldn't keep still. Icy fingers slipped under each bra cup, then he pulled the bra apart, splitting it in two. She cried out and tried to twist away from him, but he seized her shoulders again. She couldn't believe how fast he could move or his strength. No doubt he could pull off her arm or leg as easily as a boy might dismember a fly.

The cold damp air of the cellar caressed her throat, her breastbone, and her belly. His left hand kept crushing her shoulder, but the finger of his other hand pushed aside the torn cloth and traced a small circle about her left nipple. The fingernail was long and jagged. Feeling that dead thing playing with the small warm lump of flesh made her shudder, her skin prickling. She opened her mouth to scream, but managed to choke it off.

"You don't like that?"

"No." She thought of some poison, some blackness, seeping out of him and into her. "Please . . ."

He laughed. "How can I refuse so polite a request? You are, after all, my guest for the evening." He drew away his finger, but she couldn't make herself breathe right or stop shaking. "You really are frightened, aren't you?"

Again, she felt a brief anger. "Yes, damn you." She forced out a long sigh. "I'm so cold."

"Ah, yes. I'm afraid we've no central heating. Well, dear lady, how shall we pass the evening? The night is

280

young, and we must have some prelude to seduction. We want you to be able to savor our brief time together." His finger played again with her nipple.

She wanted to scream at him to stop, but she knew that was what he wanted. Normally she wouldn't scream at anything. She thought it was silly for women to shriek at bugs or scary movies, but now she had to struggle not to cry out. Perhaps there was no way to fight him, but even the devil must get annoyed at something.

"Did you . . . ?" She could manage whispering better than talking. "Did you do this to Madame Rambouillet?"

His hand jerked back, and the other hand tightened about her shoulder.

"How did she feel about your games of seduction?"

He drew his hand back, and she jerked sideways, trying to twist her face away from the blow. It never came. She turned slowly and felt his dead gray eyes on her, even though she couldn't see him.

"Perhaps you are cleverer than I thought. Actually, you did rather well this evening." His hand tightened again. "You might have killed me. She understood—that is why she sent you. The priest wanted to run away, but you remembered the stake. I wonder if she could really have been so stupid, but no, she must have known the matches would not work. She was testing you to see if you were worthy. What did she promise you? That weakling there? You know he is marked, that he is a dead man."

Mary said nothing.

"Did she promise you immortal life too?"

"No."

281

"Ah—I see. You have scruples, or . . . Of course, there is this lovely cross. You are a believer."

Mary swallowed again and wished for some water. "Why do you hate her so?" Ruthven was not looking at her, and he was silent for a long while. Mary could hear the faint echo of the wind and the occasional rattle of a window pane. One of the other vampires murmured something she couldn't make out.

"I hate her because . . . because she was a woman and because she hated me and fought me."

"But once you loved her."

The hand about her shoulder squeezed tighter and tighter, until it hurt so much she couldn't hold back a moan. "Be careful, Mary. You are on very dangerous ground. If I loved her, it was years—centuries—ago, before time began. That love was a feeble and ridiculous thing, and quite naturally it turned to hate. Then it began to grow, to flourish, until it became the sustenance for both our existences. Neither of us will rest until the other is destroyed—until *she* is destroyed."

"But she was your lover?"

"One of many, and certainly not the best. She always had a rather frigid nature, even in life, although she grew hot enough when she writhed under me."

"You . . . seduced her?"

Ruthven laughed. "Oh come now, this is becoming quite ludicrous! *Me*—seduce her? Quite the contrary. Actually, I preferred members of my own sex. We of the nobility were raised in the venerable British public school tradition, you know. She was quite persuasive though, much more so than any of the other harlots who crossed my path. However, we are discussing ancient history, something which ended aeons ago. Copulation is for the living, not for the undead. We can occasionally amuse ourselves with our victims, but it is all show. I do hope you are not a virgin and that you have had your fling. 'Ever at my back I hear Time's winged chariot drawing near,' and all that. Yes, I do hope you have sampled the pleasures of the flesh, because it will never happen for you again."

The tears trickled down her face. She remembered all the long lonely days spent indoors studying and writing when she might have been living like a regular human being. She had always thought that some day there would be another man, even children. She wouldn't look at where Steve lay in the darkness.

"Oh dear, hit a nerve, have I?" His finger touched her nipple again.

"Stop that! Stop it, for God's sake!"

He laughed.

"Leave her alone, you fucking bastard."

She could barely make out Steve standing in the shadows, a tall dark shape.

"Indeed? And why should I, Mr. Ryan? No one can stop me from doing anything I want with her, and given her apparently chaste background, something rather sordid is in order."

"You leave her alone." Mary could hear the pain and weariness in his voice.

"Really, this is quite ridiculous. I'm afraid there's nothing you can do. You're almost one of us, yourself, which hardly puts you in a position to object. When I'm done with her, perhaps she'll be willing to finish you off."

"Take your hands off her."

Ruthven shook his head. "Mr. Ryan, such dreadful cliches! This is no Gothic romance. You . . ."

Steve staggered toward them, and Mary heard Ruthven's hand strike him, a backhanded slap which knocked him sideways. He groaned and dropped to his knees. She tried to go to him, but Ruthven yanked her back. She cried out, then realized again that he could tear her arm from its socket if he wished.

"Really, Mary—there's no reason for you to behave like an idiot too."

She could hear Steve's harsh ragged breathing. "It's no use, Steve—you can't help me. He'll only hurt you."

Ruthven laughed. As with Madame Rambouillet, the laughter didn't sound right because he wasn't breathing. The air, the noise, was forced. "Listen to the voice of sweet reason. She's quite right, you know."

"You goddamn fucking rotten . . ." Steve stood, swayed, then took a step forward. She could make out his face, the rage and anguish contorting it.

"Do you really think profanity will help you, Mr. Ryan?" His big white hand shot out, grabbed Steve by the collar, lifted him off the ground, then threw him against the stone wall which was only six feet away. He cried out, then crumpled and lay on the damp earth. Mary could hear him weeping softly, as if he were only half-conscious. She tried again to break free, but Ruthven held both shoulders.

"Oh, that's quite enough nonsense for one evening." He squeezed until she moaned and wept. Her shoulders must be badly bruised—it hurt just being touched there. "So much for manly gallantry. There will be no more distractions between us, Mary my love." The edge to his voice was far beyond ordinary sarcasm, made her skin prickle again.

If only it were over with, but he would not make it easy for her. She tried not to think about what he might do to her first.

"Let me show you your future home." He led her to the grave. The flashlight still lay beside it. "Please join me." He had to hold her to keep her from fainting as they stepped into the shallow hole. "Actually your spot will be the next one over, but you may spend the first night together with me."

"Can I please . . . sit down?" The light from the flashlight wavered.

"Certainly, my dear. Please do. Pardon me, I didn't realize you were feeling ill."

She stumbled back and sat on the edge. She slumped over onto one elbow and waited for her head to clear.

"Rest for a moment. We have the entire night before us. The clouds are gone, and now mighty Orion shines high in the sky. To the west the black waters of the Pacific lie glittering under moonlight. You know, Mary, you live in an unpleasant age. I am at heart a man of the nineteenth century, but I do read contemporary books and magazines. Everything is so crude and violent nowadays, so completely lacking in subtlety or craft. Take, for instance, the matter of torture. In my day, with few exceptions, it was reserved for soldiers and other manly types. Now it is carried out on a vast scale, and everything is straightforward and mechanical—electrical prods to the genitals, various burning and cutting instruments. The torturers themselves are unrefined louts who do it so frequently that they grow quite numb. And everyone is always in such a hurry! There is no appreciation of slow torture, of psychological torture—which, after all, is what torture is all about. Wouldn't you agree?"

"Yes." She still felt dizzy and as if she might vomit.

"What can be worse then psychological torture? It lasts longer. There can be no relief, as there can be from the rack or some electrical device. That torture is best which the victim creates for himself. It seems so obvious."

"Yes," she murmured, wishing she could faint.

He reached out and took her sleeve at the wrist, then pulled it over her hand and off her arm. The front of the turtleneck and her bra were torn away, and now her arm and breast were bare. She shuddered, another chill slithering up her back.

"It's so cold."

"Soon you won't be cold. Humans are so pathetically fragile. It's so easy to kill you, to hurt you: a blow to the head, a bad fall, a gunshot, severing a major artery. Insects with their exoskeletons are much tougher. Pull off a leg or two, and they'll still survive. You're subject to the whims of climate—always putting on or taking off clothes—and your lifespan is but a moment. Pathetic, truly pathetic. Those who consider mankind God's chosen must find the Creator rather capricious. He certainly could have made you stronger."

Mary sat up. She was shivering, even her jaw trembling. Her breath formed clouds of vapor, but nothing came out of the vampire's mouth except poison. When he talked so incessantly, you forgot that his voice didn't sound quite right. How could you talk when you didn't breathe? Breathing and talking were inseparable, like breathing and living. She'd find out soon enough. She clenched her teeth hard.

"You're going to take off the rest of your clothes too." The fear tightened about her heart again. *"No."*

"Now, now, no false modesty. I am a man of the nineteenth century and do not find enormous bosoms and large pelvises attractive. Your slender boyish shape will no doubt be quite alluring." He leaned over and touched her breast. "Would you force me to undress you like a baby?"

She had to struggle not to scream at him. She needed to get hold of herself and decide how she was going to die. You call yourself a Catholic, she thought. You're supposed to know how to die. She recalled stories of martyrs burned alive or tortured. Did she have that kind of faith? Oh, God help me. Her lips moved silently.

"What are you doing?" Ruthven's tone changed.

"Praying."

"Indeed? You are becoming positively infantile. Do you think God will send a band of angels to rescue you?"

She shook her head. "No."

"Then what good is praying to him?"

"Her," Mary murmured.

"Her? What are you talking about?"

"I pray to Her."

"You would reduce the deity to one of your own miserable sex?"

"It's done all the time."

"I thought you had the brains to know better. Why does this lady God of yours stand by and do nothing?"

She was silent for a while. She could hear Steve breathing, and the sound was comforting. Fred must still be lying over by the other wall. Really, it would be better if he were dead. "We all have to suffer and die," she whispered.

"You state the obvious."

"Perhaps it's so we won't become a goddamned monster like you."

She thought he was going to kick her, but finally he picked up the flashlight and shined it into the hole. "Tell me what you see here."

Her eyes looked down at the dirt. Small black thing, glistening segments of shell and brownish forms, all moving. She didn't want to try to pick out the individual shapes.

"Bugs," she said.

Ruthven bent over, then sat down beside her and turned the flashlight on his palm. "Look at this one. Isn't he beautiful?"

Mary turned her head. Sitting in the middle of his white palm was a large slug, greenish black instead of the usual yellow-brown. By its tail was the mucousy slime. The head had antennaelike bumps, and she saw them move slowly. She turned away and tried to tell herself it was foolish to fear slugs, that Ruthven would only use the fear against her.

"Isn't he a cute little specimen? Did you know slugs have a sexual identity and mate? This one is a male. Have a good look."

"No."

The vampire's arm suddenly encircled her, his fingers closing about her bruised shoulder, drawing her closer. "Oh, but I insist."

If anyone living had touched her bare skin, she would feel warmer, but he was icy. Before when he had seized

288

her throat, the turtleneck had somewhat shielded her from his fingers. They were so hard, no give at all to them, and faintly damp, almost oily. She wouldn't look at him.

"You aren't admiring my pet. Come now, have another look. Please." His fingers slowly tightened.

"Oh . . ." She turned. He had set the flashlight on the dirt, and his hand was turned so the light caught the slug on the end of his finger. She wouldn't have thought she could shake any harder, but she did.

"You know, I don't think you like him. They are my pets, all of them. They keep me company in my grave. I really am rather fond of them. Our long association has somewhat altered them. Did you know there is some of my native soil, good English earth, in here? Rambouillet has her coffin with a handful of dirt. I prefer to lie in the earth, the place of final dissolution, of decay, but these forces cannot touch me. Why don't you take my little friend here? He wants to meet you."

Her jaw quavered, so she shook her head.

"No? I'm afraid I can't refuse him. It seems a harmless request. Perhaps you are telling yourself he can't really hurt you, that this is an irrational phobia. You are only partially correct."

He wiped his finger across her chest. For an instant, the slug was like a piece of ice, but then it smouldered, burned. She screamed and went to brush it away, but her left arm was pinned against his side, and his hand held her other arm.

"Get it off me!" She writhed and tried to break free, but he was far too strong.

"Oh dear, what can be the matter? He's only a harmless little mollusk. Let's see." She lowered her eyes. The

289

yellow light was on her breast. The slug moved slowly, behind it an inch of raw, bloody skin. "Look at that! Whoever heard of such a thing?" Ruthven laughed.

Mary clenched her teeth and closed her eyes. If only he weren't so close to her—weren't touching her. Please, God—help me. I know we have to suffer and die, but . . .

Was the pain really so bad? It hurt, but it was more the cold and darkness all around her, and the presence of the vampire. He wanted her to go to pieces—to despair—he wanted that more than anything. Well, he could kill her, he could make her hurt—she couldn't stop that—but she didn't have to yield to him. She had had a good life, she had been healthy. There were those who spent every day, every waking hour in pain, for months, for years. Why it had to be, she would never understand, but couldn't she hold herself together for one night? And if he made her into what he was, that also would end. Perhaps she would really die. Even if she existed on as a vampire, that would only be a brief nightmare before the real death came, and then she would be with God and Alex and her father and Steve. She didn't believe in a heaven with harps and white robes, but there would be something. Surely she could fight off despair for a single night, when others born into pain and suffering managed it for years.

"What are you doing?" Ruthven shook her, his voice angry.

"Just thinking. And praying."

Ruthven's fingers tightened again about her shoulder, but she held back a moan. Perhaps she was going numb there. "You disappoint me."

"That's the idea."

290

She caught a glimpse of his gray eyes raging, and he reached down into the hole and came up with another slug. Mary ran her tongue across her lips and wished for a swallow of water. She didn't feel quite so cold. Only one night, she thought.

"Fight him, Mary." Steve's voice was faint and barely recognizable.

"Be silent!" Ruthven howled, the sound making Mary wince. "You two are pathetic." His mouth twitched, then he set the second slug onto her chest.

She shuddered, but the other one still hurt so much that it was easier this time. The first one had crawled a few inches toward her bare shoulder. It felt as if someone had opened her skin with a wood rasp. She raised her head, and stared at the yellow light shining on the stone wall.

"You're . . . you're rather pathetic yourself. You're no better than all these creatures, feeding blindly. You have no will of your own. Maybe the slugs still have some real life in them, but there's none in you. You're dead. You're trapped in a rotting body, and you can't even die. You have to gorge yourself endlessly, and for what? You're nothing but a sick parody of life, a bad joke—all your feeding just makes you deader and deader."

She didn't dare look at his eyes. She could tolerate the slugs, but she wished he would let go of her. His silence was more threatening than the whiny words. She began to count slowly to herself, thinking that each number meant a second more of the night was done with.

"What eloquence. I thought you were finally worn down, and now you show this great burst of energy. It's a pity that by morning you'll be begging for death, screaming for me to kill you."

"No." She shook her head. "I won't . . . I won't . . . beg."

"Can you be so sure?" he whispered. "Perhaps lying naked in our grave with all my small friends feeding upon you will change your mind."

She closed her eyes and clenched her teeth, but the tears kept coming. It's only pain—only death—and then you'll be free forever. She thought of her father and mother, of Alex, of how much she loved them, and Steve and Fred, too. Nothing could destroy that, the bond of love between the living and the dead. Ruthven and Rambouillet had never known love. Whatever they might call it, it hadn't been love—no more than their existence now was life.

She opened her eyes. "You must . . . want to die very badly."

"So now you are a mind reader."

"You wouldn't fight against it so if you didn't long for death. Every year that passes you must want it more and more. You're neither dead nor alive, and you're trapped there in limbo. You cannot free yourself, you cannot destroy yourself. I could almost feel sorry if . . ."

He put his hand about her throat. "No more talking."

She began to choke, but then he eased up the pressure so she could just barely breath. At least with his hand on her throat, the slugs couldn't get to her face. A smile twitched her lips. His talking was unbearable, but this silence was worse. When they talked you could think of them as human, but when they were so silent and unnaturally still, you knew they were something else, something distant and dead. She closed her eyes. Only a little

292

longer. She dragged up fragments of prayers she'd had to memorize as a child.

"Mary."

Was that Steve again? She opened her eyes. Perhaps she was hearing voices. Ruthven still hadn't moved.

At last he released her and stood. "Get up."

She wanted to stand on her own, but she was shaking so he had to pull her up. He plucked the slugs off her. "I am going to finish you now." She saw in his eyes that he meant it.

"You . . ."

He could move so unbelievably fast. The blow caught her on the side of the face, and she fell over again. She blinked her eyes, tasted blood, then sat up slowly. The flashlight threw its beam of yellow light between them, and she saw her shadow alongside her.

"Let me show you what your brother and Mr. Ryan did to me." Again he hoisted her to her feet, and she moaned softly. Somehow he parted the darkness beneath the white oval of his face. His chest was smooth and hairless. She thought again of the cold smooth belly of the frog she'd had to cut open.

He picked up the light, blinked, then turned it on his chest. "Did you think your Ryan was so strong he could drive a stake through me with one blow? This was already there." She noticed something black caked under the long ragged nail of his forefinger. He probed to the left of his nipple, found a gap and slid his entire finger slowly inward. "And this." He found another wound a couple of inches away. "This." His finger sank into his belly. "And of course this." He raised his hand and tugged open the hidden seam in his throat where she had cut him. It gaped like a grotesquely smiling second mouth, opening all the way to the bone.

The impact of the wounds was visceral, her insides responding in a kind of forced sympathy. The smell of him made her want to vomit, and she wondered how many times during his long death he had been pierced or cut, how many holes he had through him. No wonder he wanted to die—he wasn't *whole*. He should have fallen to pieces long ago.

"There are more, and any one of them would kill a mortal, but not me."

No, because you're already dead. She didn't say it aloud because she knew he would hit her. She realized his British accent had disappeared, fallen away, and his voice no longer sounded even faintly human. Every time he spoke it would be an effort, another reminder he was dead.

"And now you are going to die. Soon we shall lie breast to breast, flesh against flesh." He dropped the light, then put his right hand on her shoulder, his left hand grasping her hair and yanking her head back, baring her throat.

All was blackness for an instant, and then she could see the shadowy outline of the beams overhead. She was about to close her eyes, but a piece of the darkness to her right suddenly broke loose and flew at them. She couldn't move her head, but he was so tall that she could still see the gray face hovering over her. His eyes were fixed on her, so he didn't notice the black thing and feel its dark wings until too late. The raven made a sound like someone gargling or choking, and then Mary saw the black beak rip upwards across the vampire's right eye.

Ruthven howled and clapped a hand to his face, staggering back. Mary collapsed. The other vampires were screaming. She forced herself to sit up at the edge of the grave, then she took the flashlight and crawled away. Turning, she raised the light. Ruthven stood with his gigantic hand over one eye, the red scar showing across the other eye. His bare white chest still made a V in the blackness. Mary glimpsed movement and swung the flashlight around.

Madame Rambouillet smiled at Ruthven, her eyes filled with hate. She held herself straight and tall, her chin thrust forward, emphasizing her long throat. She wore the same white gown as in the tunnel, her feet and arms bare, and behind her was Suzanne, taller and even more beautiful.

"Stop your clamoring!" Madame Rambouillet commanded, and again there was silence. "So my Ruthven, we are together again at last. You always did enjoy brutalizing women. Let's see how you deal with me."

Ruthven stared at her. His mouth twisted; his face darkened, then melted and blurred, the darkness swallowing him. His shadowy form toppled over and coalesced again. The wolf had only one yellow eye. It snarled, showing the long expanse of teeth, then turned and leaped through one of the small basement windows, smashing out the glass. Mary saw the black tail, the hind paws scrambling briefly at the stone. She swung the light about; the two women in white ran across the dark earth toward the stairs.

"Let me out!" screamed a vampire from its hole, and then they were all shouting.

Mary rose onto her knees, fumbled for her parka and put it on. Even with the coat she couldn't stop shaking—she was freezing. She stood slowly, then reached out and put one hand against the wall to steady herself. The stone felt cold and faintly slimy.

"Help me, Mary," Steve murmured.

She walked over and shined the flashlight on his face. His right cheek was bluish purple where Ruthven must have hit him.

"Help me up."

She held out her hand, and somehow together they got him on his feet. His hands were icy, but when she touched his forehead it was on fire.

"Your fever's worse."

"Let's get out of here."

"I'll need your help to get Fred. I hope . . ." She began to cry. He slipped his arms around her, then sagged against the wall, using it to support them. The vampires were quiet again.

He touched her cheek. "You were so brave. I still can't believe it. I heard your voice. I wanted to come to you, but I just couldn't get up again."

She was still shaking, but she felt so warm up against him with his arms around her.

"We'll come back for Fred," he said. "We have to go upstairs and see this through. They're up there, but they may not be for long. We can't leave until we see the end."

"What end?" she asked.

"Come on."

They walked across the basement, each with an arm around the other. She held the flashlight. The vampires cursed and screamed. One sent a white fist crashing through the plywood board. Mary nearly dropped the light, but the vampire couldn't escape while the host was there. Even on the stairs they held on to each other. They started down the hallway, but Steve turned her toward the first door.

"They're out back." He laughed. "Ruthven's afraid of her. He really is."

Mary shined the light around the ruined kitchen. Dark mold and rust stained the white enamel sink. The back door was still open.

The world opened up dramatically. The air was cold, clean and sharp, not close and fetid. The hidden moon gave the black sky a bluish cast, but there was still a multitude of brilliant stars, far more than you ever saw in Portland. Stretched out before them was the dark shadow of the house, then a blue gray expanse, and beyond that the black waters of the ocean. They couldn't see the surf, but they could hear its low rumble.

Mary felt a fierce joy which almost ached. "Oh, God—it's so beautiful, so very beautiful. After all that fog and then that evil nasty place . . ." It was as if her soul had been imprisoned in some small black box and set free at last.

On the lawn, near the peak of the house's shadow, was a white form. They went down some stairs, then Mary took his hand and started forward. She had thought she would never see the stars or the sea again. Steve's hand felt hot now. She breathed slowly and deeply, trying to flush the rotten air and the fear out of her. A thin icy coat covered the grass; it was stiff underfoot. She still had the flashlight on, but they didn't really need it.

When they came to the end of the house's shadow, they saw their own dark silhouettes before them. Mary glanced back at the moon. The white orb dazzled her eyes, but she stared, savoring its light. She thought of the virgin huntress goddess the Greeks had worshipped long ago. The cold air smelled of the ocean. Further along the shadow, about thirty feet to their left, stood Madame Rambouillet, the wind flattening her thin gown against her body. Out where the grass ended, before the drop-off, was the darker shape of the wolf. The moonlight did not glisten on its coat.

"Well, Ruthven, what now? The sea at your back and me before you. Which will you choose? Which will you face?"

The black shape blurred again, swirled upward like a small tornado. Mary drew close to Steve and grasped his arm with both hands. Ruthven's face was like a small blue-white moon, the wounded eye a dark crater, a thin black rivulet running from it. His white hand hung at his side, the skeletal fingers curving inward.

"You cannot destroy me—you cannot! Not without destroying yourself!" His voice was distorted, with no trace of an accent.

"I *know.*" Madame Rambouillet laughed. Her laughter was like Ruthven's, the pitch only slightly higher.

Mary wondered, briefly, if they had a sex anymore. *No.* No more than God or Satan would. That part of them they must have lost early on, perhaps at the moment of death. Ruthven was changing again, the black whirlwind becoming something with tattered edges flapping at the sky, blotting out the stars. It still seemed to hesitate. Madame Rambouillet laughed again, then started forward. Mary pulled at Steve's hand. She knew neither of them could run.

The black thing flittered about, then turned in an arc and, flapping its wings, headed out to sea. Steve stumbled and fell, but Mary kept going. She saw Madame

298

Rambouillet, white and brilliant under moonlight, run to the edge and hurl herself into the night sky. No human could make such a leap; she seemed to fly. Her arms caught the black thing and pulled inward, her body curling about it.

Mary stopped abruptly, the dark sheer face of the cliffs before her, the surf crashing in bursts of white foam below.

Madame Rambouillet turned as she fell, her bare thin legs twisting oddly, and the darkness she clung to howled and changed shape again and again, a writhing blur of blackness. Somehow she held on. They hit the black water a good fifty feet out, the cold depths swallowing them instantly.

Mary stared in weary disbelief. "My God," she murmured. The water beat against the rocks below, the sound of the surf rising and falling, changing constantly, and she saw the dark sea ripple and whiten as another wave swept forward and curled in on itself.

Water, she thought, remembering something about vampires not being able to cross running water. Hadn't Van Helsing said they could drown? It made sense—the sea was the source of all life on earth. But that was folklore and abstraction—she could not believe it. She kept staring at the ocean, waiting for them to reappear.

At last she turned and started back for Steve. She stopped, the fear returning in an instant. Suzanne almost glowed in the dark. She could hear Steve sobbing and Suzanne whispering to him. She knelt over him, one hand on his shoulder. Mary tried to run.

"Don't touch him—get away!"

Suzanne began to laugh. Mary opened her coat and

held out the small gold cross. Suzanne seemed to flow backwards, moving with incredible speed.

Mary stumbled onto her knees and put her hand on Steve's face. Lord, he was hot. "It's all right. It's me, Mary. I won't let her have you."

"Promise me—promise you'll burn me with the others."

She stroked his face, tears filling her eyes. "Hush. Be quiet. Just rest for a moment. You'll be all right."

Suzanne stood a few feet away with her arms folded. Like some white vulture, Mary thought.

"He won't be," Suzanne said. "He's mine. He knows it, and you know it. You can't save him."

"Wasn't Alex enough for you? Why do you hate him so?"

Suzanne unfolded her arms and made fists. "I don't hate him. I love him."

Mary stared at her. She couldn't hold back a pained laugh. *"You?* You have a funny way of showing it. You've never loved any man—you've only used them."

Suzanne stepped closer. "That's not true! Him I loved—of all of them, him alone. When I came to him newly dead, my body and mind changing, he held me—he loved me, and so I love him."

Mary pulled down Steve's turtleneck, revealing the wounds. He winced but didn't open his eyes. "Is that why you did this? So he'd be cursed like you?"

"I . . . the gift—her gift—immortal life."

Mary shook her head. "You don't need to pretend with me. I've seen all of you close up, especially those two. They were dead—you're dead—none of you are even human. They were *things,* sexless monsters, and

300

you would make him into the same thing. You never loved him."

"I do!"

"Then prove it. Prove it!" Mary screamed.

Suzanne stepped back. "How?" she whispered.

"You know how. Set him free."

Suzanne gave her head a quick, jerky shake. Mary stroked Steve's cheek softly and tried to calm her anger.

Neither of them spoke for a long while. Mary listened to the surf and felt the frigid wind on the back of her head. She began to tremble from the cold, but it was only a reflex now, not terror, only her body's way of warming her, of protecting her. The wind rose and fell, and the moon slowly climbed higher in the sky. Mary looked up from Steve to Suzanne. Suzanne was staring past them out at the sea.

"Maybe you did love him, in a way," Mary said. "I've hardly known him any longer than you, and I love him. He won't be yours, you know. He'll become like Ruthven, and you'll become like her. You'll grow to hate him and yourself, more and more, and all the time you'll become deader and less human, and . . ."

"That's enough," Suzanne whispered. Fear briefly drew her mouth back in a grimace. "You've made your point." She stepped nearer, and Mary put her hand on the cross. "Don't—*please*. I won't hurt either of you. Just . . . come with me." She walked slowly toward the cliffs.

Mary touched Steve once on the cheek. His eyes were closed. She stood and followed Suzanne.

The vampire stopped at the edge of the grassy expanse and turned. The wind blew her hair in front of her face and ballooned out the white gown. Mary was still shivering from the cold. She watched Suzanne from about fifteen feet away.

"Come closer."

Mary shook her head.

Suzanne smiled. "You don't trust me?"

"No."

"Throwing you down there would be easy for me—even before. I was very strong, you know. I could run ten or fifteen miles. I did five triathlons."

Mary folded her arms. "Really?"

Suzanne laughed. The sound was still somewhat human. "Tell me one thing: did Madame Rambouillet offer to kill me if you killed Ruthven?"

Mary stared up at the stars. "Yes."

Suzanne's face twisted, destroying the illusion of her beauty. "That scheming manipulative bitch! I served her for years! I gave her my youth, my heart, and my soul. I was willing to do anything for her. She promised power and immortal life. She was a liar! I hate her—*hate her.*

"I was so afraid when . . . I thought she would understand, would help me, but she drank and drank all the life out of me. She left me nothing. When I went to Steve I was dead, my heart had stopped, but part of me still was alive. He was so gentle, and he wanted me so badly. I felt different about him. I . . ." Her mouth hung open. "Talk is cheap—both of them could talk you to death. I suppose I did take your brother from you, even if I didn't kill him. Prove it you said. *Prove it.*"

Suzanne turned and ran off the edge. Mary rushed forward and saw her throw open her arms. She held them stiff and straight as she fell toward the black waters, then her white beautiful body vanished. Mary

302

slowly eased out her breath. After a while she walked away from the cliff. She felt relieved, but there was no exultation, only weariness.

Steve was sitting with his face in his hands. He looked up at her. "She's gone, isn't she?"

"Yes."

"Help me up. I don't feel so . . . sick."

But he swayed wildly, and they both nearly fell over. She put her hand on his face. "Oh God, you're still burning up. We've got to get you to a hospital, and Fred if . . ."

"They're not talking to me anymore, any of them. It's so quiet and peaceful, and everything looks different."

"Come on."

She had to find out about Fred, then there was one other thing to take care of before they could leave. She would drive to the hospital in Tillamook. It didn't seem probable that Fred would be alive. She had dragged him into this and gotten him killed.

Both of them hesitated at the door. "It's so clear and beautiful out here," she said. "Ruthven's gone, though. He won't be down there waiting for us."

But it was still hard. The air was damp and heavy, noxious, and the marks on her chest burned. Steve put one hand on his throat. The vampires began screaming and cursing, male and female voices joining in a terrible chorus. Mary shined the light on Fred's head. It was twisted sideways, his arms outstretched before him. The dried blood in his white hair looked almost black.

"Can you help me turn him?"

They moved him very gently. One lens of his glasses was broken, and his face was cold and still. Mary slipped her fingertips under the Roman collar and began to cry. Faintly she felt a pulse. "Oh, Fred." She put her hand on his cheek, bent and kissed him.

"Is he alive?"

"Yes." She stroked his face. "Fred?"

"He must have hurt his head. We need to get him out of here. I wish we didn't have to move him. Let me take his arms."

"You can hardly stand yourself."

"Well, you're certainly not going to lug him out alone."

It took them a long time to carry him out. Steve clasped him around the chest, and Mary lifted his feet. Somehow they got him up the stairs, then they would rest and drag him a little further. Steve wouldn't sit again. He rested with his back against the wall. They got Fred into the rear seat of the Cherokee, and then Steve started to fall.

Mary slammed against him, catching him between herself and the car. "Steve!" she shouted frantically. *"Steve!* Please don't fall—*please.* For God's sake, Steve!" She knew she could never get him back up once he was down. He must have weighed 180 pounds.

He straightened up very slowly without opening his eyes. Mary held him in place with one hand, quickly opened the front door, then slid him over, and he toppled into the front seat.

"I'm fine now, Mary. I just need to rest a little."

"That's right."

She lifted his legs into the car. His boots alone weighed five pounds each. She shut the door and stared up again at the stars. She could see the Milky Way stretching across the sky. The moon was sinking westward toward the ocean. She wanted very badly to get in and drive away, but she could never rest if she did.

She opened the back door, put her hand in Fred's overcoat pocket and found a wafer, round and whole, unbroken. She closed the door and started back for the house.

The things began screaming as soon as they heard her on the stairs. Instead of cursing, they were pleading for her to spare them. One did have a child's voice. She found the lighter and the gas can near Ruthven's grave.

The lighter worked fine now. She lit it again, bent over, and the board caught fire at once. The gasoline Fred had poured had soaked in, and the plywood became a sheet of flame. The warmth surprised her, and the fire lit up the whole basement, the stone walls and the scattered metal posts holding up the floor joists. She didn't think it could get out, but she held up the host. The board gave way, the thing underneath caught fire, and its curses became a high-pitched howl that hurt her ears. She turned away. When she looked again, something charred and black lay under the flaming wood. They burned easily.

She did them one by one, and each time it grew quieter as the voices diminished. The child was hardest. She begged, "Don't burn me!" Mary had to tell herself it was only an act. She tried to think of Ruthven and Madame Rambouillet, of their overwhelming otherness. She was too successful: the anxiety squeezed at her heart, completely out of control, and she realized she was nearly finished herself.

She walked to the last hole and held out the lighter. "You little bitch, I was the one who killed your brother! I spitted him on the stake like some . . ."

The fire turned the voice into a shriek of the damned. They sounded the same, male and female, as they burned. Mary threw more gas from the can onto the blaze, then realized that was a stupid thing to do. It nearly exploded. She fell sideways, blinded by the white-orange light. She sat up. Two flaming arms and a head came out of the fire, the O of the mouth still shrieking. Half the head was blackened and bubbly like a burnt marshmallow. Mary clawed at the ground for the host, then held it up. The thing fell back.

The silence was strange. They had been screaming at her forever. The last flames flickered quietly at the wood. The basement was getting dark again. She stood up, looked in the grave, then jerked her eyes away. She took the gas can and started for the stairs.

When you lay in bed after driving all day, you closed your eyes and saw the highway, you heard the engine and felt the car vibrate beneath you. Tonight she would see tongues of flame and sheets of fire, twisting black things that screamed as they died.

She doused gas all over the living room floor and the furniture, then lit the sofa with Fred's lighter, and went out the front door. She leaned against the car and saw fire take the house, the windows filling with orange light. She looked up at the stars and wished she had time to walk to the cliff and stare at the sea, to rest and grieve, but she had already waited too long. The Cherokee started right up, and she followed the gravel road down into the firs.

Chapter 13

In his dreams Sarah came again and again to claim him, white and cold and beautiful, but he would tell her, "I saw you die, I saw you fall."

Ruthven was a black wraith, tall and skeletal, with scythes for fingers, and Madame Rambouillet wore white like Sarah. Their naked bodies showed through the misty fabric, and all of them with eyes torn from some distant star beyond the normal universe, a strange fiery matter that was neither alive nor dead. He knew the human forms were not real. Sarah's long legs, her hips and the mound of her belly, her breasts, were dead, were rotting. He sensed something crawling beneath her, so he wasn't surprised when the flesh fell away. The shadowy skeleton wasn't shaped right, the limbs bent grotesquely.

"You're dead, you're gone. I saw you die."

Ruthven raised his arms and changed his shape. First he was a bat with great dark leathery wings and cat ears sprouting from his skull. He blurred again, then feathers appeared. His beak, feathers and legs were black, but his eyes were still gray and alien.

307

He and Madame Rambouillet were bigger with black ruffs at their throats, their cries unearthly, damned. They led a vast flock of crows, the black shapes spotting the gray white sky like some pox. The two leaders wheeled about, flew at each other, then hurtled like black meteors into the gray-green waters. The crows followed, falling, an avalanche of stones. Finally the sea was calm again, flecks of yellow-white sunlight shimmering on its surface. He heard the cry of a gull and saw a pelican flying further out. The sound of the surf grew, its roar drowning out all else.

Occasionally the darkness dissolved and faces hovered about, talking at him. He felt cold and sick. Mary was nearby, but she didn't speak. Her long straight red hair hung down on either side of her face. She looked pale and tired, sick herself.

Once he saw her sitting in the chair by his bed, the navy parka zipped up, her hands in the pockets, her eyes closed. When he woke up, the chair was empty, and he wondered if he had been dreaming. He felt lonely and sad, and then all that had happened came back to him.

He ran his tongue across his lips, felt the rough scraps of skin. An I.V. was hooked to his left arm. He touched his fingertips to his throat. A bandage covered the wounds. Tender, but at least his throat didn't hurt like it had. His cheek felt sore too.

A glass of water sat near the bed. He managed to sit up, drank half the water, then lay down and stared at the ceiling. He wondered where Mary was. A clock on the wall said 3:30, and a window somewhere let in gray light. What day was it, anyway? Abruptly, he remembered his job. He had missed a few days. His problems with Peter seemed laughable at this point.

"Awake at last. Welcome to the land of the living."

The nurse was a big, older woman wearing an old-fashioned white dress. Her hair was an unnatural light brown. Her institutional joviality grated.

"What day is it?" he asked.

"Saturday."

"I've been here for two days?"

"Yep. You were awfully sick. We might have lost you. Blood poisoning can be very serious."

A sudden, painful smile twisted at his face, contorting it.

She stared closely at him. "Are you all right?"

"Fine. I'm fine."

"Are you hungry?"

"No, but I would like something to drink." She nodded and started to leave. "Was there a woman here? In that chair?"

She laughed. "There sure was. Your wife's been here nearly the whole time."

"My wife?" He thought of Brenda, then realized she wasn't his wife any longer.

"Yes." The nurse was eying him closely again.

He forced a smile. "Oh, of course. Tell me . . . was her hair red?"

"Surely. Would you like me to get her for you?"

"Yes."

Steve stared again at the pale green enamel on the ceiling. He wondered which hospital this was. Talking to the nurse was strangely exhausting. Blood poisoning. His mouth twitched.

Mary looked very slight alongside the nurse. She had on the same blue parka, jeans, and hiking boots. Her face was very pale, her eyes shadowy and weary. A

309

greenish blue bruise marred her cheek. Her long hair was bound up in back, leaving the white lobes of her ears and the tiny gold earrings exposed. She stood on the right side of the bed and took his hand.

The nurse set another glass on the bed tray. "Don't be too long. He needs his rest, and please remember to keep off the beds."

As soon as the nurse was gone the tears began to seep from her eyes. He saw them gather, glistening about her eyelids, then the drops slipped out. A few freckles showed on her cheeks and nose, and her mouth was clamped shut.

He sat up slowly, took her hand and kissed her fingers, then her knuckles. She had freckles on the backs of her hands, and the nails were cut short. He turned her hand and kissed her palm. She stroked his cheek, then the rough hairs along his jaw. He realized he had several days growth of beard.

"How are you?" His voice was hoarse. "Wifey."

He saw the flush begin around her ears. "They started giving me such a hard time about being with you—especially that lady—that I finally told them . . ."

"I don't care about that. Where were you?"

"With Fred." She drew her hand away.

They stared at each other. "Christ, I . . . How is he?"

"I don't know—they don't know. He recognizes me, I know he does, but he hasn't said anything. They're going to send him to a neurologist in Portland. They almost flew him there earlier, but . . ."

"Where are we?"

"Tillamook." She wiped at her eyes with her fingertips. "He's lucky, you know. I'm sure he doesn't remember any of it, and if he lives it may never come back. I remember all of it—every minute—and it won't go away, it won't stop."

"You look tired. Sit down here—forget the nurse. Have you gotten any sleep?"

She shrugged. "Some."

"You look like you could use a doctor yourself."

"I'm all right."

He took her hand, put it on his chest, then put both his hands over it. They were silent for a while.

"Steve, don't feel . . ." She wasn't looking at him. "So much happened, and it was so frightening that . . . We were so alone there, and we had to depend so much on each other. Some of what happened . . . Don't feel like . . . don't feel obligated to . . . to me. We have our own lives, and if you . . ."

"Obligated?" he whispered. "What are you talking about? I owe you my life, and you tell me not to feel obligated? There are some debts you can never repay."

She still wouldn't look at him. "I just don't want you to feel . . . you were so very sick and delirious. You don't . . ."

He stared at her, the sadness closing about him. "What are you saying?" He thought of betrayals again, but then he remembered Mary facing Madame Rambouillet and her voice and Ruthven's in the darkness. "Are you trying to give me an out—because I don't want one. I remember . . . I remember you telling me that you loved me. It was in Ruthven's house just before . . . I had the stake and the mallet in my hands. Did I only imagine it?"

She stared again at the wall, and he saw the flush spread across her throat and face. His hands tightened over hers, drawing it against his chest. Her eyes had

311

such dark shadows under them, and her face was thinner than he remembered. He should never have asked—he should have kept quiet.

Her lips barely moved. "No."

He felt his own eyes fill with tears. "Good."

"Oh, Steve—it's all too close still—people don't fall in love so fast. No wonder we—but when things settle down, you'll feel differently. Men like you . . . they never end up with women like me."

"What the hell are you talking about? You think I'm some kind of yuppie jock in wingtips and a dark suit who has to marry some fashion model with big breasts and . . . ? You can't make rules about who ends up with who—you just can't! I was married to one woman who was the kind of woman who ends up with men like me, and once was enough. I don't . . . I want you, Mary—that's not going to change."

She was crying again. He kept one hand on hers, but reached out and touched her cheek with his other hand. "You act as if you were . . . ugly or something. I think you look nice. I . . . Oh, hell—come here. Please."

She bent over, and he slid his hand onto the back of her neck. Her lips were chapped too, but her mouth was warm. He opened his mouth wider and pulled her close. Finally he let her draw away, but he kept hold of her hand.

"I want to love you," he said.

"Do you?" she whispered.

"Yes. I want you very badly. I wish I felt better, and we were alone together somewhere else."

"Oh, I'd like that. I'd like that so much. If only . . ."

"If what?"

"I just—I feel so awful. I see them and smell them all

312

the time, especially when I close my eyes. There's fire and these black things screaming and screaming. I had to burn them all, one by one. And I dragged Fred and you into this, and he may never recover."

He wanted to get up and hug her, but the I.V. in his left arm restrained him. "Come here—lie down."

"Oh, I can't. You heard the nurse."

"Screw the nurse. Take off your coat and lie down for a moment. Don't talk—just lie down."

She had on a bright blue T-shirt that said, Tillamook—Cheese, Trees and Ocean breeze. He slid over to the left, and she lay down and let him put his arm around her. She didn't want to let her boots touch the bed. "Oh, don't worry about your boots. Just set them down. Now get comfortable. Just relax—that's better." He gripped her shoulder, and she winced, her eyes opening wide. "Does that hurt?"

"Yes. He . . ." The fear showed in her eyes, the sudden tension in her mouth.

He slid his hand further down her arm. "Bruises will heal, and so will you, and I, and Fred. It will be all right now. I . . . I wish I could have helped you. You didn't kill them, you know. They were already dead. You freed them. You told Suzanne she was growing deader and less human, but that's all over with. They're gone, and we're free. Don't think about them."

"I can't help it. And I can't help thinking of Ruthven, how he kept touching me—playing with me—how nasty he was. I must be going crazy or something—I can't forget it, any of it—I can't let it go."

"But you will. It will go away like everything else does, the good and the bad. No wonder you're hurting.

313

You're not God or ... Wonder Woman." She laughed abruptly. "What is it?"

"Your juxtaposition—God and Wonder Woman aren't quite in the same league."

"Well, Wonder Woman certainly didn't have much on you. Have you seen a doctor?" She shook her head. "Why not let them give you something to help you sleep?"

"No—I don't need any damned drugs."

He laughed once. "Maybe it's Rambo, not Wonder Woman. I'd hate to see you with a machine gun."

"Don't."

"I'm sorry, but you expect a lot from yourself. You don't just pick yourself up, brush yourself off, and keep going after all you've been through. It's going to hurt for a while, but you'll be all right, and now you're stuck with me. I can feel you relaxing."

"I feel like I could sleep now."

"Do, then."

She sighed and seemed to settle into his shoulder. "Oh, if anyone asks, you walked into a tree."

"I what?"

"You walked into a tree branch. That's how you got those marks."

He smiled faintly. "That was the best you could do?"

"I had to tell them something when I brought you in. We were hiking. And Fred fell down and hit a rock." She closed her eyes. He could hear her breathing deepen and slow down.

She jerked once, then said, "They do writhe around so much, and they curse me."

"Forget them. Think about ... remember when we were at Mount Hood, and I couldn't sleep? You said to

314

think about going out for Chinese food. It worked for me, and that's the first thing we'll do when I get out of here—go for Chinese food. You said you'd wear a dress."

She made a face.

"You promised. A promise is a promise. I want to get a good look at your legs and the rest of you—I want to kiss you all over your body, but I'm . . . getting ahead of things. We'll be together eating the hot food, and we'll look at each other and think how happy we are to finally be out together. Every so often I'll reach out and squeeze your hand, because I'm going to want to touch you all the time. Twice-cooked pork is my favorite. I like the cabbage. And we'll have a nice cold wine or maybe some beer. And then . . ."

He stopped talking, but she didn't move. Her breathing had quieted. The blue veins showed in her eyelids, and her lips were parted slightly. He smiled, his hand tightening about her arm. Looking at her made him want to cry.

He heard footsteps coming closer, and he shut his eyes. Maybe the nurse would leave them alone if she saw the sweet young couple together. He heard her stop at the doorway, and he breathed deeply as if he were asleep. Just keep going, he thought.

Finally she walked away. He opened his eyes. "Thank you." He gazed at Mary. She was out, and his arm was starting to go numb. He didn't care. He closed his eyes, and soon he was asleep.

HE'S THE LAST MAN YOU'D EVER WANT TO MEET IN A DARK ALLEY . . .

THE EXECUTIONER

By DON PENDLETON

Available wherever paperbacks are sold, or order direct from the Publisher. Send cover price plus 50¢ per copy for mailing and handling to Pinnacle Books, Dept. 705, 475 Park Avenue South, New York, N.Y. 10016. Residents of New York and Tennessee must include sales tax. DO NOT SEND CASH. For a free Zebra/ Pinnacle catalog please write to the above address.